Nancy –
I so Hope You Enjoy
The Story.

Beach Walk
Treasures

Best,

[signature]

Beach Walk Treasures

NANCY MOLLOY-GEIMAN

Beach Walk Treasures by Nancy Molloy - Geiman

Copyright © 2021 by Nancy Molloy-Geiman, Naples FL

ISBN: 978-0-578-91749-8

Production Management: Della R. Mancuso
Design: Donna Murphy
Copyediting: Ellen Henrie
Cover Photo: Nancy Molloy- Geiman, with many thanks to Natasha Valdes for stepping in as Jackie.

First Printing 2021
Printed in the United States of America

This book is dedicated to
my wonderful kids KJ & Katie.
I love you both more than I can put into words.
And to all my incredibly supportive friends and family;
especially my dear friends Erin and Jean
with whom I have walked the beach many times
and encouraged me to give voice to my thoughts.

Chapter One

The usual guilt started to creep into Jackie's mind—*$10 an hour times three days—that's enough to buy a case of Pull-Ups*. But as soon as she thought it, she dismissed the temptation to wallow in her guilt, because she knew that her walks on the beach were the only thing that kept her going. They were as valuable to her sanity as the extra thirty dollars was to her wallet. So, while the babysitter kept watch for an extra hour every Tuesday, Thursday and Friday, Jackie went for what she had dubbed her sanity walk.

Although she knew the stretch of beach like the back of her hand, she was continually amazed that each time it seemed like a whole new experience. Perhaps a bird catching a fish in the shallows, or a love-struck couple walking hand in hand. Sometimes the sun beat down on her with unrelenting heat, and sometimes she was caressed by a calming breeze.

Same sand, yet not. Often filled with castles and sculptures built by beachgoers, and other times strewn with seaweed, driftwood and all manner of shells that Mother Nature had deposited directly on her stretch of paradise.

Jackie loved the constant ebb and flow of not only the tide but all the everchanging nuances that lay in front of her during each one of her walks.

The one constant that Jackie always relied on, however, was the sight of the elaborate beachfront mansions that she passed about two-thirds of the way through her walk. There were about fifteen of them, but there was a special one that always caught her attention and imagination more than the others. It was magnificent in its size and architecture with columns and terraces arranged perfectly, so that even in its enormity, everything was built perfectly to scale and had the effect of making the house seem welcoming. Every passing brought the same questions, "Who lives there? What in the world do they do? And why isn't it me?"

Each time she passed by, she would imagine herself in a never-ending array of fantasies. Sometimes she would be dining in the grandness of the home or sunning herself out on the expansive deck. Often, she would see herself stepping out of the massive pool and into a towel made of the finest cotton. A well-chilled margarita sat on the bar waiting for her to take a sip. As she passed the last window of the architectural masterpiece that someone called home, she muttered "If only ... "

Then, as soon as the words passed her lips, she mentally slapped herself into reality. *Stop being an idiot and start thinking about what you should be worried about—your precious little Emily. What are you going to do to make her life better? We can't keep living in a two-bedroom bare-bones apartment that's an OK fit for a twenty-something single girl but not the place to raise a daughter. Forget the 'I wishes,' the 'how come them and not me,' and 'life is so not fair' and get a grip. This is your world, like it or not.*

Now what are you going to do about it? Always present, always there, was that nagging question.

Jackie didn't have a bad job. She was a real estate paralegal in a well-regarded and very busy law firm called Wright, Stewart & Blake. All in all, she was happy there, she liked her boss and coworkers and even considered them friends, but unlike those around her, she was a single woman with a three-year-old daughter. Not the ingredients for a great social life.

Her job was to handle all the real estate contracts that came into the firm. This basically consisted of making sure that all the things that needed to happen before the closing got done: surveys, financing, and so on. Once all was ready, she either attended the closing or mailed out the documents to be signed. Once the closing was done, she brought the file to completion. Although each file had different buyers and sellers and sometimes some drama, it was basically the same process every day. Open the file, do the work, close the file. Certainly not life on stage, but it wasn't digging ditches either.

The overriding thought that never left Jackie's mind, however, was: *I don't get paid enough. Liking what you do and who you work with is great, but it doesn't pay the ever-mounting bills that come along with a child.* Asking for a raise was out of the question as she was told quite firmly by the office manager when she was hired almost a year ago that "no increase in pay will even be considered until the second anniversary of your hire."

"I know I should have asked for more when I took the job," she chided herself, but she was so thrilled to have a real job, she settled for less and now she was stuck.

Jackie fell into one of many one-on-one discussions with herself: How am I going to make Emily's life better with rent, food, clothes, gas and the all-important childcare eating up every penny of my paycheck? I can't get another job because I'm away from my little one too much as it is. Maybe the lottery? That's ridiculous and you know it is. You can't be throwing money away on stupid lottery tickets. Well, then what? The conversation in her mind was always similar and ended the same way—Well, then what?—and then dropped until the next time.

Chapter Two

"Jackie, Mr. Wright is on his way back to the office and would like to see you in ten minutes." The voice of the receptionist snapped her back to reality.

"Thank you, I'll be waiting for him. Did he mention what it's about?"

"No, but he sounded excited."

"OK Lindsey. Thanks," said Jackie.

Excited, huh. That's odd, thought Jackie. Mr. Wright was the managing partner of the law firm. Nice, even tempered, and could be somewhat funny on occasion, but excited is not a word that Jackie would ever associate with him. He was the epitome of calm, cool and collected. Even the most demanding, crabby or ultra-emotional clients wouldn't faze him. He would just listen, nod his head, and then dispense the perfect answer to address the concern, problem or situation.

It was an amazing gift that Jackie admired and wished she could learn. She all too often found herself being emotionally connected to clients, good or bad. She would get upset when people were mean or angry with her. All it took was a raised voice and Jackie felt like she had let the whole firm down. On the other hand, she gloried in others' joy, whether it be buying the house of their dreams or selling one to free themselves to travel and enjoy. Each file felt like a personal investment to the point where her coworkers were always telling her to stop being so codependent. "I know, I care too much, but is that such a bad thing?" she'd retort when teased. She knew she could go a bit overboard, but she also knew that her caring was what made her a great paralegal.

"Jackie, please come to my office," Mr. Wright said over the intercom.

"Right away," she replied. "Do I need to bring anything?"

"Just a legal pad and pen," he instructed.

Jackie grabbed a legal pad from her desk, made sure she had her favorite pen, and made her way down the hall to the spacious corner office of Mr. Wright. "Good afternoon, Jackie," he said as she entered. "How are you today?"

"I'm fine," Jackie replied. "Thank you, Mr. Wright, and you?"

"I'm better than fine, I'm excellent."

Yes, thought Jackie. *He is excited, but why?* "That's great sir," she said.

"Yes, indeed, excellent, and I'm going to tell you why."

"OK," was all Jackie could come up with as she had never seen Mr. Wright show his emotions so candidly.

"Have you ever heard the name Trevor Harding?"

"No," she replied.

"OK, well, you've certainly heard of PPF, right?"

"Of course. Prestigious Properties of Florida. Their developments are unbelievable!"

"Well, Trevor Harding just happens to be the owner and CEO of PPF, and I just got back from having lunch with him."

He paused and Jackie didn't know whether to say something or not but decided to wait him out. He continued, "I want you to know that these opportunities don't come along every day." Another pause. *Now does he want me to reply?* Jackie thought, but again, she just sat waiting for Mr. Wright to drop some kind of clue as to why she had been summoned.

Mr. Wright put both of his hands firmly on the top of his desk and announced, "Jackie, we have been conditionally selected to represent Mr. Harding and PPF in the most exciting development ever to hit not just Naples but the entire state of Florida. And you, my dear, are going to be the legal assistant for the project."

Jackie didn't know whether to jump for joy or look for the closest hiding place, so she merely said, "Me?"

"Yes," Mr. Wright affirmed. "You are perfect for the job. Your habit of taking files and clients to heart is just what we need for this. Mr. Harding is a very nice man, but he hasn't gotten to where he is without being demanding, completely thorough, and most of all, extremely smart."

Jackie was now in the shocked world of two-letter replies, so all that came out this time was "Oh."

"Oh, yes!" Mr. Wright said finishing the thought for her. "You'll be great. Now don't get me wrong, it's going to take a huge commitment from you, lots of work, long hours, and a demanding client, but I'm absolutely positive that you're up for the challenge."

Finally, Jackie formed a full sentence and said, "Thank you for the confidence you have in me. I'll certainly do my best to live up to your expectations."

"That's more like the Jackie that I've come to know as a go-getter. Oh, and by the way, there will be a raise in your salary."

Jackie was having a hard enough time comprehending the new position, and then Mr. Wright had to go and drop the "raise" bomb on her. In the span of ten seconds, Jackie was reeling from a seesawing combination of excitement to fear, pride to panic, but the most overwhelming feeling was one of nausea.

Jackie managed to collect herself and said, "Mr. Wright, I can't thank you enough for giving me this opportunity, and I promise that I'll work diligently and give a hundred percent to this project and do everything I can to satisfy Mr. Harding and his company."

"I know you will Jackie," he replied, "but rest assured it will take all your hundred percent and more. I'll speak with Ms. Williams about your raise of $10,000, and I'll expect you in my office at 7:30 tomorrow morning to get this project going."

Again, Jackie almost lost it when $10,000 came out of Mr. Wright's mouth, but she successfully suppressed the feeling and said, "Yes, sir" and then added, "By the way, what's the name of the development?"

"Why yes, of course, that's a pretty important piece of information. Well Jackie, this development is going to set a new standard of excellence of which there will be no rival. Its name is Excelsior, as it should be."

"Wow, I'm sure it's going to be fabulous. I can hardly wait. Again, I can't thank you enough, and I'll see you in the morning." With that, Jackie left Mr. Wright's office, walked down the hall to her office, closed the door, collapsed into her chair and started to cry.

By the time Jackie got to the beach that evening, she was exhausted, but she wasn't going to miss her walk even if it was at a snail's pace. Her crying earlier was out of both joy and fear. Of course, there was a sense of pride over the fact that Mr. Wright thought so highly of her, but the tears of joy mainly came because of the extra $10,000 that she would have to make her and Emily's world better. "Ten thousand extra dollars! Ten thousand extra dollars!" she found herself repeating over and over.

Then the thought hit her that this is going to take a ton of work, unbelievably long hours, dealing with what Mr. Wright had called a very demanding client, and living up to all his expectations. Then, the tears changed to ones of fear. *How am I going to do all of this and still be a good mom to Emily?* she asked herself through the sobs.

Finally, the crying subsided, and Jackie gave herself a verbal pep talk. "Mr. Wright wouldn't have picked you if he didn't think you could do it. Right? Right! Em will be just fine. After all, lots of working women put in a ton of hours. Right? Right! It's not the quantity of time that you spend with your child, it's the quality. Right? Right! Mr. Harding better watch out, 'cause I'm going to knock this project out of the park. Right? Right!

Chapter Three

Trevor Harding was sitting on his patio as he did every day at this time. His binoculars were always handy to get a closer look at any bird of prey that might be swooping down to catch its nightly dinner of fish fresh from the Gulf of Mexico, or to hone in on a pod of dolphins casually swimming by the beach. Lately, however, Trevor's sights had been distracted from the wonderful Naples wildlife because his eye was always drawn to her.

He was forever asking himself, "Who is this woman who mesmerizes all of my attention?" He came to anticipate her appearance like a schoolboy waiting at the front door of his date's parents' house. He learned her schedule and found himself planning his evenings around her. Unless it was storming, he was guaranteed to see her Tuesday, Thursday and Friday at 5:40. When storms would come, he was genuinely disappointed that he wouldn't get the dose of medicine that seeing this enchanting woman provided him.

Trevor acknowledged to himself that this borderline obsession with a total stranger was not only odd, but totally out of character for him. In every other aspect of his life, Trevor was in total control of his actions and emotions. Whether he was sitting at a negotiating table with an adversary, presenting a project to a boardroom full of investors, or managing the ups and downs of a personal relationship, Trevor Harding was a master of the ability to portray exactly the right persona to achieve his goals. He didn't consider it devious, just smart. So why on earth did this woman unsettle him so?

She was not "knock you dead" gorgeous but had a beauty that he found magnetic. About five foot nine inches tall, light brown hair, and legs to die for, thanks in part to her regular beach walks. Her not being perfect was what he found so perfect. He'd had enough of the artificially proportioned women that were a dime a dozen in Naples. Implants everywhere, Botox, and enough collagen to plump up a skeleton. Combine that with the must-have Mercedes, BMW, Range Rover or Audi, the ever-increasingly larger diamonds, and the prerequisite multimillion-dollar home, and you have the Naples social scene. He had been there, swam with the well-manicured sharks for a while, but then realized that deep down, even though he must live in that world to a certain degree, it was not what he was looking for.

Then he admonished himself saying, "Trevor, you are one big hypocrite. Just look around you." His home was one of Naples' finest. A magnificent mansion that Gatsby himself would find quite to his liking. Three stories and over 12,000 square feet of palatial luxury situated directly on the beach overlooking the Gulf of Mexico.

If the interior was impressive, the outside patio had no rival, with its expansive deck surrounded by cozy seating areas. Of course, every detail was top of the line in its placement and its quality. This outdoor space was just as perfect for entertaining dozens as sharing a private evening with someone special.

The true focal point of the patio was the magnificent pool and spa. Not only huge, it was exquisite in its beauty. The water was not the normal aqua color found in everyday pools, but had more of a green tint to it that replicated a pristine tropical hideaway. The tranquil flow of water started at the marble steps leading into the pool then headed twenty-five yards past rock formations, flowering plants and lush greenery, to then disappear over a false edge that made it appear like a horizon in a foreign land. However, if one was in the mood to exercise, a retractable wall could be brought up at the false edge to create a lap pool. Midway through the journey, a cutout led to a ten-person spa. Again, the spa was surrounded by a perfect combination of rocks, bushes, flowers and trees, but the real highlight in this haven was the multitude of orchids. Something about the hot, humid air created by the steaming water made these flowers flourish. Too many varieties to remember, but the canvas of purples, yellows, pinks and whites was breathtaking.

Yes, this was the house that Trevor called home. A 39-year-old bachelor with a home that a dozen people could live in and certainly not step on each other's toes. As he did with almost all his acquisitions, Trevor bought the house because he knew it would be a good investment. Naples beachfront property was almost nonexistent, and he owned one of the most sought-after locations in the entire town—a can't-miss bet. While waiting for the real estate market to soar (because it would soar), Trevor lived in the house, sat on the patio, and waited for the first sight of her.

Chapter Four

As always, Jackie changed from her work clothes into running shorts, a tank top and sneakers in the public bathroom at the beach. She could change at work, but she didn't think it was professional to be seen leaving her place of employment in such casual attire. So, she took the extra five minutes to do her changing here and then brought her work clothes back to her car. Five minutes of wasted walking time, yes, but important to keep up her appearance at work. *Now, it's going to be super important!* she reminded herself.

She had the routine down to a science. Leave work at 5:15, drive to parking garage by 5:22, change and bring clothes back to the car by 5:27, take her first step on the beach by exactly 5:30. This precise exercise left her exactly thirty minutes of "sanity" before getting back to her car and driving home to arrive at 6:15 on the dot. She often had to convince herself that the extra ten dollars for an additional hour of babysitting was worth it, but these walks were her salvation. And now with this new position and all the responsibility that would come with it, she would need her walk even more to decompress.

So, Jackie took the first step of her walk that evening with a new future ahead of her. As her foot sank gently into the sand, so did her anxiety give over to the beautiful scene before her. The water tonight was so incredibly calm that it gave the appearance of a sheet of glass. This too helped to calm her, as did the gentle breeze that carried the scent of salt. She started slowly walking down the beach that was always familiar, but never the same.

The sandpipers were doing their never-ending dance down the sand when the water receded only to scamper away when a wave came back ashore. All the while, they'd search for a tiny morsel of food beneath the wet sand. Back and forth, back and forth. The sight of them always made Jackie smile.

The sun was still pretty high in the sky, but because the water was so calm, it created a sheen that almost made it look like the water was on fire. "That is one of the coolest things I have ever seen," Jackie heard herself say out loud.

Yes, the beach had worked its magic again. Jackie was no longer in the world of business suits and corporate pressures or, for that matter, diapers and parental responsibilities, but in her own world filled with peace of mind and wonderment in all that surrounded her.

Then, she looked up from the imaginary flames that were licking the gulf waters and took in the vision of that breathtakingly beautiful house. She saw it on every walk and every time was just as amazed that this magnificent structure was real and not just some mirage at the edge of the sand. Again, the questions came: *Who in the world lives there? What could they possibly do to have all that money? My giant $10,000 raise* *probably doesn't even cover the cost of mowing the lawn.* She joked with herself as she did every time she passed by, saying quietly, "Yoo-hoo, whoever you are. I'm nice—I could be your friend and share your world. I'm a very good friend." Then she allowed herself to go mentally into the realm of friendship with the owner of the beach mansion.

This time, she was sitting at the perfectly set dining table with two other couples. She and her beau were at a small yet elegant dinner party hosted by the owners of the house. The funny thing about these imaginary events in Jackie's life was that she never pictured what this beau of hers looked like. There was always a feeling of comfort and caring from him, but never a concrete vision. For that matter, she never had a clear image of the others there either. Just some representatives of your typical Naples people: tan, slim, well dressed, but nothing detailed.

Instead, she saw the beautifully appointed room. Mahogany-paneled walls, with brushed iron sconces framing a modernist painting that showed an array of greys, blacks and whites. The value of the artwork alone in the home was probably in the millions. The table was also mahogany as was the other perfectly proportioned furniture. Nothing too big and bulky, but every piece certainly making a statement. The chandelier matched the sconces in look and added the final ingredient to an exquisite setting.

Jackie and the other guests talked casually with the hosts as friends do, discussing the charitable endeavors that each was involved in. One saying, "I just got finished helping with a great event for Special Olympics. I donated money for a banner that was hung at a swim meet that these amazing kids competed in. It really puts our lives in perspective when you hear about the challenges that these kids face every day."

"Yes," her friend chimed in, "I know. When I was at the Make-A-Wish Ball, I couldn't believe some of the stories that these kids with cancer told. It just breaks your heart."

Jackie just nodded her head and said, "It isn't fair," but inside she was wanting to challenge these "do-gooders" for what they were constantly patting themselves on the back for and perceived as giving back. Donating $800 for a sign or buying a $1,000 ticket to a ball is not the same thing as rolling up your sleeves and volunteering. Why don't they get out there and be a timer at the swim meet or drive a young kid with cancer to her chemo appointment instead of just writing a check? Jackie kept her thoughts to herself, however, took a sip of the vintage cabernet that was served to pair perfectly with tonight's Chateaubriand and continued the small talk—the state of their tennis games, where each was traveling next, the newest trendy restaurants that have opened, on and on—all very pleasant, but never anything meaningful. Such are the concerns of the social elite in Naples.

Even in her fantasy, the "rich Jackie" was still true to herself and reminded herself: *You aren't that shallow, you do care, not just with your wallet, but to put in time and effort to the causes you support because you know what it's like to have lived in a world of struggle, deal with hardships and overcome adversity. Of course, thank God, I never had a disability or, God forbid, cancer, but being a single mom, whose bum of a boyfriend left at the first mention of my pregnancy with Emily has allowed me to know what depression and desperation feel like. As hard as it's been, it has made me who I am today.* With that, Jackie left her make-believe mansion existence and was back to the reality of her world in her two-bedroom shanty-like apartment.

Chapter Five

Jackie had barely put her key in the door, when she heard the shouts of "Mommy, Mommy!"

"Emily, my sweet, give me just a sec to get the door open for goodness sake." As soon as there was just enough room for Emily to squeeze her little body through, she wrapped her arms around Jackie's legs and squeezed as tight as she could. "Oh, my precious Em, I missed you so much," Jackie said as she bent down, pried the arms off of her legs and picked her up. "I can hardly wait to hear all about your day, but first let me talk with Miss Maria."

Maria was Emily's babysitter, and even though the $10 per hour put a significant dent in Jackie's wallet, she was worth every penny. A wonderful older woman who had raised six children of her own and treated Emily like her seventh, Jackie was so lucky to have her. What made it even better was that Maria came to the apartment, which saved Jackie time in the mornings and kept sweet Em out of the factory-like daycares. A huge financial sacrifice, yes, but Jackie was adamant that her daughter was not going to be herded around with thirty other kids just to save a few dollars. Just the germs alone made Jackie cringe.

Maria also felt that children needed to be at home, preferably with their mother, until they were at least four to receive the proper love and attention. Obviously, Jackie couldn't stay home, so Maria felt like she was the next best thing. This common belief shared between Jackie and Maria was the foundation of their relationship, and Emily certainly received the benefits.

"So, Maria, how was our princess today?" Jackie asked.

"An angel, as usual," replied Maria. "And how was your day?"

With that question, Jackie's face broke into a giant smile, and she answered, "Oh Maria, you'll never guess what happened to me today."

Maria pretended to frown, "You know I hate guessing games, but from the look on your face, it has to be something major. Did you meet a man?"

"No," Jackie firmly replied. "Why does everything related to being happy have to do with stupid guys? This is much more important, especially for my precious little girl."

"Silly me," admitted Maria, "you're right. The last thing you need right now is to add a relationship to your already way too complicated life. So, what is it then?"

"I feel that if I say it out loud, I might wake up and it's just going to be a dream."

"Wow, that big, huh?" said Maria. "Just take a deep breath and spit it out. You wouldn't have that gigantic smile on your face if it weren't great news."

Jackie gathered herself and excitedly blurted out, "I got a promotion and a $10,000 raise today!!" With that, Maria and Jackie hugged each other and started jumping up and down.

In the midst of their jubilation, Emily kept pulling on Jackie's leg and repeating "Mommy, what? Mommy, what? Mommy, what?"

Jackie looked down and swooped her up into her arms and said, "Mommy won a big prize today, and we are going to have a party with ice cream after dinner."

"Yay!!" exclaimed Emily.

Jackie realized that Maria had to get going, so she quickly synopsized the meeting with Mr. Wright, the new position and all that would come with it, including the extra hours. "I have to meet with Mr. Wright at 7:30 tomorrow morning. Will you be able to get here early?" Jackie asked pleadingly.

"Of course, honey, but we'll have to sit down and have a chat about how all of this is going to work out. I'm here to help in any way I can, but I'm no spring chicken."

"Thank you so much, Maria. I don't know what I'd do without you and I promise, once I have this meeting, I'll have a much better idea of what my schedule is going to be like and we'll figure it all out. Can you believe it though—$10,000?"

Maria looked at Jackie as a mother would her own child and said, "Absolutamente! I do believe and I know you deserve it. Congratulations, and I'll see you tomorrow morning at 7:15." Then, Maria gave Jackie and Emily a kiss and hug goodbye and shut the door.

The words "Mommy, I'm hungry" brought Jackie back to the reality of life with a three-year-old wanting dinner.

"Of course, you are Em. I'm pretty hungry myself. What should we have tonight?"

"Mac and cheese, mac and cheese," Emily repeated as if it were a chant.

"Now, Em," Jackie protested. "I know it's your favorite, but we shouldn't have it all the time."

"But you said that we were going to have a party, Mommy," Emily retorted.

"You're right Em, yes, I did say it's a party. So, OK, let's live large and party down with some mac and cheese." Jackie then started laughing at how ridiculous her version of partying had become. Forget the Jell-O shots, shooters of tequila, or glasses of champagne—her throwdown now consisted of mac and cheese and ice cream with a preschooler. "Ain't life grand," is all she could manage to say.

Chapter Six

Trevor Harding was sitting down to a dinner of chicken piccata over linguini, a mixed green salad with a bright Italian vinaigrette, and lovely glass of pinot grigio. Although Trevor liked to dabble in the kitchen from time to time, almost every dinner was made to order by his personal chef, Andre.

Andre wasn't needed for breakfast, however, because it was the same routine every day. Trevor would seat himself at the table in the kitchen at exactly 7 o'clock, the housekeeper would serve him half of a toasted whole wheat bagel with cream cheese, some yogurt (choice of flavor rotating—peach, strawberry, blueberry, blackberry, raspberry) with granola added and coffee. As Trevor ate, he read his usual complement of papers—*New York Times, Wall Street Journal* and, just to keep up to date on the local goings-on, he read the local *Naples Daily News*. Then he would go over Andre's offerings for dinner, which were printed on a card that replicated a room service order form.

If he had plans to go out, he would always make sure Andre knew at least the day before. This way, food wouldn't go to waste, but more importantly, Trevor felt that it showed respect for Andre's time and acknowledged that the chef's meticulous attention to detail wasn't being taken for granted.

Trevor's meal tonight was a perfect example of Andre's special talents. Not just your finest Italian restaurant-quality chicken piccata, but always a five-star Zagat review. The organic free-range chicken was pounded to the point where it still had texture to the tooth, but then it almost melted in your mouth. The accompanying sauce was the perfect balance of acid from the lemon and astringent from the capers, which were blended expertly with the silkiness of butter and rounded out by a wisp of white wine. Simple yes, yet done to this standard it was extremely difficult, and Trevor truly appreciated Andre's art.

So there Trevor sat, savoring each bite, letting the crisp pinot add its own dimension to the budding flavors on his palate. Suddenly, Trevor was taken back to a similar dinner, one that was shared between himself and his father.

* * *

The dinner was almost fourteen years ago. They were at the Manhattan Athletic Club and were together to catch up after not having seen each other in almost a year.

Trevor's father, Pierce Harding, was a man of the Wall Street establishment and possessed all the ingredients that are a must for such a place in financial society: pedigreed lineage—at least one Harding had always held a chairmanship position at a major brokerage house on Wall Street since 1875, and even through the horrible trials of the Great Depression, the ups and downs of the bulls and bears, the Hardings were a constant. Of course, he was a prep school alum and boosted an Ivy league education—

BS from Harvard, MBA from the Wharton School at Penn.

Most of all, Pierce Harding had an unmatched stock market savvy. It's one thing to have the name and the degrees, but what really made the financial pundits call Pierce Harding an absolute genius was his attention to every bit of minutia that was in each stock offering, his all-consuming research into every company and their finances, and finally, his amazing innate ability to pick out which companies were going to be the supreme winners in the stock market. Some people admired him, some even revered him, some people envied him, some even hated him, but all acknowledged that he was, without a doubt, one of the most formidable powers in the high-stakes world of corporate finance.

"So, how's life in the swamps, Trevor?" Pierce asked his son reproachingly.

"We're doing OK. As you know, any startup company takes time. We have almost all of our approvals in hand, and we're about to start on the infrastructure."

"I still don't understand why a smart talented boy like you wanted to go down to that sweltering place and build things? If the mosquitoes and alligators don't get you, the hurricanes will. You know, you could have come on board with me and had a proper and, might I add, very profitable career here."

This jab was always how their conversations started. It took different forms, but it always had the same intent—to reinforce the fact that his father thought his Florida real estate venture was absolute folly and to remind him of all that he gave up chasing this fantasy.

Trevor just sighed and said, "Haven't we gone over this enough, Father? Why can't you just let it go? I like what I do, and mark my words, I will make a lot of money. Now, can we please just enjoy dinner?"

"As you wish, but I still have my concerns," Pierce said dismissively.

Trevor internally acknowledged that his father was partially right. He did give up a guaranteed position in one of the nation's top brokerage firms, an easy seven-figure income, and the security of the known. All things Wall Street had been ingrained in him since he was a kid. He knew the ins and outs of the financial markets just by listening to his father throughout the years. He also had the formal education of a Harvard degree and an MBA from Wharton. Just like his father.

That was, however, the crux of the problem. Everything he ever did was "just like your father." From day one, he was groomed to be a Wall Street ace, but he never really wanted it. Facts, figures, projections, margins, stock splits, prospectuses— none of it was real. Trevor wanted to be involved in a career that made real products, not money off of others' products.

So, after his graduation from Penn, Trevor decided that he was finished doing everything just like Pierce Harding and he was going to go his own way. He wanted desperately to have a hands-on career and be responsible for bringing something to life. What better way than entering the world of real estate development, and what better place than in the quickly awakening real estate market of the Sunshine State—Florida.

Breaking the news to his father was no easy task, but Trevor knew that he could no longer play the "follow in your footsteps" charade. He strategically went to his father's office because he knew Pierce would never lose his temper and decorum in this setting. He sat down across from his father, swallowed hard and blurted out, "Father, I've decided to buy a piece of land on the west coast of Florida and develop it."

His father replied, "Son, you're just out of school, don't you think you should work a few years before building a second home?"

It was hard enough saying it the first time, but Trevor realized that his father had no idea what he meant, so now he was going to have to restate it, present it again, and wait one more time for the dreaded reaction.

"No, Father, you don't understand. I'm buying 200 acres of land in Florida and building a housing development."

"What in God's name does that mean?" His father tersely questioned. "What the hell do you know about land development?"

"I took some classes that certainly do apply, and I've done a lot of research on my own. You've said yourself that I've got a great business sense, and Florida is ripe for development."

Pierce's voice started to rise and have that clipped cadence that emphasized every word. "Business sense, yes, as it applies to markets and finances—not dirt, cement and lumber!

Plus, you're just out of school and you're about to start working here, so how the hell are you going to oversee a project that's 1,200 miles away?"

Trevor tried to keep his voice very calm and give each word importance so his father would know that he was serious. "That's why I'm here—to tell you that I'm not going to work here after all. I really appreciate all that you've offered me, but it's just not the right fit. I've never really wanted the Wall Street life. I want to be a part of building something from scratch, and real estate development is just the thing. I'm closing on the land on Friday and moving to Florida in ten days."

Very rarely did Pierce look perplexed because he was always the one to have it all figured out before everyone else, but after hearing his son's words, he had a look of complete bewilderment on his face. "I just don't understand" came rather meekly out of his mouth.

Seeing that his father's fury had abated, Trevor continued as calmly as he could. "You see, Florida is just waiting for someone smart to come in and turn it into a developer's dream come true. That someone smart is me! All that undeveloped land is a huge opportunity for turning into retirement communities for all the baby boomers. Do you know how many people will be retiring in the next twenty years? Thousands upon thousands looking to get out of the snow and cold and move to the Sunshine State."

"But Trevor, this is so sudden!"

"Sudden for you, but this has been at least five years in the making for me. I know it's not what you had hoped for, and I don't even feel right asking for your support, but at least don't hinder me. That's all I ask."

Pierce looked down his nose as he often did to his son when he was going to say something that he wanted Trevor to take very seriously and said, "I obviously have no option here, but I caution you that this is not just a game of Monopoly where you can buy and sell properties and land on "Go" and collect money. The real world that you are so eager to join is brutal. Those good ole southern boys are going to look at you like a babe in their swamps and, believe me, they will try every way to take advantage of the slick kid from New York who knows nothing. However, the biggest difference between working here and going off to Florida for some pie in the sky dream, Trevor, is that your daddy will not be the fool to come to your rescue.

You, my son, are on your own!"

Almost a year later, those completely dismissive words still rang in Trevor's ears as he tried to make small talk with his father while dining on the Manhattan Athletic Club's merely adequate version of chicken piccata.

* * *

Now, almost fifteen years later, "You, my son, are on your own!" still stung as much today as they had the minute they left Pierce Harding's mouth. Trevor remembered that he had to summon all his resolve not to respond emotionally to such a harsh and severing statement. He merely got up out of the plush leather chair, buttoned his suit coat and said, "Father, you mark my words, I will make you proud and I will make a lot of money." With that, Trevor Harding left his father's world and entered a new one all his own.

The first few years were certainly tough. Trevor had to tap deeply into his trust fund to capitalize his inaugural 200-acre venture in the sleepy Florida town of Arvida. Planners, engineers and designers all had to be paid to put Trevor's vision of baby boomer heaven into a real plan of action. Lawyers were brought on board to get the land rezoned and obtain permit upon permit upon permit. Then, the construction process had to be funded. It took an exorbitant amount money just to get the sewers, roads and infrastructure completed before the first housing slab was even poured. Trevor could have easily obtained financing for his project, but he instead chose to fund it all on his own.

"I'm willing to take on the debt, and more than willing to take in the profit" was his ever-repeated motto. This strategy also had a lot to do with the grudge that he held against his father. He didn't want some buttoned-up investor making money off his hard work. "Let them ride on someone else's coattails, but they're not going to make one dime off of mine!"

Eventually, all fell into place—the marketing campaign to sell property at Trevor's first foray into real estate began, and it was an overnight success. He named his project Eclat because it sounded foreign and distinguished. No matter what you're selling, Trevor believed that buyers wanted to feel like they were getting something special. More to the point, however, Trevor picked the name because it meant brilliance of success and reputation. That summed up Trevor's burning desire. Not only to be an amazing success, but also to have a reputation for doing things beyond reproach.

Eclat's homes and amenities were far superior to any other product at the same price point. Trevor figured that if he spent a little more on the front end of the project, it would set him apart from all the other developments and translate into his selling out faster. Less profit maybe, but a much quicker turnaround, which in Trevor's mind was just as important, because when capital is realized quicker, it can then be used to propel the next development, continuing his "more boom for your buck" strategy.

Even fifteen years later, with countless developments under his belt, Trevor was still abiding by the mentality that he launched with Eclat and always provided more to the consumer than what was necessary. He was the wunderkind of the Florida real estate boom, and every article written about him pointed out that he was the groundbreaker when it came to changing the meaning of the bottom line from one of "let's make as much profit as we can by cutting corners" to one of "let's make a fair profit by giving the consumer real value for their dollar and providing them with more than expected." This seemingly upside-down way of turning a profit worked tremendously for his first project, Eclat, and he was supremely confident that it would work for his latest, most ambitious project—Excelsior!

Chapter Seven

Jackie's alarm clock didn't need to go off, because she was up an hour before she needed to be. "Oh my God, what is today going to bring?" she said to herself.

Then, as if she were a third person giving sage advice, she answered, "You just need to take things one step at a time, trust your abilities, and everything will work out fine. It's not like you're starting a brand-new job. It's the same place with the same people."

Back to the panicked Jackie, "Yeah, but it's not the same, it's a whole new ball game. New development, new files, new issues and, most of all, a new client who happens to be one of the most powerful and successful people in all of Florida!"

"OK, but getting yourself in a tizzy is not going to win him over or impress him in the least," she admonished herself.

So, Jackie put both feet on the floor, got out of bed and said, "OK, Trevor Harding, get ready for Jackie Summerville to be the best damn legal assistant that you've ever had. I'm going to make Excelsior the smoothest-running project there has ever been, and you will be so impressed you might just give me an amazing offer to leave Mr. Wright and come work for you!"

With that, Jackie took a shower, got dressed and went into Emily's room to say good morning to her darling daughter. Before she woke her up, Jackie stared at the little figure all curled up under the covers. *What would I do without my little princess?* Jackie asked herself. The answer to that question always had two replies—on one hand, Jackie knew that Emily was the best thing to have happened to her. Before she was born, Jackie was without purpose. Yes, she always had a job, but she would float from place to place, never really latching onto any one job in particular. She tried her hand at banking—so boring; retail—too up and down; restaurant—too seasonal. Once Jackie found out that she was pregnant, she knew she had to buckle down, so she signed up for classes to become a real estate paralegal and finally found her passion. Not only did she love it, but she was really good at it. And look where she was now: a good job with benefits and a new position with a $10,000 raise. All thanks to Em!

On the other hand, Jackie knew that having Emily shut the door to the many extracurricular activities that are enjoyed by most single young women in their late twenties. No more long weekend trips to the Keys just for fun, or taking a trip anywhere, for that matter. She had to save every dime she could to put food on the table and pay the rent. No more happy hours with her buddies that would turn into a night of dancing. She had to get up at 6:30 on weekdays for work and rarely got to sleep in on the weekends because Emily would be pulling on her pajama sleeve to get up so they could watch Sesame Street.

Most of all, no more relationships with guys. She was far too busy with work and raising a daughter to give any energy to the thought of a date. Plus, when her ex up and left upon hearing that Jackie would not have an abortion, she swore off all things that had to do with the male species. She would recount to her girlfriends, "Funny, how he was so 'into' me until I dropped the P word. Then he became the most self-centered creature I have ever met. He had the nerve to ask me to get an abortion, so he wouldn't be burdened by a kid. He sure didn't seem burdened when he was making the kid. I can't believe I fell for such a jerk. I'm actually happy he took off. We're better off without him."

Jackie whispered, "Yes, we're way better off," as she bent over and kissed the soft, smooth cheek of her baby girl. "Good morning, my sweet."

"Morning, Mommy," yawned Emily.

"Mommy has to go to work early today, but Maria will be here any minute, and she'll make you some breakfast when you get up, OK?"

"OK Mommy. I'll see you later. Love you," Emily said and then rolled over and nestled back under her blanket.

Jackie looked at her beautiful daughter and replied, "I love you mostest." It was their made-up phrase to exceed the common "I love you more." With that, Jackie tiptoed out of the room and into the kitchen where Maria was making them both a cup of coffee.

"Well, today's the big day! How are you feeling?" prompted Maria.

Jackie sighed, "I don't know. I'm excited, but all jittery. Not so sure I need the extra caffeine in that coffee."

Maria used her most comforting voice possible and said, "Oh my dear, you were born for this job. You just have to trust yourself and everything will be fine."

"I know. I'll feel much better about everything once I meet with Mr. Wright and get an understanding of exactly what I'm going to be responsible for and how demanding it will all be. Until then, I feel like I'm facing the unknown, and you know how my control freak self hates not knowing."

"Yes, I do. So the best way for you to know is to get yourself out the door and meet your future head-on."

"Oh Maria, I love you! Thank you so much for all that you do for Emily and me. I don't know what we'd ever do without you."

As she'd done hundreds of times, Jackie gave Maria a hug, took the cup of coffee out of her hand, grabbed her purse and briefcase, and breezed out the door to face her future that was to begin in fifteen minutes in Mr. Wright's office.

Chapter Eight

Jackie knocked on Mr. Wright's door and heard his baritone voice answer, "Come in." She pushed open the heavy oak door to see the office in a state that she had never seen it in. Maps and drawings were everywhere. Papers were piled in countless stacks on every available spot—not only his desk but also the credenza and meeting table. This was certainly not his normal "place for everything and everything in its place." Mr. Wright always prided himself on control and order.

"Well good morning, Jackie," he greeted her.

"Good morning, Mr. Wright," she responded. She had handled projects before but never anything close to this magnitude, so she was going to let him totally take the lead.

"This office is quite a mess, don't you think?"

How should I answer that one? she thought. *Let me throw him a compliment.* "Well, it certainly looks like you've been very busy since yesterday."

"Yes, this opportunity has me so excited that I decided there's 'no time like the present' so I called Mr. Harding after we met and had him deliver all of the pertinent documents to me last night. Of course, I had to sign an ironclad confidentiality agreement before they were released to me, but here, in this office, is our future. Mind you, I've only had time to review a handful of documents, but this project is going to be unlike anything you, or anyone else for that matter, could ever dream of or imagine. It's sheer genius."

Just at the sight of it all, Jackie was teetering on the verge of panic. Then after the buildup that Mr. Wright just gave it, she fought the urge to scream that she was not the one for the job, that she's just a lowly legal assistant, and to run back to the safety of files entitled "Jones sale to Smith." Instead, however, Jackie swallowed hard, took a deep breath and surprisingly found herself saying, "OK, Mr. Wright, what would you like me to do first?"

"Nothing yet, Jackie. First, I have to brief you on what exactly Excelsior is so you can understand the scope of the project. But before I say a word, you must sign this confidentiality agreement. The privacy of all things related to Excelsior is of the utmost importance. You may not discuss any details or information regarding this with anyone, under any circumstances. Do you understand?"

She nodded her head convincingly, "Of course, Mr. Wright. I absolutely understand." She took the document placed in front of her and again gathered up her courage and asked if she could read it first.

"See, I told you that you were exactly right for this type of work! Of course, you can and should read it before you sign. Isn't that rule number one? Always read—and reread—everything that we prepare, produce or sign."

"Yes, I know, Mr. Wright. Thank you." She then read the three-page document that addressed all the parameters that controlled her and the law firm's actions as they related to their representation of Mr. Trevor Harding, individually, and as owner and CEO of Prestigious Properties of Florida. It also included language that extended the confidentiality to all agents and employees of Mr. Harding in all business matters, but especially those having to do with Excelsior. It was all very detailed and thorough, but nothing jumped out to her as being excessively burdensome. Working in a law firm, one learns that confidentiality is the cornerstone of your business and reputation.

"May I ask if this is the same agreement that you signed Mr. Wright?"

"Another astute question, Jackie. Yes, it is, and by your very logical thought process, you will now be comfortable signing it, having read it yourself and knowing that I read and signed it as well."

"Yes, that does make me feel more confident. Thank you," Jackie said, and then signed her name to the bottom of page three, which Mr. Wright then notarized.

Mr. Wright filed the document away and said, "Well, now that's out of the way, let's get started. You'll see as we go along, Jackie, that Excelsior is not just a development that has 'top of the line' and 'state of the art' everything. That has been done before. This project is going above and beyond anything that anyone has ever seen. I used the word ingenious earlier, and here's why Excelsior is light-years ahead of its time.

It's going to be an all-inclusive community that has every product and amenity that an aging population is looking for, no matter their needs. There will be small homes, condos and villas just like every other community from here to Tallahassee, but these will all be assisted living to some degree. All the residents can still live in a comfortable setting that suits their needs but are assisted by the community staff offering an array of functions.

Some may want cleaning services; some may want someone to take them shopping, while others want the shopping done for them; a wife may be fine doing all the household chores but needs help to bathe her husband who has had a stroke; a husband might still love to work in the yard but needs help with trimming the bushes. Whatever your personal needs and wants are, you name it, and Excelsior provides it to its residents.

Then, once a person isn't able to handle independent assisted living due to poor health, he or she then transitions into Excelsior's full-time medical care facility where there's 24-hour care by the best-trained and qualified team of doctors, nurses and therapists possible."

Jackie was listening and was impressed but had to ask, saying, "I'm sorry to interrupt, Mr. Wright, but don't these types of places already exist? I know of a couple in town that sound similar."

"They sound similar maybe, but they can't hold a candle to the standard of excellence that Excelsior will have in everything that's provided, whether it be in the construction, the amenities, the maintenance, the services, the healthcare and the quality of life. With our population, you can't ask for a better package. But the true genius of this plan lies in the next feature that I'm going to explain to you."

Mr. Wright took a deep breath, smiled, and continued, "You

see Jackie, once you buy in Excelsior, you never have to worry about selling your residence, regardless of the transition you're making or the market. Trevor Harding will guarantee that your home will be bought back from you at either the current market rate (and you are able to provide your own appraisals) or, at the very least, the amount that you paid when you bought it. With your sale guaranteed, you don't have the stress of selling or being at the risk of a down market. You can then move smoothly on to the next phase of your life and the next Excelsior product. The homes that are returned to the company then get upgraded or remodeled if necessary and put back in inventory for sale. That way, all the homes are at one point or another maintained by Excelsior management and are put back in tip-top condition, so the value is always preserved. Pure genius, I tell you!"

While Jackie was trying to wrap her brain around all of this and how it could work, all she could come up with was, "That's certainly a novel concept."

"Novel, groundbreaking, cutting edge, whatever you want to call it, nobody has even come close to this all-encompassing lifestyle. Excelsior is going to set a new standard that others will try to emulate, but by the time that happens, Excelsior will be far and away in the lead. Trevor Harding has made a fortune on foreseeing what the baby boomers will be needing as time goes on, and he has hit on his next goldmine."

Again, Jackie felt the need to say something, so she asked, "What's the timeline for all of this?"

"Good question, Jackie. Mr. Harding told me at lunch that the land has been cleared, the infrastructure is done, and the models are progressing. He has purposely kept the marketing of Excelsior under wraps because he wants to make sure that all the pieces are a hundred percent in place for the sale and closings of the products so that when the dam is opened, we all don't get washed away."

"Yes, I one hundred percent agree," Jackie said as she started to allow herself to imagine the magnitude of the work related to all that was Excelsior.

Then, Mr. Wright put on his "I'm the commander of the ship" attitude and semi-bellowed: "Being that we ARE going to be the closing end for all of this, we need to get to work! We have exactly one week, from now until next Friday to A) thoroughly familiarize ourselves with the sales contract and digest every clause and requirement therein, B) develop a timeline and checklist for each contract so that all deadlines are met without fail, C) organize our files so we have a separate category for every type of residence, D) personally review the title and issue a title report so you'll know exactly all the title requirements needed for each closing, E) draft the usual correspondence— letters to buyers, realtors, buyers attorneys, banks and mortgage companies—and there will most likely be an F, G, H and maybe more as I work my way through all of this."

Jackie was writing as fast as she could to keep up with what Mr. Wright was saying. Most of it was part and parcel to the normal requirements of any closing, but this was on such an enormous scale that she could feel herself start to panic again and had to ask, "Mr. Wright, you said we had until next Friday to get all of this done? Why, may I ask? What's happening then?"

"That's when Mr. Trevor Harding will be paying us a visit to introduce himself, see how well prepared we are to represent him and handle his closings, and sign off on our agreement."

Jackie couldn't help but question, "You mean, this is not a done deal yet? If I don't live up to his expectations, we could lose this client?"

Mr. Wright could see that she was getting overwhelmed, so he calmly said, "You'll be just fine. One of the reasons I chose you is because you work so well under a deadline. I know it seems like a lot, but you just have to take it step by step. Mr. Harding will be so impressed, he'll sign on the dotted line without hesitation. I have full faith and confidence in you."

"Oh, thank you Mr. Wright. That means a lot. I'll work diligently to make sure it's all done by next Friday," Jackie said as her boss's calming nature did the trick again.

"Good Jackie, I'm glad you're ready for the challenge. Oh, and you know the step-by-step process that I just spoke of?"

"Yes," she answered,

"Mind you, my dear, those steps do have to be taken at a fairly quick pace." With that, Mr. Wright let out a little chuckle as he always did when he thought he was being funny.

"Of course, Mr. Wright."

Then he pointed to a tall stack of papers on his meeting table and said, "That pile is yours to start. In it you'll find a copy of the sales contract. As you know, this is the most vital document, and therefore it is critical that we know it inside and out. You must go through it with a fine-toothed comb and commit it to memory. I don't want us to have to visually reference it if Mr. Harding shoots us a question. I want every answer on the tip of our tongues so we can answer all questions or concerns without any hesitation whatsoever."

"Yes, Mr. Wright. I'll get right on it. I love dissecting con-tracts," said Jackie excitedly, as she really did enjoy the process of reading and understanding the minutia of real estate contracts. "May I ask, what are the rest of those papers?"

"They're the sales brochures for all the products and informational guides for the development. In them, you'll learn about each type of home and all the amenities available, from pools to beauty salons. I expect you to become an expert on all this as well. Even though the sales contract is already signed by the time it gets to us, we are still part of the team that brings each sale to fruition, and Excelsior deserves this absolute attention to detail. Therefore, I want us to thoroughly know each type of residence, its floor plan, its features—everything. I also want us to know all there is to know about the various offerings at Excelsior from manicures to occupational therapy and everything in between. There's a lot to digest, but we both are going to become Excelsior experts!"

Jackie walked over to the table, put her legal pad on top of the file and then wrapped her arms around the cumbersome pile. She bent her knees as if she were about to pick up a barbell stacked with weights and lifted the load.

"Put that down, Jackie!" Mr. Wright exclaimed. "That's way too heavy for you to lift. Just take the contract on top, and I'll have Ryan bring the rest down to your office. I don't need you throwing your back out and being laid up."

"Good point, Mr. Wright," said Jackie who was relieved that she didn't have to lug the giant pile to her office. "Is there anything else you'd like to go over?"

"No, Jackie. I think you have the picture of what we have to do, how pressing the timeline is, and how extremely important our role will be in assuring that Excelsior is a success beyond anything the real estate market has ever seen."

That's an incredibly high bar, thought Jackie, but responded with an enthusiastic "Absolutely, Mr. Wright. Again, I thank you for the confidence that you have in me, and I'll make every effort to live up to this fantastic opportunity."

"Great, now let's get to work. Next Friday will be here before we know it," he replied and then pushed his reading glasses down on his nose, picked up a file and opened the cover. This was Jackie's signal to leave, so she gingerly picked up her legal pad and the Excelsior sales contract and tiptoed out the door.

Jackie got to her office and shut the door, but instead of collapsing in her chair, this time she sat down with confidence, placed the all-important sales contract on her desk and muttered to herself, "If I do say so myself, I am damn good at breaking these things down and understanding what needs to get done— what's important and what's just boilerplate language that's in there to cover everyone-under-the-sun's behind. So, Ms. Jackie, let's go!"

Then, Jackie picked up her phone and dialed her assistant's extension. "Karen?"

"Yes, Jackie," came the reply.

"Please do not disturb me unless it's absolutely necessary. I'm going to be deciphering a 25-page contract, and I have to be totally focused."

"Wow, OK. I'm guessing that has something to do with your meeting with Mr. Wright this morning. How did it go?"

"It went fine, but get ready to work your butt off. We're going to be busier than we've ever been."

"OK, but what's this all about?" asked Karen, who had no clue about Excelsior and the magnitude of the project.

"I can't let you know yet, but it's going to be big. Look at it as job security," Jackie said with a quick giggle.

"All right Jackie, I trust you. Change of subject—after plowing through that contract all day, you'll probably need a drink. We're going to happy hour after work. Care to join us?"

Jackie sighed knowing that she always seemed to have to say no for various reasons, "I'd love to, but I'm already paying Maria extra today because I had to be here so damn early. Next time."

"OK Jackie, if you say so," Karen kidded, knowing full well that Jackie's "next time" would never happen.

The girls in the office often talked about how hard Jackie's world was. Almost 30 and being a single mom with a demanding job left her no time for anything fun. The comments always went something like "With her looks, she could land a man in no time if she ever went anywhere but home." Or, "She's still young and so attractive. I feel so bad that all she has is her daughter and her work." On it went, Jackie's coworkers always including her in the invitations to happy hours or parties and Jackie always declining with the promise of joining in "next time."

Jackie knew that she was missing out on a lot of fun, but she had no choice. As her late mother would always say, not knowing that it would apply so harshly to her daughter, "Well Jackie, so-and-so made her bed and now she has to lie in it."

"Yes," said Jackie, "and here I lie." Then she stared at the contract and said kiddingly, "You're mine now. Tell me everything about you," as she picked up page one and started to read.

There was a thump, thump, thump on her office door. Jackie looked up and realized that over three hours had passed, "Come in," she answered. The door opened and Ryan, the office clerk, was standing there with his arms full of the other documents that Jackie had to know like the back of her hand by next Friday.

"I don't know what these are," said Ryan with a strained voice, "but they're heavy."

"Here, let me help you," Jackie said as she jumped out of her chair and rushed over to the door.

"No, it's OK. Just tell me where to put them. If you touch one, they might all start falling."

Jackie hadn't thought about where they should go, so she replied, "Ahhh, OK, ummm ... "

"Please hurry," squeezed out of Ryan's mouth.

"Yeah, sorry, just put them on the floor in the corner for now. I'll figure out a permanent place later."

Ryan walked over to the corner that Jackie was pointing to, stooped over and let the pile drop with a thud. "I came here to learn how to be a lawyer, not a weightlifter, for God's sake. What is all this stuff?"

"I know, Ryan. I'm sorry you had to carry all that, but Mr. Wright didn't want me to throw my back out. It's all related to a new project that I'm not at liberty to discuss yet."

"Whatever! I guess your back is more important to the boss than me getting a hernia," Ryan countered jokingly.

Jackie laughed and replied, "You're a gem, Ryan. Has anyone told you that lately?"

"Yeah, yeah, I'm a precious gem that gets treated like common colored glass," he said with a bit of an edge.

"Oh, come on now Ryan. You knew coming into this that part of what clerks do is law related, but a lot of it is just grunt work. It's the same everywhere."

Ryan smiled and said, "I know, but it's just such a waste of my brilliant mind."

Jackie laughed again and sarcastically said, "Oh brother, here we go again. Listen, I'd love to chat about all things Ryan and how incredibly gifted you are, but as you can see, I have a ton of work, so off with you."

Ryan walked toward the door, "Thank you for acknowledging my genius. I wish others would see the light."

Jackie let out another giggle and ended the conversation with, "All in good time, my pretty, all in good time. Now, shut the door."

Jackie walked back to her desk, opened the left-hand drawer and pulled out a granola bar saying, "This will have to do for lunch, I have way too much to do." She ripped open the wrapper, took a bite and flipped the contract to page ten.

Another four hours later, Jackie had finally finished her initial reading of the contract with copious note taking. Her yellow legal pad was filled with jottings of all her thoughts, questions and concerns. The next step was to go through it again to make sure she had digested every detail, addressed every aspect of every clause, and then commit it all to memory. But first a bathroom break.

Jackie emerged from her office to face an office filled with curious looks. Karen asked the question that was on everyone's mind, "What in the world have you been doing?"

Jackie didn't realize that she looked like an exhausted college kid who had just pulled an all-nighter, so she replied, "I told you, I've just been reading a contract, that's all."

Karen whistled and said, "That must be one hell of a contract. Have you looked in the mirror lately?"

"No, why? Is there something wrong? I'm going to the ladies' room now."

"Let's just say, you've looked better. I hope whatever this new project is, it isn't going to take it out on you like this every day."

Jackie was shocked. "Do I really look that bad?"

Karen thought it best not to answer, so she merely said, "Go to the bathroom and take a look. Oh, and try not to scream."

Jackie pushed open the ladies' room door and hesitantly looked around the corner to catch a glimpse of her reflection. Karen was right. She looked like she had just taken the red-eye from L.A. to New York and hadn't slept for a wink of it. Her eyes were bloodshot, her face pale, and the frown line that she always tried to hide was creased to the point of her being scared that it may never uncrease. Jackie's hair, usually perfectly in place, was every which way from her running her hand through it as she read line after line of the contract.

"Holy crap!" she said out loud. "I do look awful. No wonder everyone was looking at me like an alien." She turned on the faucet and threw some cold water in her face. "That's not going to do much, but at least it feels good."

Jackie came out of the stall and walked slowly back to the sink. She looked in the mirror again and asked herself, "Is this all going to be worth it? If this is the toll that just the first day is taking, what am I going to look like a week, a month, a year down the line?" Then, she admonished herself a la her mother saying, "Jackie, you know better than to worry about the future and things you can't control. What you can control is doing the very best job for Mr. Wright and Mr. Harding, no matter the effects. Now, get your act together and get back to work."

With that, she washed her hands, smoothed out her hair, tried to uncrease her frown line, and walked back out to the office.

Karen greeted her with, "Well, that's a little better."

"All right already" Jackie said exasperated. "I admit that I look a bit frazzled, but I have a lot to get through and not a lot of time to do it. So, my appearance will have to take a back seat for a week until I meet our new client. Then I have to look totally put together, calm and one hundred percent composed."

"My, my!" said Karen "Who might this new client be?"

"Again, Karen, I'm sorry to be evasive, but I can't let you know yet. Let's just say that if all goes well, we'll have hit the big time. No more piddly little closings on houses in run of the mill neighborhoods. Now, please don't ask any more questions. I have to keep all of this very hush-hush until the deal is sealed and Mr. Wright gives the go-ahead to let the cat out of the bag."

"OK, boss," Karen said sarcastically.

Jackie went back to her office, shut the door and walked over to the pile of documents in the corner. There were sales brochures for Excelsior the development, copies of floor plans for all the residences, bylaws and homeowners' documents for all the communities within Excelsior, and contracts for the services that Excelsior could provide to each homeowner. "How in the world am I going to get through all of this by next Friday?" Jackie questioned and then immediately answered, "Because you have to. That's all there is to it. Now, back to that blasted sales contract, so you can at least get to the point where you can go for your walk and not feel guilty."

Chapter Nine

It was Friday evening and Trevor knew that she would appear any minute now. He had memorized her schedule and found it intriguing. Most people who did things three times a week would go Monday, Wednesday and Friday, but not her. For reasons that only she knew, she walked the beach on Tuesday, Thursday and Friday evenings. Trevor liked to imagine why. Maybe she was taking a graduate class on Monday and Wednesday. He loved a woman who was looking to improve her knowledge. Or maybe she had an exercise class those days. A body as flawless as hers certainly had to take a lot of work. Or, when Trevor was in a funk, he would allow himself to believe that she had a boyfriend who she met for drinks and dinner on Monday and Wednesday evenings, but then he'd snap out of the funk with confidence saying, "Once she's met me, anyone else doesn't stand a chance."

It was all part of the game that Trevor played—*Who is she? What does she do? How can I meet her?* Going down to the beach and just bumping into her was out of the question. She would think that he was some sort of crazy person. He continued thinking, *Maybe I should pretend that I'm looking for something I lost in the sand and ask for her help? Not a bad idea, but she always seemed so lost in thought that he'd hate to interrupt. Oh well, I'll come up with a great idea one of these days, but it has to be ironclad because I'm not going to blow my chance at meeting her and asking her out. For now, I'm just going to watch her do her thing and hope that she is single for as long as it takes for me to figure out the perfect way for us to meet.*

As expected, Jackie came walking along the sand right at 5:40 like clockwork. He put his binoculars to his eyes and was a bit taken aback by her appearance. Instead of her normal put-together self, she looked somewhat disheveled and lacking the normal spring in her step.

I wonder what went on in her day to make her so tousled and tired? I hope she's just having a bad day and there's nothing really wrong. What if she has a major problem that will prevent her from taking her walks. That can't happen!

Trevor then realized how ridiculous these thoughts sounded and gave himself a reality check. *You need to get a grip buddy. First, who the hell knows why she looks a little wiped out today, and you have no say-so in any of it. She doesn't know you from Adam.* Trevor agreed with his assessment, but added out loud, "No matter. She's still gorgeous and totally captivating."

Down on the beach, Jackie was pushing herself to get her walk in and decompress while conducting one of her many internal conversations.

She lectured herself thinking, *Now Jackie, we are going to have to establish some ground rules to manage this new undertaking of yours. Number one: You positively, absolutely cannot take your workload and responsibilities to the beach with you. This has always been sacred ground for you, and you will not tarnish it just because you have this new project.*

She laughed out loud, took over the other side of the conversation and admitted, *Easier said than done, but OK, I promise, I'll try my best.*

OK then, rule number two: You positively, absolutely cannot let this project adversely affect your job of being the best mom ever to Emily. She will certainly benefit from the extra money, but all the money in the world can't give her the love and attention that you can and should be providing.

Back to the other side. *Again, easier said than done, but I hereby do solemnly swear that I will always put Emily first and foremost in everything I do, so help me God!* Jackie then looked at the sky and verbally added, "And, God, by the way, I will desperately need your help, so don't let me down."

Jackie laughed at the ridiculousness of this back and forth, but it really did allow her to go through the thought process from both sides. With all that she had on her plate, it was far too easy to let the stresses, emotions and irrational fears take hold. When she talked to herself in the third person, it was much easier to take the rational approach, put things in perspective, and remain somewhat calm.

By the time Jackie was done with her talking-to, she had passed "The House" and was at the end of the beach. Time to turn around and head back. As always, she was in a much better state of mind by this time in her walk—thus the sanity part of the sanity walk.

She picked up her head and started to take in all the constants in her walk, yet also every nuance of difference that this evening presented to her compared to all the others. To Jackie this was the most magical thing about her walks. Sure, the stretch of sand was the same, the condos were all finite in their locations, and the mansions, of which "The House" was one, were always majestically looking down from the same spots. But during each walk, Jackie always experienced something new. None was ever the same. One evening she would see a school of dolphins frolicking in the shallows while a flock of pelicans would swoop so low to the water that their bellies were almost touching. On a different walk, the pelicans would instead be climbing high only to dive straight down to pluck a fish from the Gulf, and instead of dolphins, Jackie would spy a nurse shark stalking the shoreline.

"What show will I be treated to tonight?" Jackie questioned. Instead of looking out to the water, Jackie decided to check out the land side where "The House" laid claim over the multimillionaire landscape. First, she eyed what appeared to be just a bunch of thorny weeds, until she noticed the most delicate yellow flowers peeking up from the tangled brush. *Just amazing how something so beautiful can whittle their way through the prickers and scrub to totally change the image of that otherwise nasty-looking plant.*

Then she looked upward, and her eye caught the faint outline of a bird on the very top of the highest chimney of "The House." Like the owner, an osprey had staked out the perfect lookout to survey his surroundings both on land and, of course, the sea, where the perfect dinner was waiting to be snatched by vise-like talons and devoured with a beak that systematically disassembled the whole into perfect bite-sized pieces. Trying to be as quiet as possible, Jackie walked closer to get a better look. The magnificent bird was born to hunt and exhibited the perfect balance of Zen-like patience combined with every nerve on edge so that when the timing was right, it would spring off the peak and throttle down on its unsuspecting catch of the day, which would be exceedingly fresher than any $39.99 fish so proudly offered at every local restaurant. This thought made Jackie giggle, and she turned her attention back to "The House."

Just then, she saw another figure, but this one was of the human variety—a man up on one of the many balconies with binoculars held up to his eyes. In all the many times that she had walked by, she had never seen, or perhaps never noticed, anyone living in the mammoth home. "So, you do exist," Jackie muttered. But the same old questions remained: *Who the heck are you? Why do you have so much, and I can barely make ends meet? I've said it before, so one more time might just add the right amount of karma to the universe: I am a fantastic person who has morals, a very rare trait these days. I'm a loyal friend who will not dime you out on social media, another rarity. And I'm actually sorta funny. Aren't those all the qualities that you want in a friend?*

Then, in a rare moment of rashness that was born from the immense fatigue that she was feeling, Jackie shouted "I BET YOU NEED A FRIEND! WHY NOT LET ME BE YOUR FRIEND? I'M A GREAT FRIEND!!"

The second the last exclamation came out of Jackie's mouth, she became instantly mortified. She spun around to see if anyone was near, and to her great relief, she was all alone on the sandy patch of beach that had become her soapbox. *Thank God! I so hope what's his name up there is hard of hearing and I can keep this little outburst to myself. Now, let's get a move on, I have only seven more minutes to get this walk finished, back to the car and home to the only person that really matters: my beautiful girl.* With that, Jackie started jogging down the beach to make up for the time she had just spent in fantasyland.

Up on the balcony, Trevor was trying to figure out what the hell just happened. At first, he admonished himself for being seen. Every other time he came out to take in the beauty of his mysterious walker, he made certain that he positioned himself perfectly so he could eye her but never be seen from her angle. What made him change his failproof strategy, he wondered. *What's wrong with you. That's risky and reckless behavior. She now knows that A) I live here, B) I look out with binoculars, and perhaps C) I look at her. Just unacceptable!*

However, the next thoughts that Trevor had were more to the emotional side of his personality that he rarely let see the light of day. *She did seem interested in me, too. Could this be a sign that it's meant to be? Couldn't quite make it out, but she seemed to be shouting something about a friend. I have no idea what that was all about, but it's a start. Yes, this screwup of yours of being in the wrong spot, although highly undisciplined, could be a blessing in disguise*

"Or," Trevor somewhat joked aloud, "I'm going to be arrested for stalking. Now that the cat is somewhat out of the bag, I definitely must come up with a plan of action to see that my budding romance is just as successful as everything else in my life."

Trevor put down his binoculars, walked in from the balcony, and readied for Andre's delectable offerings for dinner. Tonight, it was sea bass, accompanied by haricot verts and a mushroom risotto. Add a lovely sauvignon blanc, and life is good—and hopefully going to get a whole lot better.

Chapter Ten

Jackie got home just in time, rapped on the door in rhythm, and said, "Knock, knock … knock, knock, knock," and waited for the reply. Not five seconds passed when she heard "knock, knock" from the other side, and with that the door swung open with little Emily was jumping up and down excitedly waiting for her mom to swoop her up in her arms like a bird, but this one made of all love.

"Good evening, Jackie," called Maria from the kitchen. "How did your big day go?" Without waiting for a response, Maria peeked her head around the corner and said, "Dios mio! What kind of day you must have had to look like that!"

"I know, believe me, you're not the first one to point out my less than cover girl appearance. Yes, saying that it was quite a lot to take in is very much an understatement, but I plowed through the most important document today and feel like I have a good handle on it. But let's not talk work. How was your day? Did my angel live up to her billing?"

"Why, yes she did, with the exception of not wanting to

take a nap." Then, Maria turned her attention to Emily and said, "I explained to you, though, that you have to take your daily siesta so you can grow and become as beautiful as your mother, didn't I?"

Emily jutted her lower lip out a bit, but then shook her head up and down repeatedly while saying, "Yes, Miss Maria. I'll take big girl naps from now on, Miss Maria, and will grow up to be just like my mom."

Maria gave her a big hug, kissed her on the forehead, and gently said, "That's a good girl. Miss Maria loves you and your mom very much. I hope you both have a great weekend, and I'll see you on Monday." She then directed her attention to Jackie saying, "You try to rest and recharge your batteries, OK? You're going to be no use to anyone, not that highfalutin law firm, not that mystery all-important client, and especially not to your precious little girl. Oh, and I almost forgot, you also owe it to that other precious girl—you!"

Jackie hugged her saying, "Oh Maria, I love you and thanks so much for all you do to help both in actions and very valuable words. I promise, I'm going get it all figured out, and we'll be just fine. I don't have to be at work at 7:30 on Monday, but is 8 possible? We have a huge make-or-break presentation next Friday, and I need to put in some extra time."

Maria gave her a look that spoke a thousand words of admonition, but conceded, "OK, I'll be here at 7:45 all week, and then we'll have another chat. Deal?"

"Deal! Thank you, thank you, thank you! You enjoy your weekend too, and we'll see you Monday."

Maria closed the door behind her, and Jackie turned her attention back to her daughter.

"OK, Miss Emily, what do we want for dinner tonight?"

"Mac and cheese, mac and cheese!" shouted Emily, while twirling around like a jewelry box ballerina.

"Absolutely not!" Jackie said sternly. "We just had that last night, and it was only because we were celebrating my great news."

"Aren't we still celebrating?" Emily asked coyly to see if she could perhaps work the deal to get another bowl of cheesy goodness.

"Well, of course, we are still very happy, but you know we can't eat that stuff all the time. Now let's think. I know, how 'bout we make breakfast for dinner—pancakes and sausages? I know how much you love that, and you can help too, like a big girl."

Emily jumped up and down again, saying "Yay! I am the bestest stirrer in the whole world, aren't I Mommy?"

Jackie laughed and said, "Well, that's a lot to live up to, but let's get to stirring and see if you can be the World Champion Stirrer."

With that, Jackie and Emily started taking out the items needed for real pancakes: flour, baking powder, salt, sugar, eggs, milk, butter, and Jackie's secret ingredient, vanilla. *None of that boxed mix crap for us. First, they all include extra mystery stuff to extend freshness or to enhance flavor. What a bunch of hoo-ha. Plus, you save so much money when you make it yourself, and that's certainly a major bonus when you're on our meager budget. It's not like I'm making some fancy-schmancy haute cuisine delicacy. That's Mr. Beach Mansion's style, not mine.*

Jackie chuckled to herself as she thought of the image of her mystery man while measuring the dry goods. She then added the egg because she was always paranoid about Emily getting salmonella, but the rest was all Emily's.

"OK, here we go, is my first mate ready to carefully pour in the milk?" Jackie asked Emily in her favorite sea captain's voice.

"Aye-aye Captain!" shouted Emily.

"Commence pouring! Perfect. Now the most important ingredient of all. Are you sure you're up to the task?"

"Yes Captain, yes Captain!" exclaimed Emily as she played along with the imaginary roles they were acting.

"Very well, easy does it. Here's the magic serum that adds the deliciousness beyond all deliciousnesses to our pancakes," Jackie whispered as she held out the measuring spoon filled with a mere quarter teaspoon of vanilla for Emily to pour into the bowl.

"Well done, my fine young matey!" Jackie bellowed in as low a voice as she could muster. "Now take the tiller and stir away until we have a golden sea of beautiful batter, and you may become the World Champion Stirrer!"

Jackie giggled as she handed Emily the wooden spoon for her to stir, but Emily was all business. Her little cherub face was scrunched up with all the concentration that a three-year-old can summon as she went to work.

Switching back to her regular voice, Jackie instructed, "Now remember not too hard or too long though. We want our pancakes to be light and fluffy."

"OK Mommy, I won't," replied Emily.

Jackie then went to the refrigerator and took out a box of "all natural" sausage while internally chiding herself thinking, *Sure, you save some money on the pancakes and then blow it on these ridiculously expensive sausages. Wouldn't plain old Jimmy Dean do? Stop it! Of course not! Nitrates, sodium, God knows what, and preservatives out the wazoo. I will not let my little girl be filled up with all those chemicals that will come back to haunt us both. If that's being irrational and stupid, then so be it. We both had enough yellow dye #2 with that mac and cheese yesterday to last us awhile."*

Once the pancakes and sausages were both browned to perfection, Jackie prepared their plates with two apiece of each and drizzled some warmed maple syrup (of course, 100% natural) over it all. She cut Emily's into bite-sized pieces and then set the plates on the table.

Once seated, Jackie reminded Emily saying, "First, napkins on our laps." Then mother and daughter held hands and said the blessing that they say every night, "Thank you God for this day, thank you God for this meal, and especially, thank you God for each other. Amen!" With the blessing over, Jackie and Emily dug into their dinner, which was really breakfast.

Chapter Eleven

The Saturday morning sun shone through Jackie's window, and she turned away to get in a bit more relished sleep on her day off. As she was adjusting her pillow, she saw her little girl in the doorway.

"Well, good morning Sunshine," Jackie said as she had a million times before.

"Morning Mommy. Can I come in your bed?"

Unless she had a really bad dream or there was a violent thunderstorm, Jackie only let Emily into her bed on the weekends. She felt it was important for Emily to learn to be independent and self-reliant. Sometimes it was a struggle when Jackie wanted Em in bed with her almost more than Em did, but she knew it was the right thing to do.

"Climb on in my little one, but Mommy wants to sleep some more, so you try too, OK?"

"I will Mommy. I still tired too."

Always a stickler for speech and grammar, Jackie wasn't going to let Emily's mistake go, so she gently said, "It's 'I'm still tired,' not I," and then she brought her arms around Emily, pulled her close, and they both drifted off into a wonderful slumber.

Two hours passed and Jackie awoke with a start. "Oh, good Lord, it's 9:30! I can't remember the last time we slept this late. I must have been exhausted. But enough about that, we have things to do today."

"What Mommy?" Emily drowsily asked as she wiped some sleep from her eyes. "What do we have to do?"

"Well Em, you get to come with Mommy to her big office building and see the cool place where I work," Jackie said in a voice that was meant to sound like it would be a grand adventure.

"But Mommy, you never go to work on the weekends. I don't want to!" Emily said with a tone of finality.

Feeling like a lawyer instead of just a legal assistant, Jackie started to plead her case saying, "But Em, you can bring whatever toys you want, and I'll give you a very special yellow pad just like mine. You can draw on it as much as you want and, best of all, my office is waaaaaaay up on the eighth floor, so you can look out the window and see all around at the trees and birds and who knows what else. You'll see, it'll be loads of fun."

"OK, I guess," Emily gave in. "I want to see a pelican!"

"That's my girl. I can't promise, but I do see pelicans sometimes, and if we don't, I promise that we'll go to the beach afterwards where we are guaranteed to see them."

"Can we go to the beach no matter what, Mommy, please?"

"That's a deal," Jackie said as she gave Emily a big kiss on the cheek and jumped up out of bed. "Let's get a move on. Work time and beach time's a wasting," Jackie said as she assumed the voice of a southern cowgirl.

"Let's go!!!" exclaimed Emily as she ran toward her room to get dressed.

The parking lot was completely empty except for Jackie's and one other car, which belonged to Mr. Wright. Jackie was a bit hesitant as she unbuckled Emily from her car seat thinking, *I hope Mr. Wright doesn't mind me bringing her here. I have no other option, and he'll certainly appreciate my dedication on coming in. Right?*

As usual, then the other side kicked in. *But a law office is no place for a child, no less a very active three-year-old.* Back to the positive. *He made it clear that the files can't leave the building, so the only way to get work done is to come here, and Emily coming with me is the price he'll have to pay for me to get things done. Right? Right! I'm glad that's settled.*

Jackie put Emily down and held her hand as they crossed the parking lot to the big doors leading into the lobby. "Wow, Mommy, you really work here?" Emily asked as she stared up at the big office building.

Jackie was relieved that Emily seemed to be on board with the visit and answered in an excited voice, "Yes, I do, waaaaaay up there, and we're going to get to take an elevator ride up there."

They entered the building and Jackie said, "Here are the elevators. Why don't you press this button, and we'll see which one gets here first?"

Emily pushed the up button, and the right elevator dinged as it opened its doors to the lobby. Just like the parking lot, the office was a ghost town, so Jackie and Emily had the elevator to themselves. "OK, now you get to push the eight button, but let's count first."

Jackie pointed to each button as they both said out loud, "One, two, three, four, five, six, seven and then eight."

"That's the one," instructed Jackie, and Emily firmly pressed the eight button, the doors closed, and the elevator started moving up.

"Wheeeeeee, this is almost like a ride Mommy!" cried Emily with excitement.

Jackie was amazed at how a normal daily routine like riding the elevator became a magical ride when seen through the eyes of her beautiful girl. *I will have more of her enthusiasm from now on,* Jackie pledged while saying, "Wheeeee" out loud, too.

The doors opened at the eighth floor, and Jackie and Emily stepped out into the office reception area. *I guess it's best just to get this over with from the get-go,* thought Jackie as she grabbed Emily's hand and started heading toward Mr. Wright's wing of the office.

After a few steps, Jackie stopped and leaned down to Em's height and said, "Before Mommy shows you her office, I want to introduce you to my big boss. He's a very nice, but very important man, and I need you to be on your best behavior. OK?"

Emily nodded and said, "OK Mommy, I'll be good."

They continued down the hall to the double set of doors leading into Mr. Wright's office. Jackie knocked gently and said, "Hello Mr. Wright. It's Jackie. I thought it would be a good idea to come in and get some extra work done for our meeting on Friday."

In his normal well-measured voice, Mr. Wright said, "Ah,

so glad you're here Jackie and, yes, I thought the same thing. Extra hours this weekend will be critical to our success with this project."

Not wanting to be left out, Emily excitedly piped up, "And I came to help my mommy!"

Jackie awkwardly coughed as she finished pushing open the door and said, "Yes, Mr. Wright, may I introduce my daughter Emily, who, as she proclaimed, has agreed to come in and quote "help me" today."

"Well now," Mr. Wright said as he softened his tone, "how lucky is your mom to have such a special little helper. It is so very nice to meet you."

"Thank you," Emily replied and then added, "You're not as scary as I thought you'd be. Mommy is always talking about her big boss, so I thought you'd be way more bigger."

Rattled by her daughter's opining, Jackie quickly took her hand and said, "Well, I'm sure Mr. Wright is very, very busy, so we will be going now. Off to Mommy's office to get lots done. Say bye-bye."

"Bye-bye!" Emily shouted as she waved her hand back toward a widely grinning Mr. Wright.

"Bye Emily," Mr. Wright replied as Jackie closed his doors and walked to the other end of the hallway where her office was. A most relieved Jackie said, "Thank you for being such a good girl. I'm sure Mr. Wright likes you a lot. Now, I'll get you that special yellow pad that I told you about, and you can get out your crayons."

"OK, but can I please look out the window first, Mommy? It's soooooo hiiiiiigh up!"

Knowing that this whole day would be a giant balancing

act between getting work done while also not allowing Emily to get bored and cranky, Jackie agreed, "First, it's 'may I please look out the window,' not can I. But sure, you may for a while, and then I need you to be my best girl and sit down and color. First, how about we play a game?"

"A game Mommy! I love games. What is it?"

"How about you look out the window for fifteen minutes, and every time you see something special, you shout it out—a bird, a flower, an animal, a car! Even a person if you see them walking down there. Every different thing you call out, I'll write down and then we'll see how many we have at the end. Doesn't that sound like fun?"

"Yes, yes Mommy!" Emily said excitedly. "Let's start."

Jackie sat down at her desk and took out a blank legal pad for chronicling Em's finds and her other one that was filled with her jottings and notations from yesterday's digestion of Excelsior's contract. "Let's both get to work," Jackie had no more said when Emily shouted "A big black bird, Mommy!" With that enthusiastic claim, so began their day at the office together.

Jackie had a list of twenty birds (but no pelican), ten trees and bushes, three animals, and six different people: two bikers, three walkers, and another that was most excitedly announced, "Mommy look, its another mommy pushing her baby!" This proclamation was only about ten minutes into their day, but it was the end of Emily's interest in the game. "What can I do now, Mommy?" Emily asked.

Jackie looked up from her work and patiently replied, "Remember, you're going to do some special drawings on your yellow pad, just like mine. OK?"

"OK, Mommy, I'm going to draw pretty." And then she went to work on her masterpieces. Jackie also went back to the masterpieces that were Excelsior's floor plans.

There were eight units in all: three each in the single-family home and villas categories and two condos. Buyers had the choice of two bedrooms, two bedrooms plus a den, and three bedrooms. The condos had two designs; one bedroom or two. *Nothing so extraordinary about that*, thought Jackie, but as Mr. Wright loved to say, "the devil is in the details," and the more Jackie examined the plans, the more she beheld the genius of Trevor Harding once again. As was the usual Florida standard, all homes and villas were single story, and the condos were four stories high. However, because of its older population, the Excelsior models were fit with extras that would make their owners' lives much more enjoyable.

All the units had extra-wide hallways and doorways just in case the owner had to use a walker or wheelchair, either now or in the future. The same width was used for the shower door, and there was a large built-in bench to make showering easier and safer. Instead of a normal horizontal bathtub, all the tubs in these homes were an upright design for ease of getting in and out and to remove the dangers of slipping. Of course, they were also equipped with the most cutting-edge therapeutic jets to soothe achy muscles and joints. Perfect for a physically compromised older person, but also very appealing and practical for one who was still fit and able.

The kitchen was also masterfully laid out to appeal to anyone's ability, but more so for the elderly. No cabinet or counter set too high or too low, all flooring made of nonslip tile, all appliances featuring alarms if left on or open too long.

The lighting in the kitchen and throughout the home provided extra visibility for aging eyes, but none of the harshness of a too-bright bulb.

The rest of the floor plan followed suit with every attention to safety and comfort. There weren't any carpets to snag a foot or cane, no raised thresholds, every lighting switch and door handle within reach. The washer and dryer were easily accessible with a feature that made Jackie utter, "So cool!" under her breath. There was a chute from the extra-large master bedroom closet that was set at just the right pitch so the clothes would tumble into to the laundry room, where they would land in a perfectly elevated bin for ease in putting in the machine. No stooping, bending or lifting of cumbersome baskets. Once dried, the clothes would be folded on a "measured to height" table, so again, no strain to backs, knees or necks. *So simple, yet so amazing.*

Just then, Emily announced that she was done coloring and showed Jackie her scribbles. "How beautiful!" gushed Jackie at the mish-mosh of colorful swirls, twirls and dots. "I do believe you'll be a world-famous arteeest someday," laughed Jackie in a very bad French accent.

"Can you keep it on your desk, Mommy?"

"Mais oui, but of course. I'd be tres honoured to showcase such talent," Jackie continued in her pathetic attempt at sounding French.

Emily was used to her mom being silly, so she just yawned, pulled her favorite blanket to her chest, curled up in the corner and said, "Mommy, I'm going to take a nap now, just like Miss Maria asked me to."

"Great!" said Jackie as she relished the idea of some real "alone" time to continue studying the floor plans. "You take a nice nap and when you wake up, we'll go to the beach to finally see a pelican." Jackie got up from her chair, leaned over her little girl, and gave her a gentle kiss on the cheek. "Have a nice nap, my Em. Mommy loves you." Emily had already drifted off to sleep, and Jackie went back to work.

She had finished examining the homes and villas, and now onto the condo plans. Again, on the surface it seemed like your normal four-story condo with twelve units on each floor. But the master had done it again by adding not one elevator access, as is required by law, but four. *What the heck! That's soooooo much extra money,* thought Jackie as she tried to figure out why the need for so many elevators. *Oh my, I get it now. These are going to be the most elderly self-reliant residents, and they need to not have a long way to walk to get groceries and themselves to their units. Who'd a thought? The answer always comes back to Trevor Harding.* Jackie turned this thought over in her head as she continued examining the plans.

An hour passed, and Emily stirred awake. "Hi, Mommy. Are you done yet? I want to go now."

"Yes, my very good girl. I'm done for today. Let's gather our things, and it's off to the beach to track the long-awaited pelican," Jackie said as she put down her pen and closed the latest document that she was digesting.

"Yay!" exclaimed a now fully awake Emily. "Let's go!"

Mother and daughter packed their belongings and headed down the hall. Jackie stopped and called out, "Enjoy the rest of your day, Mr. Wright," to the still shut doors of his office and proceeded to the elevator while hearing a faint "You too, my dear" from Mr. Wright.

"You know what to do," Jackie reminded Emily, which

prompted her to push the button. The elevator dinged, the door opened, and Emily and Jackie stepped in. They arrived at the bottom and quickly left to enjoy the beautiful beach that was a mere five minutes away from the seriousness of law, contracts, floor plans and profit. They could hardly wait.

Jackie pulled into the parking garage and was amazed at how full it was. Normally she never had a problem finding a spot, but that was always on a weekday in the early evening. This was a Saturday midday, and the place was jam-packed, so she circled round and round until she finally found a parking spot on the top floor. "Wow, I've never been up this high in the garage."

Emily pipped in, "Yeah Mommy, we're waaaaaay up, but not as high as your elevator took us."

"True, but it looks like we have another ride coming our way," Jackie said as she unbuckled Emily from her car seat and pointed to the parking garage elevator.

"OK Mommy, but that one isn't as nice as yours."

"Now, I own an elevator," Jackie chuckled while she and Emily made their way to the bare-bones one that serviced the county parking garage. "Just so long as it does its job, I don't care what it looks like," Jackie muttered as they stepped onto the sand-covered floor and pressed one for the beach.

Jackie and Emily exited the elevator and started walking toward the beach. Now she was on familiar ground, but this time she had her little daughter in tow. This was an unplanned visit, so they didn't have any of the beach essentials with them: no bathing suits, no chairs or umbrella, no cooler or beach toys. Jackie did find some sunblock in the car that she smeared all over Emily and herself, but that was it. She was fearing that

Emily would become upset without all of their normal beach stuff, so she came up with a quick plan to reroute Emily's attention, by saying, "Hey Em, let's go on a pelican hunt and play that same game that we did at my office here at the beach. Doesn't that sound like fun?"

"Sure Mommy, I betcha there's lots of cool stuff here at the beach," Emily agreed to Jackie's great relief.

"Fantastic! Let's start our adventure by heading this way," Jackie said as she turned in the direction of "The House."

Jackie and Emily strolled hand in hand down the white sandy beach, weaving around the many sun worshipers who had staked out their territories with blankets, towels, chairs and various other beachy paraphernalia.

"Look Em, there's some cute little birdies called sandpipers over there. See how they run like they want to go swimming and then run away when the water gets close. It reminds me of you the last time we were here."

"Yes, Mommy, they are silly, but I did go in the water," Emily said proudly.

"Yes, you did, like the big girl swimmer you are."

Then Jackie raised her glance to the pristine aqua blue water that always made her realize how lucky she was to live in such a tropical paradise. *People pay beaucoup bucks to come here to enjoy what we have so close to home. Don't you ever forget to appreciate that or take it for granted,* Jackie chided herself silently as she scanned the beautiful waterscape in front of her.

Just then, the water parted, and she spotted the head then the fin of a dolphin. First one, then two, then three, then four. "Emily, Emily!" she shouted and pointed excitedly as the dolphins dove back down into the gulf. "Look over there!

There's a family of dolphins!"

"I don't see anything! Where did they go?" Emily asked pleadingly.

Jackie used her most patient mommy voice and said, "Just keep looking very carefully where I'm pointing, and they should come up again." Then she picked Emily up so she'd have a better view.

A few moments later, the dolphin pod resurfaced, letting out showers of spray from their blowholes, arched up and then forward in their never-ending rollercoaster ride through the water.

"Oh Mommy, I see them, I see them! They are soooooo cute!" Emily exclaimed. "Will they come up again?"

Jackie replied, "They will come up again, but we probably won't see them. It all depends on how long they stay under and how far they swim. Let's just be happy that we had a very special treat in seeing them at all."

"Yeah, that was super special," Emily agreed.

Jackie turned her attention to the land side of the beach and got her bearings as to where they were in relation to "The House." She debated with herself if she wanted to go down to where it was and show Em her dream home. As always, she went back and forth in her mind, making arguments for and against. *It would be cool for her to see such a magnificent home and see what you can achieve if you're successful.*

On the flipside, *Why in the world would I risk making Emily feel disappointed in where we live, once she sees the grandeur of "The House" and all the other homes that lay just down the beach? Part of my job is to keep her feeling loved and secure no matter where we live. More to the point, she didn't want her innocent daughter to be exposed to the questions that had teased Jackie relentlessly for years: Who lives there and why isn't it me?*

Of course, the second argument won the day, so Jackie turned herself and Emily around and was about to start convincing Emily why the walk had to end when a shadow passed overhead moving in the direction back to the parking garage. Two pelicans had saved the day.

"Hey, Em! There are the friends we've been looking for. They're probably flying home for the night and are showing us the way back home, too. Come on, let's follow them."

"Yay, hi Mr. and Mrs. Pelican! We're coming!" shouted Emily as if the pelicans could understand.

Jackie knew that Emily was probably nearing exhaustion and that meant the onset of crankiness, so she reached down and picked her up, put her on her shoulders, which she knew was one of Emily's favorite things, and started the walk back down the beach toward the car, home, and the last day of her old existence.

Starting Monday, and until the all-important meeting on Friday with Mr. Trevor Harding, she was going to be full-on Excelsior obsessed.

Chapter Twelve

Again, no need for an alarm, as Jackie was already up, showered and dressed, with makeup perfectly applied a half hour before her normal Monday wakeup time of 6:30. "Now what to do?" she asked herself. She couldn't leave early because Maria wasn't going to be there until 7:45. Her darling little Em was still sound asleep, and Jackie was a big believer in letting sleeping dogs and children lie. She didn't have any work papers with her because they were under lock and key at the office.

"What the heck am I going to do for the next hour and fifteen minutes?" she pondered. "I know—a checklist. I'm going to come up with the most precise checklist for everything that has to happen on each file so that every "t" is crossed twice and every "i" is dotted three times. It'll be generic in terminology so I'm not revealing Mr. Harding's version of state secrets, but it'll be essential in making sure each file is handled in the most careful, professional, efficient and cost-effective manner ever. I'm going to knock their very expensive socks off," Jackie giggled to herself.

She took out her legal pad, put her head down, and went to work until she heard a key turning the front door lock. When she looked up, she saw Maria entering with her usual big smile on her face. "My, my, Miss Jackie, you look like you're ready and raring to take on the world this morning. As a matter of fact, you look like you've already gotten a head start."

"Good morning Maria. Yeah, as you can see, I was up pretty early and thought why not get some work done."

Maria gave Jackie a nod and said, "I know you're excited and I know this is a great opportunity, but just as I tell little Emily, you too need your sleep to remain as beautiful as you are. You can't burn the candle at both ends and expect to stay in good health. I don't need to remind you that your little girl needs a happy, healthy momma, and you need to take care for your own sake, too."

Jackie nodded her head in what she hoped was a convincing fashion and replied, "I know Maria. I'll make sure I keep a limit on my obsession with this project."

Maria laughed and said, "You used the word obsession, not me. Now get going so you can enter your future. God bless you, my dear."

Jackie gave Maria a kiss on the cheek and said, "Oh thank you Maria, I am already so blessed to have someone as special as you in my life. No walk tonight, so I'll be home right after work. Love you!"

Jackie closed and locked the door, got in her car, and sped down the street to the office.

The elevator doors opened to the lobby of her office just like they did every Monday since she started working there, but today was different. Today, she made very quick work of saying hi to her coworkers, she grabbed a cup of coffee from the breakroom, and went immediately into her office to get right to the Excelsior project.

Before starting, however, she buzzed her assistant Karen and told her that they'd both be working on their own this week. She needed Karen to follow through on the existing regular files to make sure things were progressing as they should. She told her that she was only to be disturbed if it was completely necessary and something was truly blowing up.

She emphasized her instructions by saying, "And that doesn't mean when some overbearing, excitable real estate agent who thinks the world revolves around their piddly little deal starts jumping up and down over some minor hiccup. It has to rise to the level of a true emergency, Karen. We've done a million and one closings, and I have faith that you can handle almost everything that comes along. I'm going to be immersed in this new project and need absolutely every second possible if I'm going to get this all done. Got it?" she added.

Karen replied, "You got it, Jackie. I'll try to run interference as much as possible so you can hammer your brains out with whatever this monstrosity of a project is. I just hope the client isn't a monster to go along with it."

Jackie thanked her and truly hoped so, too.

The checklist that she had started at home was the first order of business as she now had the actual documents in front of her to double-check that she hadn't missed anything.

Jackie started talking to herself, "Let's see, I've done this checklist so it's in chronological order from the first viewing of the models, to the selecting of a lot/unit, to the floor plan, to the boilerplate contract terms that are included in all contracts, to the custom arrangements and personal selections for each buyer, to the financing terms, the inspection periods, the title commitment and its requirements, to the actual closing, post-closing and, in another stroke of Harding brilliance, follow-ups with the purchasers at one month, three months, six months, and a year after closing to ensure that they were satisfied and pleased with their new home. Did I get everything?"

Just then, Ryan poked his head in the door and asked, "Who in the world are you talking to?"

Jackie jumped a little as she was startled out of her thoughts. "Oh, hi Ryan," she replied. "I'm just talking to myself. Don't you know that all geniuses talk to themselves? I recommend you try it if you want to get past hauling files," Jackie joked.

"Well, Miss Mumbles, I also heard that most mass murderers heard voices in their heads and talked to themselves too, so which is it?" Ryan retorted.

"I'll stick with genius, and if talking to myself helps Trevor Harding, I will never shut up with this verbal dialog because he is the Albert Einstein of real estate development."

Ryan looked at her quizzically and said, "Trevor who and why do you look so enamored?"

Quickly realizing that she had said too much, Jackie waved her hand casually and said, "Oh, he's just some big-shot real estate guy in Australia that I've been following, and I'm certainly not enamored—just an admirer of his brain, nothing more," Jackie lied somewhat defensively.

"OK, whatever. I'm around enough brainpower here during the week. The last thing I'm going to do is waste my free time on real estate mogul mania, especially those from different countries. The playoffs are going on for God's sake."

Jackie was relieved when she realized that Ryan's obsession was not work-related in the least but the world of sports, which he followed like a total groupie. She thanked her lucky stars that her slip of the tongue wasn't damaging and vowed not to let any other detail, no matter how small, come out of her mouth until after Friday. Hopefully, then she and Mr. Wright could announce for the whole world to hear that they were the sole closing agent for Trevor Harding's latest and most impressive development to date—

Excelsior!

Jackie looked up at Ryan and teased, "You have your interests and I have mine. That's what makes the world go around. Now, scram! I have lots to do as I trust you do too, oh law clerk extraordinaire!"

Ryan sighed and said, "Yes, today's very challenging mission is to update the law library. What a totally archaic job. Has anyone ever heard of the ability to access case law online? However, as we know, Mr. Wright is an old-school kind of guy who likes things the way he's used to them."

Jackie cringed at Ryan's impertinence and replied, "Mr. Wright can have things any damn way he wants them. He does write your paycheck, and your future employment with this firm depends on his opinion of you and your work, so I'd button your somewhat overactive mouth and do your job, no matter what it is. Now out with you!"

Jackie put her head down dismissively toward Ryan so he'd realize that the conversation was over and turned to her computer screen. Talking to herself again, she said, "OK, now let's put all these items on a spreadsheet so each file has a common corresponding tracking system of things that must get done and the timeline associated with each."

An hour or so had passed, and Jackie was pleased with the system that was starting to take shape. As her mother used to say, "A place for everything and everything in its place." This was just her version for Excelsior—meticulous, exacting and complete.

She reviewed everything again and noticed that she had missed a very important category—the clients' color selections for each room in the house. At first, she thought this was total overkill and outside of the realm of her work. However, after reading the material on this, she realized how important it was to each home and, more importantly, the experience of the elderly homeowner.

It's called color psychology, and Mr. Harding was a big proponent. Every color has a big effect on our brain and mood and can set the stage for a wonderful living experience or a total disaster.

As she looked through the guide for the colors allowed in each room, she learned that every color had an impact, negative or positive, and the selections were regulated to this end. For example, red was not allowed to be used in living spaces as it has been shown to raise people's blood pressure, respiration and heart rates. A kiss of perhaps literal death when dealing with an older population. Crimson is attributed to triggering anger, which could certainly exacerbate this common side effect of stroke or Alzheimer's disease.

Jackie continued reviewing the guide and learned that quite the opposite to red, warm hues of blue achieved a completely different reaction. Blood pressure went down, as did heart rate and respiration. It also instilled a feeling of calm, relaxation and serenity. Dark blue was totally nixed though, because it made people sad. *How perfect is this plan for our clients*, thought Jackie, who was again amazed at the complete thoroughness of each detail of the Excelsior master plan.

Yellow was permitted, but only in small rooms like a kitchen where it would exude happiness, but not larger rooms like living rooms because then it totally flipped its effect and solicited frustration and maybe even a temper.

Jackie smiled to herself and muttered, "Mr. Harding and Excelsior are all about keeping the peace."

Thus, the bedrooms were to be either the warm blues she had already read about or soft greens, which prompted feelings of restfulness, lower stress, and relaxation. Soft grey was also an option, but not too steely, as that made one feel cold, a chronic condition among older people. It also made people feel not engaged, another all-too-often feeling with seniors that could lead to isolation.

For those units with dens, lavender was the highly suggested color because it contributes to serenity and mindfulness—a perfect setting for reading, keeping up on emails, or doing whatever personal hobby they may pursue.

Beiges, tans and browns were only to be used in very small doses because, although calming, they can also go toward nondescript, which could make the owner feel the same way.

The verbiage read: "Here at Excelsior, we know every aspect of your home is a part of your living experience. We are 100% committed to providing everything we can to allow every owner the means to live life to the fullest, to ensure that with each day your living experience is an amazing one that completely satisfies your needs and provides an atmosphere in which you will not only live, but thrive. Our scientifically based color selection process is another cutting-edge advancement that we provide to make the quality of your life better than you ever could imagine."

Jackie leaned back in her chair, sighed and said, "Damn, don't I wish I could live there. I'd be happy, serene and, the thing I dream of most, stress free! A money-back guarantee, Mr. Harding. Right?"

Chapter Thirteen

Trevor Harding had already been on site for three hours and it was only 10 o'clock. He had spent most of the first hour in the construction trailer going over plans for the next phase of Excelsior. The infrastructure and utilities had been installed, and now it was time to get building. This was when Trevor really came alive, when he could start seeing the hands-on fruits of his vivid vison for a community unlike any other. He relished the intense planning for everything from the models to the clubhouse, to the medical center, to the wide-ranging amenities.

These concrete, solid, real-life assets were what made Trevor never doubt his decision to turn his back on the Wall Street life that he had been destined for. Where his world was filled with buildings made of wooden trusses, cement blocks, drywall and clay tiles, the make-believe financial world was based on speculation, projections and theories. Sure, both can make you a lot of money, but Trevor wanted nothing to do with what he considered the shell game sham of the bulls and bears.

"Good morning, Pete," Trevor said cheerfully to his project manager when he walked into the trailer at exactly 8 o'clock. "This is certainly an exciting day. Looks like we're ready to start building our model homes and condos."

"Yes, sir, Mr. Harding," answered Pete. "The lots for all three single-family homes and the other three villa lots have been cleared and filled, and we're ready to lay the slabs. As you instructed, the condos will be in the next phase and will be sold now from floor plans."

"Correct, Pete." Mr. Harding then explained, "The permits for the condos are taking a bit longer than anticipated, but I don't want to wait to get the other buildings completed ASAP. As you well know, floor plans and drawings don't get the job done; they rarely clinch the deal. People like to see and touch the real thing, and I don't blame them. When it's real, they can wrap their brains around imagining themselves living in whatever home they're buying. Especially with the older population who's our target market. They're not prone to taking risks this late in life, so we need to make them feel confident and secure that Excelsior is going to be the last but best major investment of their lives."

Pete had been working for Mr. Harding from the very beginnings of his foray into the world of real estate development and had heard this or very similar sermons from his boss a million times, but he convincingly bobbed his head up and down as if it was a moment of epiphany and said, "You are one hundred percent right, Mr. Harding. People that age aren't even going to buy a tomato unless they go to the store, pick it up, feel its ripeness, maybe give it a smell, and then they'll drop the 69 cents for it. They definitely are less likely to drop hundreds of thousands of dollars on a home, no matter how fantastic the floor plan and brochure make it sound."

Mr. Harding laughed at this very accurate analogy and said, "That's why I keep you around, Pete. You see it like the average Joe without the all the BS. Now, a lot less talk and a whole lot more action. Let's go."

With that, Trevor and Pete walked down the trailer steps, hopped into Pete's company-owned heavy-duty pickup with all the bells and whistles, and headed out to the building sites.

The first ones they pulled up to were the sites for the single-family homes. There were three options, and the lots were sized according to the type of home and the ever-present reality of an older population. Some may need three bedrooms and two baths because they have family who make frequent visits, so there was a plan for them, all functionally designed in a manageable 1,600 square feet, where there were no wasted areas that in a traditional home became unused and cleaning nightmares. The two-bedroom, two-bath plus a den was a bit more scaled down at 1,500 square feet, and the final two-bedroom, two-bath model was 1,400 square feet of efficiently placed rooms, hallways and closets, which gave the owner a feeling of totally manageable space.

The lots were also designed with the single-family mentality in mind, but such that they would never become a maintenance burden. Each homeowner got to choose the ratio of lawn to garden and plantings. If one liked the exercise of mowing, their lawns would be ample, but not overwhelming. If a garden was more to your liking, the lawn area would be smaller and more beds would be allotted to accommodate the plants, flowers and shrubs chosen by the individual to suit their tastes and needs.

The villa lots were of a similar design, but even more scaled down because these owners most likely did not like yardwork and so it became a necessity, not a pastime. Thus, they were designed for esthetics only and ease of care for the homeowner or landscape company.

Right now, however, these promising pieces of framed-off dirt were exactly that—dirt—and Trevor wasn't fond of dirt, so he looked at Pete and demanded, "Where are the cement trucks? They should be here by now!"

Pete tried to calm him down by replying confidently, "Mr. Harding, I was told by Tom at County Cement that they would have twelve trucks here by 8:30. It's only twenty after, so please let's just wait a few. Tom has never let us down before, and he knows there are at least fifteen other companies that would die for this contract. I mean who uses two trucks for every slab, so it's poured faster and ready for construction in half the time?"

Trevor looked sternly at Pete and said, "I do, and I pay for it. That's why they had better not be late! I have a very strict timeline to adhere to."

As soon as the words left Trevor's mouth, the loud noise of tires rolling and metal banging echoed down the road followed by a caravan of a dozen huge cement trucks with their gigantic containers whirring around, mixing the soon-to-be foundations for Excelsior's first model homes.

"Well, it's about time!" shouted Mr. Harding to the lead truck in which the supervisor was a passenger. "Come on, get out," he said as the man opened the door. "Time's wasting. Two trucks to every lot and start pouring. Tell your men to be quick about it, but I don't want them to be sloppy. We pride ourselves on doing things right around here and now that you're

FINALLY here, you will do the same."

The supervisor looked a bit shell-shocked but started calling out orders to his crew, basically regurgitating what Mr. Harding had just said.

Trevor looked around, put his hands on his hips, and uttered in a satisfied way, "Yes, this is the real beginning of my dream and the dreams of all who will live here, who will grow old here and, yes, will most likely die here. Excelsior, it is time to come to life!"

Chapter Fourteen

The days at the firm that week went by in much the same manner every day. Jackie went over and over every detail of the mighty Excelsior project so that by Friday she would be ready. The contract, floor plans and brochures all had to be committed to memory. The requirements to be fulfilled regarding title must be understood like a well-versed poem. The documents to draw up, surveys to review, punch lists to prepare, closing statements to calculate all contained variables, depending on each file, but the process that accompanied each had to be drummed into Jackie's brain to the point of it becoming an integral part of her being. She must be relentless.

Every day at 4:45, Mr. Wright came into Jackie's office and asked the same question, "So Jackie, on a scale of one to ten, where are you in your knowledge and confidence about Excelsior?"

Jackie knew better than to exaggerate her grade to Mr. Wright, so she was very prudent in her assessment each day.

Monday she replied, "Mr. Wright, I do feel like I'm getting

a good grasp of it all, but I'd only give it a four."

Mr. Wright nodded and replied, "Well, that's better than a two, but we both know that we need a ten if not a twelve by Thursday afternoon before our Friday meeting."

"I know sir. After my work on Saturday and today, I really feel like I'm turning a corner with all of this, starting to understand the guiding principle behind this amazing project. Mr. Harding and Excelsior are always looking to do things better and provide more than has ever been experienced before, and I want to show him that our firm is the perfect complement to his vision."

"Well said, Jackie." Mr. Wright nodded again. "We have to convince him through our extra due diligence and dedication that we also share the same convictions to the highest standards. I'm certain you'll be there by Thursday afternoon when we meet for the last gauging of your confidence."

Tuesday, Jackie reported that she had climbed the rating ladder to a six but decided to forego her beach walk so she could use the extra hour to prepare more. Wednesday, she told Mr. Wright that she was a strong eight, to which he replied, "Sometimes the last two steps in any journey can be the hardest, but also the most satisfying. I know you'll push yourself to the proverbial top." He gave her a pat on the shoulder, nodded his head in encouragement, left her office, and left her immersed in her thoughts, which turned to those of self-doubt and alarm. *What the hell was I thinking when I took on this monster. I have one measly day left to get this all hammered out and look like an Excelsior master. Can I really pull this off?*

As usual, her debate then went in the other direction, and she chided herself like a school marm. *What do you mean, can you pull this off? Not only can you do it, but you will do it. You know all this stuff like the back of your hand, and the presentation video is awesome, so stop the nonsense. The only thing that stands between you and success is self-belief. Now stop being a Debbie Downer and start jacking it up like the Jackie you are.* She laughed out loud at her silly pun, closed the files on her desk, and finally got up to go home to the light of her life, little Miss Emily.

Chapter Fifteen

Trevor Harding was also just finishing up his day, except he really didn't have anyone or anything to go home to. Remembering that it was Wednesday, he couldn't even look forward to watching "her" walk the beach and try to think of ways to transform their brief, weird, yet somehow promising last encounter into a longer, more sane and assuredly more promising relationship. Tonight, however, was not one of her beach nights and, regrettably, he'd had to work late yesterday so he missed her then, too. *What should I do now?* he thought as he got behind the wheel of his matte gray Tesla sports car.

I could go to the office and get more work done. There's always plenty of that. Then, in a high soft voice that mirrored his mother's when she would admonish his father, Trevor said, "Now, that's enough for the day, dear. You can't solve all the world's problems in one day. It's time for you to put work on the back burner and do something else. Why don't you take a nice swim and then we'll enjoy a lovely dinner. Then, you can relax with that book you've been enjoying."

Trevor smiled at the thought of his demure, calm, and oh-so classy mother. If his father, Pierce Harding, exemplified the steely cold and calculating focus and determination that personified his being a pillar of the Wall Street establishment, his mother, Elaine, was the perfect foil and counteragent for him. She was gentle, warm, understanding, a bit on the silly side, and everyone's soft place to fall if necessary.

"God, how I miss her!" Trevor said achingly for the umpteenth time. *She would have loved Excelsior with all its features, which are people oriented, not just profit driven. I so wish I could share my dream that is finally becoming reality with her.* Trevor then dropped his head and sighed, still grieving for his mother who had passed away eleven years before.

He remembered that she hated the fact that Trevor and Pierce were at odds, and even though outwardly she had to support her husband's decision to let Trevor succeed or fail on his own, she inwardly hoped and very often literally prayed that her son would prove Pierce wrong and exceed beyond anything he or she could dream of.

Of course, she had been as initially shocked as her husband when Pierce came home from the office, bellowing about "How dare their son turn away from his rightful place on the Street! Doesn't he know that he's throwing away his future? He doesn't have the first clue what he's getting into!" How "the way things are done in God-forsaken Florida are going to make Trevor's eyes spin!" How "I am not going to be part and parcel to this guaranteed train wreck."

Then he stopped flipping through the mail, looked at Elaine, and sternly said, "I know you're not going to like this, but it had to be done." Then without letting his wife respond, he finished his pronouncement, "I told Trevor that he is on his own."

It took all of Elaine's self-control to not become emotional, but she knew that showing concern or care would not get her anywhere with Pierce because he would view it as illogical, weak, and merely acting hysterical. So, she swallowed hard, looked her husband in the eye and said, "Pierce, I'm sure that this news of Trevor's is not what you wanted to hear, and I'm taken aback by it as well, but he is such a smart boy. I'm sure he has thought this through."

"I don't give a damn what he thought or didn't think, I will have nothing to do with it."

"Now Pierce," Elaine said in her most comforting, yet not condescending voice, "Trevor didn't ask you for any money, did he?"

"No," Pierce sharply replied. "That's not the point. His money or my money doesn't matter. This is a bad investment, plain and simple."

"Well dear, you always say that someone has to take the risks that others won't to really make it big. Maybe our boy is that someone."

Pierce just harrumphed and muttered, "Doubt it and won't be associated with it."

Elaine knew that the subject was now closed and there would be no further discussion about it, so she calmly told her husband what was for dinner and left the room.

Elaine—the mom, not the wife—then quietly went about reassuring Trevor that all would be all right, that it would just take time, but that his father would come around. Then she added, "And the best way to make your father come around is to carry out this dream of yours in the most successful way possible. Do everything right, aboveboard and, most of all, make money and lots of it!"

Those words guided Trevor from the moment she gave voice to them to this very moment as he drove home. Tragically, she only got to see the beginning of all that he would do and succeed at with his Florida developments, which ended up being acclaimed throughout the real estate world, because she was diagnosed with lung cancer just when his first community Eclat was coming to fruition. Nonetheless, she was always supportive, forever positive and had an abiding faith in him that made him strive harder, be more focused, push the boundaries—all to make his mother proud. By the time he was what the real estate periodicals called an "overnight success," Trevor had been slaving away every day for three years to make his dream a reality, all while his beloved mother, his constant cheerleader, was wasting away with cancer and finally passing away.

The funeral for Elaine Margaret Whitehead-Harding was held at Saint John the Divine with the bishop of the Episcopal Diocese of New York presiding. Father and son, Pierce and Trevor, were sitting dutifully together in the first pew. The service and it's gathering afterward were the height of propriety and decorum with both Harding men playing their roles accordingly.

"Yes, she will certainly be missed," Pierce Harding said genuinely for the thousandth time, as he, indeed, would miss his wife's company. Somehow, she always knew how to deal with the demands of being his wife. She overlooked the long hours, the constant pull of work over family. She even had a way of handling her high-pressure husband that allowed him to decompress, almost to the point of relaxing. The true magic of it, however, was that she weaved her spell in such a way as to make Pierce think that he was in charge and that it was his own doing.

Across the room, Trevor was shaking hands with his cousin, Mark, whom he hadn't seen since he moved to Florida. "I'm so sorry for your loss, Trevor. Aunt Elaine was always my favorite. She had such class but also an incredible warmth. She will certainly be missed."

Trevor nodded and tried to stay composed. "Thanks Mark. I know what you mean. She was an amazing lady and such a great mother."

"I'm sure it was hard for you being all the way down in Florida. By the way, how's all that going? You sure sent your father for a loop when you decided to go out on your own."

Trevor knew that the subject of his leaving the eternal Harding march of success through the streets of lower Manhattan and moving to Florida would come up, so he had some prerehearsed lines ready. All of them purposely ignored any query into the Pierce-Trevor relationship.

"Thanks for asking, Mark. Yes, it was hard not to be here in person for my mother, but we spoke every day and I'm so thankful for that. As far as my Florida developments, they're doing very well. We've wrapped up my first project, Eclat, and it's exceeded all expectations. I'm now turning my attention to the next one in our pipeline. If you're ever in Florida, I'd be more than happy to show you around, but right now, I have to make the rounds here. So many people taking the time to pay their respects. Mother would have loved that."

Trevor patted Mark on the back and headed into the sea of relatives, business associates, club members, socialites, and neighbors from both the city and out east who had all gathered at Elaine's funeral for many different reasons. Some to perhaps just make an appearance out of obligation, not only to Elaine but certainly also to Pierce—one did not want to be counted among the missing when Pierce took a tally of the crowd. Some came because they, too, thought of Elaine as a favorite aunt or cousin. Some showed up because of loyalty and love for a dear and trusted friend. For whatever the reason, over a hundred people came to say their last good-byes to Elaine Margaret Whitehead-Harding.

The two people who didn't have to construct a reason to be there were Pierce and Trevor Harding. They were there because the one person who meant everything to them was no longer. That single common ingredient should have been enough for them to throw away their need to be the one who wins, to let her love for both of them thaw the cold war that was in its third year of conflict, to bring them to their senses and show them that when it comes to life and death, who's right and who's wrong becomes irrelevant and meaningless.

This detente, however, was not to be for Elaine's beloved husband Pierce and dearest son Trevor. Of course, they carried out their bereaved husband and son duties faithfully and without incident, but they moved around each other as if there was a foul circle painted an arm's length away from each other and there would be a penalty flag thrown if it was invaded. Handshakes were given, but nothing more. A few words exchanged about what a wonderful woman Mother was, but nothing that would let the other see their true feelings and love for her. The stiff upper lip had never been so rigid when it came to them showing their grief around each other, with only a bowing of the head or a nod when discussing their loss.

When everyone had left the reception and there were only the two of them in the cavernous banquet room, Pierce walked over to his son and said, "Well Trevor, I think she would have been happy with how things went."

Trevor did one of his nods again and said, "Yes Father, I think it was a lovely way for all to say good-bye. There are a lot of people who will miss her."

"True," Pierce said stoically. "Now, if I'm remembering correctly, you have an early morning flight back to the land of sunburns, snakes and swamp holes."

Instead of nodding, Trevor just shook his head and said, "Yes, your memory is ironclad, as usual. I'll be leaving early tomorrow morning." Then Trevor decided to test the waters by saying, "By the way, our development Eclat is completed, and the numbers are very positive. We'll begin our next project shortly."

Pierce looked his son in the eye and said, "Not bad, but long term is the true litmus test for any investment, not just one lucky fluke. I'm not sold yet." He then put out his hand for one last shake, walked to the elevator, and left Trevor's life again.

Chapter Sixteen

"Mommy, Mommy, Mommy! I'm sooooo happy you're home! I missed you soooo much!" Emily exclaimed as Jackie walked through the door.

"Hi Em! Wow, what a welcome! I missed you too!" replied Jackie as she folded her daughter into a big hug. Then she looked up to see Maria smiling at them.

"Nothing is as sweet as a mama and child embracing," Maria said and added, "How are things at the office? One more day until it's showtime!"

"AHHHH, don't say that!" Jackie quickly snapped.

"Oh, I'm so sorry Jackie. I didn't mean to upset you," Maria said while rubbing Jackie's back.

"No, I'm sorry for overreacting. It's just all coming to a head, and even though I have a really good handle on everything, I'm still so stressed out about Friday."

"What's Friday, Mommy?" Emily piped in.

Jackie tried to come up with a way to make the enormity of Friday's meeting make sense to a child, so she sputtered out,

"Well Emily, remember how we went to mommy's office last Saturday and how I had all those papers and things I was looking at?"

"Yes, Mommy. That was also when we counted all those things and we rode elevators and we went to the beach and saw dolphins and pelicans. We had lots of fun!"

Maria and Jackie both smiled at how Emily had just taken an overwhelmingly burdensome thought in their adult minds and transformed it into a day of fun. So with a much lighter attitude, Jackie continued, "Well, all those papers are super important, and Mommy has been reading them a lot so I can remember what they say. On Friday, I'm going to be meeting with a man to show him how well I remember everything."

"Oh Mommy," Emily laughed, "You'll do great. You never forget anything. Even when I forget to brush my teeth, you always remember."

Jackie and Maria both burst into laughter, and they all gave each other hugs. Then Maria said, "OK ladies, it's time for Miss Maria to say adios for the evening." She gave each of them a kiss on the cheek, gathered her things, and closed the door behind her.

Jackie turned to Emily and said, "What are we having for din-din tonight?"

Emily rubbed her tummy and said, "That's another reason why I'm so happy that you're home. Miss Maria made my favorite—chicken fingers and sweet potato fries. I can hardly wait to eat them."

"Yummy!" agreed Jackie and continued, "Now go wash your hands, let's say our blessing, and then we'll get to work polishing off those crunchy morsels of deliciousness."

Jackie and Emily did exactly that. Every last chicken finger was dunked into either honey mustard (Jackie) or ketchup (Emily) until all sixteen were history. Same went for the fries, which weren't fried at all but baked to Jackie's healthy standards. Of course, they also nibbled on the carrots, celery, cherry tomatoes and cucumber slices that Maria prepared to add the required vegetable portion to their meal.

Having finished, Jackie picked up the plates from the table and went to the kitchen sink, while Emily continued to sit at the table. "Come on, Em, you know the deal—if you have enough energy to eat, you have enough energy to help clean up."

"I know Mommy, but I was just thinking. Why do all the other kids have a daddy and a mommy, and I only have you?"

Jackie stopped in her tracks. She had always known that this question would come one day, and she'd gone over a million ways to answer, but now that Emily had actually uttered the words, Jackie was at a loss for what to say. She suddenly felt a shame that she had never thought would be associated with the birth of her beautiful baby girl. It was guttural rather than emotional, like someone had knocked the wind out of her. She took a long, deep breath to regain her composure, put the plates down on the counter, and walked over to Emily and sat down.

"Here Em, come sit on Mommy's lap," she said as she patted her legs. Then she swallowed hard and continued while Emily was climbing up. "You're right. A lot of other families have a daddy and a mommy, but there are some that only have a mommy and some only have a daddy. There are many reasons why, and everyone has their own story, just like your books have lots of different stories."

As she always did when she was deciding on or trying to

understand something, Emily scrunched her nose and asked, "I guess, but what's our story? Why isn't our daddy here with us?"

Again, Jackie felt the pit of her stomach lurch, and all those chicken fingers and fries started to seem like a really bad idea. She didn't want to lie, but to tell her precious daughter that her father didn't even want her to come into the world was not happening. She also had to somehow figure out a way to explain away the fact that her father had never even tried to see her or be involved in her life one iota.

She decided to take the middle ground, semi-truth path and started to gently explain. "Well, Em, you know how much I love you and you know how we just said 'especially, thank God for each other,' in our blessing?"

Emily nodded up and down, so Jackie haltingly continued. "We have each other and love each other the mostest, right?" Again, Emily nodded. "Well, sometimes mommies and daddies don't have that same love. They don't get along well, so it's best that they aren't together." Jackie looked at Emily who still had her nose crinkled, so she carried on. "You know when we're watching The Katie and Cassidy show and sometimes the twins don't get along and their mommy has to put them in timeout where they go to different rooms?"

Emily nodded, but added "Yes, but that's because they were bad. Is my daddy bad?"

Jackie thought to herself, *Oh Lord, now what do I say?* but continued on, "Well, no, he's not bad, but he and I were like the twins, except we didn't get along at all, so it's best for all of us for him to be on his own and you and me be together. Remember, there are lots of families just like us."

Much to Jackie's relief, just like that, Emily hopped off

her lap, said "OK, Mommy." She then picked up her plate and walked to the kitchen to help clean up.

Jackie, on the other hand, felt as if she had just finished a marathon. She was exhausted not only from work, but from the even greater stress of the dance that she just performed through the minefield of the truths, half-truths, and lies that she wove so Emily could start to understand her life's story. Jackie knew that this was only the beginning of that journey, and she hoped with all her heart that she handled it OK, and as Emily grew, Jackie, too, would grow in her ability to explain the painful truths of the past.

Chapter Seventeen

Trevor was still reminiscing about his mother when he pulled into his garage. "What I would do to meet someone half as wonderful as her," he thought out loud. Then he followed it up with another of his mother's sayings, "When it's meant to be, it will show itself. In the meantime, to thine own self be true." He climbed out of his car, shut the door, and sarcastically said, "I know Mom, but thine own self could use a little company."

Then he went upstairs to find Andre at work in the kitchen. Tonight's dinner was shrimp and scallops served with a Mediterranean sauce of fresh tomatoes, artichokes, onions, basil, garlic, and finished with a hint of white wine. This light but flavorful dish would be served over homemade pasta and accompanied by Trevor's favorite salad. Unbelievably simple but supremely delicious, it consisted of arugula, olive oil, lemon, salt, pepper, and shaved Parmigiano-Reggiano.

"Now Andre," Trevor said as he took a seat at the counter, "You know that I'd be a very happy man if all you served me was that amazing salad."

"I know, Mr. Harding," Andre replied. "But I have to make myself look worthwhile. Plus, with all this work you've been doing, you've lost weight and can't afford to drop any more."

"Why Andre, I never knew you cared," Trevor said teasingly. They both laughed and Trevor inquired, "What time should I plan on eating this magnificent creation of yours?"

"Whenever it suits you Mr. Harding. It's 6:30 now."

"OK. I'm going to swim some laps, then take a shower, so let's plan on 7:30."

Andre nodded and said, "You got it. If it's OK with you, I'm going to pair tonight's meal with a lovely sparkling wine from California."

"Sounds great. Thanks for respecting my wishes and only serving American-made wines in my home. I understand that France, Italy and other countries have marvelous products, but we have to support our own."

"Yes, Mr. Harding. Our vineyards are certainly improving in quality and variety, so I'm not as stubborn as I used to be. I'll meet you in the dining room at 7:30."

Trevor went to his bedroom and changed into his bathing suit. As he looked in the mirror, he did notice that he had slimmed down some and agreed with Andre that any more weight loss would be too much, thinking, *After all, part of the model of being a successful businessman is having a healthy and vigorous body type that portrays strength and confidence.*

Trevor loved to swim, not only because it was such a total body workout, but more so because it was so serene. The water blocked everything else out, and it was just him and his thoughts. Surprisingly, the water also had a magical way of blocking out negative thoughts. Trevor never thought about his father when he was swimming, nor the latest problem with permitting or schedules or whatever. When in the water, all his thoughts were focused on what's next, how to make things better and more appealing to his customer, more successful—not in a dollar-and-cents kind of way, but in ways to meet his residents' needs. Trevor looked at the pool as his Menlo Park, his laboratory for the experiments of his mind. Many of his best ideas—his perfect laundry chute, his use of color psychology, his radical idea to guarantee that no one will ever take a loss on their property— all came to him as he followed the line on the bottom of the pool back and forth for thirty minutes each day.

However, as he jumped in to start his routine of swimming while pondering, he made an executive decision that from to- morrow on, his swim would be cut to fifteen minutes, because it burned too many calories. It would also be on the tail end of his workout so he wouldn't be tempted to cheat and do more, because dinner would be waiting. The first half hour, he would now go to his very underused gym and work on strength training. More lifting and less aerobics, so his frame would fill out again to its impressive form that most took notice of and helped him command whatever setting he found himself in.

I have to bulk up a bit to fit the bill of man in charge, he thought as he made a flip turn. *So, you had better make good use of the fifteen-minute brainstorming session you're going to give yourself every day in the pool,* he chided to himself and then turned out those thoughts and let himself fall into the world of his underwater think tank.

Thirty minutes later, Trevor emerged from the pool with what he thought could be a groundbreaking idea for how the medical care aspect of Excelsior was going to develop. This part of the project always gave him fits because it had nothing to do with what he was an expert in. He knew all about dirt, fill and lots; all about plans: site plans, architectural plans, floor plans, marketing plans; all about concrete, lumber, drywall, trusses, windows, roofing. Everything that had to do with seeing a real estate venture come into being, he was at the top of his game, but this community was to have a medical care facility that residents would move to when their health was such that they couldn't live on their own and they needed more advanced care. This he knew nothing about, and Trevor hated the feeling of not knowing.

Tonight, while under the water, an idea struck him that was so obvious he couldn't believe that he hadn't thought of it before. *I will retain the nation's most preeminent authority on medicine and aging, and we will form a joint venture.* "It's brilliant!" Trevor announced out loud to no one while toweling off.

Chapter Eighteen

Thursday morning arrived, and Jackie was up an hour before her alarm again. She was thinking about what was on her agenda today and trying to come up with a schedule that would maximize each minute of her last day of preparation before meeting with Trevor Harding on Friday. *Let's see, first things first, what am I most unsure of? I know the contracts down pat, I might as well live in each of the floor plans I know them so well, the title requirements are seared in my brain, the presentation video is perfect, what's missing?* she asked herself again, and then it hit her. *Tomorrow, I'm having a meeting with probably the most important person I've ever met, and I virtually don't know anything about him except that he is the owner of Prestigious Properties of Florida and he's the developer of Excelsior.*

Then she used her third-person voice and said, "Jackie honey, you had better do some serious research today and, as your mother always told you, know your audience so you can wow them."

The door opened and Maria stepped in as Jackie simultaneously stepped out. "Sorry I don't have time to chat. Gotta get going, Maria. I've got some very important work to do," Jackie said as she gave Maria a glancing hug.

"I know, I know, you always have something important to do, and this is the last day to prepare, so off with you, but make sure you don't use your extra hour today at work. You need to take your walk more than you need to review those papers for the millionth time. Do you have your walking clothes?"

Jackie came to a halt, turned around and ran past Maria saying, "Oh crap! How in the world could I forget them? They're on my bed." She raced into her room, grabbed her gym bag and ran past Maria again, while Maria laughed and said, "You forgot them because you're so wrapped up in your work world that you're missing what's around you." She poked her head out of the still open door and called, "Hopefully, after tomorrow you can pick your head up and start enjoying the rest of life again. Love you!"

Jackie didn't have the time to address Maria's concerns, so she rolled down the window and quickly replied, "Love you too!" and then pulled out of the driveway and drove to work to start her thorough investigation of Mr. Trevor Harding.

Once she briefly said her hellos to the office staff and poured herself a cup of coffee, Jackie closed her office door, situated herself behind her computer and went to Google, because she thought that was always the best and easiest place to start when you wanted to learn about something or, more to the point, learn about someone. She typed in Trevor Harding, took a deep breath and hit enter. Google did its usual lightning-speed magic and hundreds of postings appeared before Jackie's eyes. "Holy smokes!" Jackie muttered to herself. "This might take all day to get through, and I don't have all day. Let's start with the Wikipedia page first, and we'll go from there." She double-clicked on the entry, and a lengthy article came up with the history of, facts about, and even a photo of Trevor Harding.

"Wow, I so didn't expect him to be so good looking," Jackie said to the screen as she took in the shot of him dressed to the nines in a perfectly tailored business suit. His hair was jet black with just the hint of some gray starting around the temples. He was holding blueprints of something, which gave him the air of a man in charge. "Boy am I glad I'm doing my recon now because if he walked into tomorrow's meeting without me getting this preview, I'd be totally blindsided. He certainly is a charmer."

Then Jackie started to read: Trevor Alexander Harding, Real Estate Developer. Owner and Chief Executive Officer of Prestigious Properties of Florida; 39 years old; born and raised in New York City; only son of Pierce and Elaine Harding; educated at Avon Old Farms Prep School, Harvard and Wharton Business School. "What a pedigree," Jackie said out loud and then had another thought. *Weird that someone with such an upper-crust New York upbringing would come down to Florida. You'd think he'd be selling stocks and bonds and working in the market. Who knows though, and as Mr. Wright is forever reminding me, I shouldn't really care. All I need to focus on is what is, not what isn't.*

She continued to assemble her dossier on the man that she was to meet and, hopefully, thoroughly impress tomorrow. His first project, Eclat, was fourteen years ago and was groundbreaking at the time. Mr. Harding had marketed a product that focused on fulfilling the purchasers' needs and offered more substantial upgrades at the base price than any other developer at the time. He turned the business model upside down and threw away the normal cost-cutting, bargain-basement way of turning a profit. Instead, he built things better, with more extras, and watched as droves of customers competed to get in the door. Less profit per unit, yes, but a quicker sellout and a much happier clientele, who would create the most valuable commodity of all in business—word of mouth.

Of course, there was no mention of Excelsior. His latest, greatest project hadn't hit the airwaves yet, but the article did briefly describe the three other Trevor Harding/PPF developments to date: Essorant (which means soaring), Elan (brilliancy/vivacity), and Epos (epic poem). All names carefully selected to convey something a bit foreign, worldly and special. *After this, I have to put some time into researching each of these projects to see what they were all about,* Jackie planned as she jotted down each name.

Then, her eye was pulled to the very short sentence headed by "Personal Life," and she read: Single, no children. "What the heck," Jackie said surprised and then made a judgment call. *He's probably a self-absorbed egomaniac who is a workaholic to boot. No time in his oh-so powerful world for a relationship.*

Chapter Nineteen

Trevor didn't go to the job site because he had made it very clear to Pete what he expected to be done and knew that Pete would definitely see to it—he hadn't kept his position working for Mr. Harding by being anything less than exacting in carrying out orders for his boss. With this confidence, Trevor instead went to work in his office to begin brainstorming how he would assemble the greatest minds who deal with healthcare for the aging and then convince them to work with him on the medical facility that would be a main anchor and certain draw for those purchasing at Excelsior.

Trevor sat down at his desk and pondered, *I've made a commitment to having each element and aspect of Excelsior meet the highest and most innovative standards, so it is essential that it carries through to this extremely vital piece of our puzzle if it is to be the masterpiece that I've dreamt it to be.*

Of course, Trevor knew quite a few local doctors and healthcare administrators. At first, he thought that maybe he'd chat them up a bit but then realized that their purview was too narrow for what Trevor needed. At a minimum, he wanted a nationally, if not globally, recognized expert. So, like Jackie, Trevor turned to his computer and Google to start the search for his dream medical partner.

He typed 'best geriatric hospital in United States' and hit the search button. Up came the U.S. News Report article that ranked hospitals in this field, and Johns Hopkins University Hospital received a 100%. Trevor read the write-up thinking, *Wow, it can't get any better than a perfect score, so Hopkins is where I start my search.*

"OK, now let's check out who's in charge up there," Trevor said as he hit the website icon for the hospital. Up on the screen came a somewhat dizzying display of all the services offered there for geriatric patients. Trevor was impressed but glanced over the specifics and went to the tab that indicated 'Meet our Team.' He immediately scanned down the list for the Department of Geriatrics and Gerontology and saw this Associate Professor of Medicine and that Assistant Professor of Medicine, but he only stopped to read the descriptions for those who were full-fledged Professors of Medicine. There were six, so he tapped on each name and read each one's superstar resume, each seemingly more complete and spectacular than the former.

The fifth doctor he clicked on was Michael B. Worthington, and when his page came up, it blew Trevor away. Although young compared to most of the others, the list of achievements, accolades, research projects, and published articles was almost jaw dropping, and Trevor knew immediately that he was the one to get on board at Excelsior. Trevor drummed his pen on his desk and said out loud, "Now, how do I go about convincing good Doctor Worthington that Excelsior will be an opportunity that he cannot pass up? The first step is to find out more about this fine fellow."

Again, just like Jackie had done to research him, Trevor went to the Wikipedia article and started to read: Michael B. Worthington, Medical Doctor specializing in Geriatrics and Gerontology. Currently practicing at Johns Hopkins University Hospital, Baltimore, MD, (2015–present). Also, practiced at the Mayo Clinic, Rochester MN, (2009–2015), Mount Sinai, New York, NY, (2005–2009). Trevor recalled the list of the nation's top geriatric hospitals, and Dr. Worthington had spent time at all of the top three. "Bingo! Just what I wanted to see," Trevor said excitedly as he continued reading.

Born in Danbury, CT, son of Kenneth and Katherine Worthington. Youngest of four children, two brothers, Andrew and Brian, one sister, Kathryn. Educated at Avon Old Farms Prep School, Yale University, and Johns Hopkins Medical School.

Picking up on the common link at Avon, Trevor tried to jog his memory by repeating aloud, "Michael Worthington, Michael Worthington, maybe Mike Worthington." Then he threw his hands up in the air and shouted, "I've got it, this guy is little Mick Worthington! *Boy, talk about a drastic change! He used to be the shrimpiest kid in class, never said a word, and certainly wasn't anyone's first pick to be on your team. What do ya know, now he's some hotshot doctor. I can't remember too well, but I hope I didn't pick on him or anything. Now, let's figure out a way to reconnect with my old buddy Mick and persuade him that his next goal in life is to head up the amazing medical care that we will provide at Excelsior.*

Chapter Twenty

Jackie heard the knock on her door and knew that it was time for Mr. Wright to get his final progress report before tomorrow's meeting. "Come in," she said with more confidence than she was actually feeling.

"Good afternoon, Jackie," said Mr. Wright. "Well, tomorrow is when all the hard work and long hours that you've dedicated will pay off. For the final time, I'm asking, scale of one to ten?" He no longer needed to complete the sentence as they both knew all too well what they were measuring.

"Mr. Wright, I'd be lying if I said that I wasn't nervous, but I really feel like I know this project inside and out, and I am very pleased with how the video turned out. I even broadened my research and familiarized myself with Mr. Harding and PPF's four prior developments, just so I have a complete understanding of how things started, how they progressed, and how they compare to Excelsior."

"First Jackie, being nervous is not a negative, it's a positive, if you tap into your nerves to heighten your senses. Don't you think world-class athletes have nerves before competition? Those who use their nerves to be more alert, more aware, and more focused are maximizing their performance. Now, the difference between this high-functioning nervousness and being a nervous nellie is trust. If you've done your preparation well, you've trained better than your competitors, you have more knowledge and expertise than them, then you know that you can trust what you do and you don't have doubt."

Mr. Wright looked Jackie in the eye and continued in his best coachlike voice, "Your going the extra mile and educating yourself on the four prior developments, plus all of your work in learning every aspect of Excelsior, shows me that you fit the bill for our legal version of a high-performing athlete. You can, without a doubt, trust yourself to present, defend, convince and, most importantly, prove to Mr. Harding that you, my dear, score a ten out of ten, and we are the law firm that is the perfect match for his exacting and superior standards."

Jackie finally felt the boost of confidence and sense of ownership that she had been waiting for, so she nodded and replied, "Yes, Mr. Wright. I know all the material, I've memorized every floor plan, I've gone over the contract and title work a million times, I know the deadlines for all the paperwork, and our video presentation is ready to go. I've even looked at Mr. Harding's Wikipedia page and read all the trade magazine articles about him."

Mr. Wright smiled and said, "My, my, Jackie that is quite impressive. Our work and how we conduct business are always a byproduct of our upbringing and personal life. Is there anything of which I should be made aware?"

Jackie didn't want to sound trivial and certainly wanted

to keep the conversation on a completely professional level, but she felt that she needed to let Mr. Wright know about her thoughts as to what led Trevor Harding to Florida and real estate development, so she decided to risk telling him her premise. "Well, there is one thing that has me curious. It may not be a big deal and it's a little bit of conjecture on my part, but it seemed odd to me that someone with Mr. Harding's upbringing would wind up building houses in Florida."

Mr. Wright just stared at Jackie and replied, "What do you mean?"

Jackie swallowed and continued on, "Well, he went to Harvard and Wharton, and his father is one of the most powerful men on Wall Street. But, instead of going the normal, follow-in-your father's footsteps route, Mr. Harding leaves the big city, moves down to Florida, and strikes out on his own. It just seems very unusual."

Mr. Wright looked somewhat disapprovingly at Jackie and responded, "Yes, Jackie, but that has nothing to do with business. Our job is not to play psychiatrist and delve into people's motivations. We are here to do as he asks, represent his company, close his deals, and help him make profits. Now I've always admired how you involve yourself in your work and how you see the personal side of our business, but Mr. Harding is a very private man, and you and I are going to keep it that way."

Then he looked her square in the eyes, raised his voice a bit and said as more of an order than a question, "Understood?"

Jackie snapped up from her chair and confidently answered, "Yes sir, I completely understand."

Mr. Wright nodded and resumed his coach's tenor.

"Good! Again, an excellent job in becoming so well prepared for tomorrow. You will do a wonderful job. Now, just like any elite athlete, please make sure you get a good night's sleep, eat smart, and be ready to give the performance of your life." He turned around, walked out of her office and closed the door.

Jackie plopped down in her chair and moaned, "That was going so well until I had to be an idiot and bring up the personal thing. When am I going to know better? Lawyers and especially Mr. Wright could care less about their clients' personal lives. It's all black and white for them. Why do I always gravitate to the gray?"

* * *

Thank goodness it was Thursday evening because Jackie needed a double dose from her sanity walk after the week she was having. She stepped onto the sand and looked out over the expanse of water that had a little chop to it today, which made the variety of blues change as the waves bobbed up and down. Some you could almost see through and appeared like a light blue looking glass. Others were cloudy because some sediment had been kicked up from the bottom, so they looked more like a foggy lens that distorted your vision. Some had a distinct touch of green to them because strands of the seaweed had been captured in the wave cap. The one thing they all shared was how amazingly beautiful they were. All just waves, but all so magical in their own way.

Jackie shook her head to break the trance and started to walk down the beach. There were a fair number of beachgoers, but nothing compared to Saturday, so she took her usual line of passage. She always tried to walk where the tide had gone out and the sand was firmer, but not too close to the water where she would have to run away from the surf coming ashore to avoid getting her sneakers wet. It was a well-versed ritual, but almost every other aspect of her walks changed from one evening to the next.

Tonight, she noted two sails on the horizon, which made the view look like one of those cheesy paintings that tourists bought at the local art fairs, but there was nothing fake or put on about this. It appeared by happenstance, and that's what made Jackie's wonderment with what she encountered at the beach never ending.

Those boats are in the gulf at the exact time when the sun is in the perfect position to shine off their sails and create an almost unworldly reflection. Almost like a halo is beaming around them. So unbelievable, but so absolutely real, and right in front of my eyes. I pray that I never get callous and world beaten to the point where I lose sight of how incredible life is and how lucky I am to experience such miracles.

Then she started her usual back and forth. *So, I'm poor. So what? I'm healthy. I'm a single mom. But, so what? I have my precious Em. I'm overworked. But, so what? I'm going to meet Mr. Trevor Harding tomorrow and all my hard work will pay off.*

She turned her attention from the water and looked at the row of beachfront houses that had this view of the water 24/7. She focused in on "The House" and gave herself a very different speech than usual. *You know what, whoever you are? I don't care who you are or what you do! I might be poor and not have all your all-so important things, but they are just that—things. I'll take my life and all that I hold dear and wouldn't trade it for whatever it is that you have.*

She turned around and started to walk the other way when she stopped and glanced one more time at "The House" and giggled to herself and said, "Now remember, though, Mister Bigshot, I could still be your friend and keep all that I hold dear. Sounds like a great compromise."

Chapter Twenty-One

As usual, Trevor was up before his alarm and had finished reading the *Wall Street Journal* before it was necessary to start the day. His meeting with Mr. Wright's firm was at 9 o'clock, so he certainly had time to read and digest the remainder of his morning briefings: *The New York Times* and *The Naples Daily News* joined the *Journal* in good old-fashioned print versions. He then turned his attention to his email postings of Morning Brew and the daily report from Pete addressing the latest updates about Excelsior.

Trevor already knew all that Pete wrote about, but he thought it important to have the activities and progress documented so it all would be memorialized by someone other than himself.

Today's report read: All projects are on schedule and moving along as planned. Models have all been blocked and are on target to be framed and roofed by midweek. Have cleared and surveyed site for the clubhouse and medical center. Condos will be ready for foundation to be poured also by midweek. All necessary permits are in place and moving forward.

Trevor turned off his phone, took a sip of his coffee. *I am so confident of this project. It's going to be a groundbreaker for how we care for our elderly. Of course, I want it to be a success for me, but unlike my other properties, this one has a larger mission. I hope this law firm will share my vision, and we can partner to make this dream of mine a reality. If they aren't in it for the right reasons, I'm going to have to start my search all over, and I don't have time for that.*

It was still only 7, so Trevor showered and picked out the appropriate clothes for his 9 o'clock meeting. He surveyed his closet. *I don't want to be too formal but want to show some authority—blue suit, not black. Don't want to seem too power hungry but in control—navy and white tie, not red. White shirt, not light blue, as it gave a much crisper look and would set off the tie.* Even though it was now the style to pair brown shoes with navy, he was still old school and went with a sleek pair of black ones to complement his hair.

Once dressed, he still had an hour and a half, so he got into his Tesla and drove to Excelsior. He didn't go to his office, didn't stop to talk to Pete, didn't check on the specifics of the day-to-day activities and their progress, he just drove around and took it all in. The image of the original piece of land was still impressed in his memory, and it was gratifying to see how it was starting to morph into his idea of a first-class community that would serve the elderly Florida population and allow them to live and, yes, die in a way that had never been imagined before. He saw the models mentioned in Pete's report and how they would be ready for potential buyers within a few weeks.

He saw the land that had been cleared for the clubhouse and allowed himself to imagine all the activities that would be going on in each. The clubhouse filled with seniors engaging not only the usual mahjong, bridge and canasta, but also ones that would benefit them even more—yoga, Pilates, painting, music classes and so on.

Then he turned his attention to the raw land that would eventually be the site of the medical center, and he got a bit emotional. *Even though my mother isn't here to reap the benefits of a place like this and my father is too much of an SOB to ever ask for assistance, this is going to set the world on its ear when it comes to treating the elderly. We'll design a system that will only utilize the best and newest ways to meet their needs. Just as important, we'll give them the respect they deserve, not only in healthcare, but in everyday living.*

Then he picked up his phone, dialed his travel agent, and told her to book him a flight, car and hotel for Baltimore so he could meet and woo good old Mick Worthington, so he could stop dreaming about the medical center and make it come to life.

* * *

Jackie was also up and at 'em and looking in her closet to pick out the perfect outfit for the biggest meeting of her life. She pushed one hanger after another examining each: *Not black—too formal; not red—too pushy; light lavender—too wishy-washy.* She finally settled on a blue suit that wasn't navy, but a bit lighter. She paired it with a floral print shirt so that the crisp lines of the suit were softened by the flowing patterns of the flowers and vines. After dressing, she examined herself in the mirror and completed the look with a silver necklace and moderate hoop earrings. Then, she held out her right hand and put on her mother's platinum and pearl ring that gave her the comfort her mother was no longer there to provide in person. It also had become somewhat of a good luck charm.

Jackie closed her eyes and whispered, "Mom, I know you're watching out for me, and you know that this is a ginormous opportunity today. Please, please, please help me to stay calm, be confident, and show this big-shot guy what a great job I'll do for him. Please Mom, this is the chance that I have waited and prayed for. I know you'll send me your guidance and support. I love you and miss you so much."

Jackie opened her eyes, looked one more time in the mirror, nodded her head, and said in her best coach's voice, "All right it's game time, let's make this happen!" She gave herself a fist pump, turned around and walked out of her bedroom to the kitchen where she put on an apron to protect her perfect outfit if a mishap occurred, filled the coffeepot with water, and poured it over the brewer so she could administer her much-needed first dose of caffeine before Maria arrived.

Although her stomach was gurgling, Jackie wasn't the least bit hungry. She forced herself to look in the fridge—nothing. She eyed some English muffins on the counter but decided that it took too much effort, then she opened the snack cabinet and next to Emily's assortment of organic cereals, cheese crackers, and chewy granola bars (her favorite), Jackie spied a breakfast bar. "I guess that'll do," she said as she tore open the wrapper and took a forced bite into the square made of oats and apples with cinnamon and brown sugar—a concoction that was supposed to be healthy while tasting like apple pie. She chewed and swallowed the bite, then pitched the remainder in the garbage saying, "I just can't do it. Tastes like cardboard that's been sprayed with apple juice." Instead, she poured herself a steaming cup of strong dark coffee, took a sip and said, "Forget booze, this is my liquid courage."

She sat at the table, savoring her coffee and reading her notes for the millionth time when she heard a soft whisper. "Hi Mommy. I know I'm supposed to be sleeping, but I had to get up to wish you good luck today. I know you'll do just great."

"Why Emily, my sweet. That is so nice of you to get up special just for me." She tapped her lap, so Emily knew to have a seat. Once Em snuggled onto Jackie's lap, she continued. "Ya know, I just know that your extra wishes are going to be what it takes to wow everyone. I'm so sure of it, how 'bout we plan on a special dinner out tonight to celebrate?"

Emily's eyes widened with excitement because dinners out were almost unheard of, outside of someone's birthday. "Do you mean it, Mommy?" she asked, and then before Jackie could confirm, Emily added, "Can we go to Charlie Cheese, Mommy? Can we, can we?"

Although this was the most repugnant idea that Jackie could imagine, she gave Emily a kiss on the forehead and replied, "Well, you know I'm not a big fan of that place, but I guess just this once, we can." Even as she was uttering her consent, Jackie's mind went to the awful image of preservative-laden pizza, artificially colored and flavored candies, and overpriced games that kids just HAD to play "One more time, Mommy please!!"

Emily was completely oblivious to her mother's imaginings and bounced up and down on her lap excitedly saying, "Oh yay Mommy! I can hardly wait. You go to work and then we can go to Charlie Cheese. Yay, Yay, Yay! I'll even be extra good for

Miss Maria."

With that, Jackie picked up Emily in her arms, carried her back to her bed, and tucked her under the covers while gently saying, "You can start right now by going back to sleep for a little while longer for Mommy and Miss Maria."

Emily gave Jackie a kiss, said "I love you Mommy" and rolled over. Jackie kissed her tenderly on her cheek, said their own personal tag line "I love you the mostest," then she pulled up the comforter around Emily's little shoulders and tiptoed out of the room.

Jackie was just reentering the kitchen when Maria came through the door. "Buenos Dias, Jackie," said Maria as she swept through the kitchen already tidying things up.

"Buenos Dias, Maria," replied Jackie and continued, "and what a fantastic day it is going to be. No more time for doubts, no more worries about whether I know it all, no more fears about Mr. Big-Time Developer not being impressed. Today is the day that I have been waiting for, and I'm going to grab it by the horns and show them all that Ms. Jackie Summerville, legal assistant extraordinaire, is the perfect person for the job to help bring Excelsior to life!"

Maria looked at Jackie as if she was watching a politician give a campaign speech and clapped her hands quietly when she was done, but still inquired, "Wow, aren't you Miss Confident. Are you really that calm?"

Jackie laughed and said, "Hell no, but I figure the more I say it, the more I might believe it."

They both laughed together, and then Jackie gave Maria a kiss and a hug and said, "Wish me good luck. I never, ever thought I'd say this, but I hope things go great and we get to go to Charlie Cheese tonight."

Maria looked flabbergasted, so Jackie just said, "Ask Em. She'll tell you all about it. Goodbye Maria. Love you!" Jackie grabbed her things, went out the door, got into her car and said a short but heartfelt prayer, "Please God, let this be a good day. Please let me live up to my potential. And please, please, let Mr. Harding be a decent guy." She turned the key, put the car in drive and headed to the office.

Chapter Twenty-Two

At precisely 8:55, the elevator doors opened and out stepped Trevor Harding. Mr. Wright was waiting for him and extended his hand.

"Mr. Harding, we're honored by the privilege of demonstrating what an exceptional partner we plan to be with you and your superb development, Excelsior."

"Yes, Mr. Wright, I'm here with great anticipation, but, first, let's dispense with the formalities better suited for the stuffy offices in the Northeast. Please call me Trevor, as Mr. Harding is still reserved for my father."

Mr. Wright laughed slightly and said, "Absolutely, and call me Alan, but please not Al as, like you, that is reserved for my father."

With that, Alan escorted Trevor down the hallway to the conference room and opened the double doors.

The conference room was staged with all things Excelsior. Floor plans, sales brochures, drawings and designs, and a large screen for the all-important video presentation, which would act as a visual flowchart of the closing procedure from start to finish. This was Jackie's idea, and Mr. Wright bought in completely.

Mr. Wright then turned to his left, put out his arm and said, "Mr. Trevor Harding, I'd like to introduce you to my assistant, who has been and will be my right hand during this project, Ms. Jackie Summerville."

Trevor could not believe his eyes. Standing not ten feet away from him was the beach-walking woman, the one he had spent countless thoughts on various ways he could meet her. Here she was.

Very seldom in his life had Trevor not been in total control of his composure, but it took every one of his well-developed disciplinary skills to keep focused and play the part of man-in-charge, when all he really wanted to do was let his guard down and say, "I can't believe I've finally met you. I've been dreaming of this for so long."

Instead, he took a deep breath, walked across the room, held out his hand and said, "So very nice to meet you, Ms. Summerville."

Jackie was also finding it hard to keep calm. Not only because it was the culmination of all her hard work, but more so because the Wikipedia photo that she had seen of Trevor Harding paled in comparison to the real man who stood in front of her.

Tall, but not towering, fit but not bulky. The grey at his temples was more pronounced, but only added to the appeal. He was also impeccably dressed, which always got bonus points in Jackie's assessment of a man.

She accepted his handshake, tried to still her voice and

replied, "I very much admire your work, Mr. Harding."

They engaged each other's eyes for a moment, and then Mr. Wright proclaimed, "We know how valuable Mr. Harding's time is, so let's proceed with our presentation."

Jackie broke her eyes away from Trevor and agreed, "Yes, of course Mr. Wright."

She walked over to the video player, nervously put her finger on the play button and said another quick prayer.

Mr. Wright turned to Trevor and asked if he would like anything to drink, to which Trevor shook his head and said, "No, thank you."

Mr. Wright continued by firmly saying, "We've prepared a video for you that will highlight all that our firm is prepared to do in our representation of Prestigious Properties of Florida as it pertains to Excelsior. We're very confident that after viewing, you'll know that we are not just seeing this as a legal and business opportunity, but as an all-encompassing partnership that is knowledgeable, involved, and invested in the total one hundred percent success of Excelsior." He then turned to Jackie and instructed her, "Please begin."

Jackie swallowed hard, exhaled deeply, and hit play.

The video came to life with the Excelsior logo emblazoned on the screen. Then it flowed to a shot of Mr. Wright behind his desk. He looked directly into the camera and said, "What follows is just a small sampling of the services that Wright, Stewart & Blake will provide to ensure that we not only live up to our very high standards but more so all that Prestigious Properties and Excelsior have come to define."

The image changed to another shot of Mr. Wright poring over documents while a narrator explained that he was reviewing the title to the property from the beginnings of its existence back in the 1700s up to Prestigious Properties of Florida purchasing the land just last year.

The explanation continued saying, "Back before computers took over everything, this chain of title was actually documented in a paperbound book called an abstract. In it, one could see and examine all the deeds, government limitations, environmental issues and so on that pertained to the property. A good title attorney was like a detective in making sure all the previous documents that affect the property were prepared and executed properly. It was also vital to make sure that nothing in the annals of time would put a restriction on the proposed use of the property."

Next, the video showed Mr. Wright eyeing his computer while jotting items down on a legal pad. Then it faded out and back in to show the title report that Mr. Wright had issued that would be used to close all the Excelsior deals.

The narrator added, "In the title report, there is also the legal description of the individual properties that will be sold to the purchasers. It is vital that these descriptions are correct." The video showed Mr. Wright studying surveys to ensure that they jibed with the written language in each report.

After this mini primer on title law, Mr. Wright looked into the camera again and expertly stated, "My thorough review of the title to the Excelsior property proved to show nothing out of the ordinary, with your usual restrictions and easements. Chain of title shows the normal warranty deed to warranty deed passage without issue." Then, he smiled slightly and added, "Mr. Harding, I'm not sure if you are social with the Colliers, but I would venture that you are familiar with their ownership of most oil, gas and mineral rights in Collier County. That is also the case here, but, again, this is common and nothing to cause concern. Therefore, once some small and very mundane requirements are cleared from closing to closing, our firm is prepared to issue title insurance policies to all purchasers of Excelsior properties."

The screen faded from Mr. Wright and continued with a montage of photos showing the timeline for the closing process: One of Karen acting the part of a real estate agent handing a widely smiling Jackie a contract. Another of Jackie behind her desk on the phone with the appearance of complete competence. The next a photo of contently smiling buyers looking over the floor plan for their home. The following one showing construction workers diligently building the buyers' dream home and then flowing to a decorator reviewing personalized selections for the homeowners. On it went until the video concluded with a photo of the buyers beaming at Jackie as they shake hands across a closing table—an indisputable image of a job well done.

The picture faded again and returned to the Excelsior logo, then it showed the Wright, Stewart & Blake firm logo, and finally both logos intertwined with a tag line that the narrator reads, "Superior alone—Excelsior together."

Throughout the viewing, Trevor couldn't help but stare every time Jackie came up on the screen. He forced himself to concentrate on the question of whether to finalize the hiring of Wright, Stewart & Blake and asked himself, *Are they impressing me on a business level as much as Jackie impresses me on a human level?*

As another photo of her appears, he is lost in the loveliness of her demeanor—the way she cocks her head when on the phone, the quirky way her left upper lip goes a little higher when she smiles, and her impeccable choice of exactly the right outfit for each setting, a definite plus with him.

Mr. Wright interrupted Trevor's thoughts by saying, "We trust we covered all of the vital areas and considerations, but if you have any further questions, Ms. Summerville and I would be pleased to address them."

Trevor looked at Mr. Wright and then to Jackie, collected himself and said, "No, that was a very concise yet complete overview of what my expectations are. I'm especially thankful for the concise part, as most of these presentations drag on ad nauseam." Then, he allowed himself a little chuckle.

"Well Trevor," Mr. Wright said. "I can't take any of the credit for the video. I'm an old lawyer who, as you saw, started out my career with paper abstracts. I'm not terribly comfortable with all the new technologies. The video is entirely Jackie's creation."

Trevor looked at Jackie, nodded and said, "Very well done. I might have to have my marketing people pick your brain."

Jackie couldn't control a blush that warmed her cheeks, nodded back and said, "Thank you, Mr. Harding. I'd be happy to talk with them, but my main goal will be to get your closings done in as efficient manner as possible, so your residents can start enjoying the amazing lifestyle available to them at Excelsior."

At once, she realized that she made it sound like this was a done deal and immediately backtracked by quickly adding, "Of course, I mean, to be clear, that is if we are fortunate enough to represent you."

Trevor looked at her sternly and then broke into a smile that made her a little wobbly in her knees and said, "You don't know me, but I like people who speak in an affirmative manner. None of this wishy-washy 'this is what we may do or could possibly do or think we can do.' No, I got this far by saying 'this is what we are going to do, and this is how we are going to do it!'"

Then he turned to Mr. Wright, put out his hand and said, "Well Alan, we have a deal. Let's get to work."

Mr. Wright shook his hand vigorously and replied, "Thank you Trevor. Yes, let's get to work."

Trevor turned to Jackie, smiled, nodded and said, "It truly has been an unexpected pleasure." With that, he opened the door, saying, "You both have a good day" and exited the room.

Mr. Wright let out a big sigh, looked at Jackie, clapped his hands together and said, "What a splendid job you did, Jackie. I don't think that could have gone any better. I knew you could do it!"

He then did something he had never done before. He reached over and gave her a big hug. Jackie was shocked, but so elated that she hugged him right back until a few seconds passed, and he abruptly let her go, went back to his normal formal self and said, "All right, enough celebrating, back to work."

He opened the doors of the conference room to be greeted by everyone in the firm smiling and clapping. The two walked out, and Jackie heard Karen saying, "Boy, that guy is super good looking." Ryan then piped up adding, "He's not bad, but it's easy to look good when you have that kind of money."

Mr. Wright held up his hands, smiled and said, "Thank you all for your congratulations. Yes, we are now the sole closing firm for the unprecedented community of Excelsior, an exclusive

Prestigious Properties of Florida development. Our Jackie did an outstanding job, and I'm certain she and all of you will continue to do so. Now, as I just told her, there's a lot to do, so that's quite enough self-congratulating. Let's all get back to work."

Jackie went to her office and virtually fell into her chair while uttering, "I cannot believe that just happened!"

Ryan peeked his head around the corner and said, "OK, I give. Maybe talking to yourself out loud does get you places. I've never seen the old man beam so much about any of us."

As usual, Ryan's choice of words got Jackie perturbed so she replied, "Look Ryan, as I've said a million times before, his name is Mr. Wright, and he deserves to be addressed with respect. As for me, an opportunity presented itself to me, I seized it, worked my ass off, and it paid off. I know it's somewhat of a foreign concept for a lot of you millennials, but I don't have the luxury to flit from job to job trying to find my passion."

Ryan scoffed and replied, "Hey, wait a second. Stop being so defensive. I just came by to congratulate you and now you're giving me a sociology lecture!"

Jackie looked at Ryan and quietly said, "I'm sorry. I'm just super exhausted. Elated, but exhausted. I really do appreciate you stopping by Ryan."

He laughed saying, "No offense taken. I've also busted my ass for good old Wright, Stewart & Blake, but it's been researching mundane case law, writing nonessential memos, and let's not forget the always popular law library supplement. I do believe the firm would cease to exist if it weren't for me."

They both let out a shared laugh and then Jackie said, "You're doing the right things. Hang in there and you will be rewarded."

Ryan waved his hand and retorted, "Yeah, if I live that long. Again, major congrats. What are you doing tonight to celebrate?"

Jackie hesitated, fearing his response, but inhaled and answered, "I'm having a major throwdown with my daughter at Club Charlie Cheese."

Ryan laughed again and said, "I'd say that you're pathetic, but, somehow I think you already know that. Say hi to the stupid mouse."

Then he disappeared and Jackie was once again alone. She looked around her office at all the files and documents, plans and piles that all had to do with Excelsior. She got up, closed the door, and then put her face in her hands and started to cry softly, saying, "I did it. I'm going to get that raise that will allow me to do so much for my darling Emily."

As she touched her ring, she continued, "Thanks so much Mom for seeing me through all of this and for being there with me today. I miss you and love you so much." Then she broke down into sobs.

Chapter Twenty-Three

Trevor usually didn't mind traveling because the only thing tying him to Naples was Excelsior, but now he was regretting his decision to take a 12:30 afternoon flight to Baltimore.

Having finally met her and knowing that she'd be walking the beach later, he was annoyed that he wasn't even going to be here. "Talk about crappy timing," he muttered out loud. "I could have conveniently bumped into her on the beach tonight."

No more had he said it, he reconsidered and realized that it was best to be gone so he wasn't here to be tempted to do something irrational. "Yes, Trevor," he admonished himself. "If you're away, you won't have even the slightest opportunity to be rash. Remember, she is technically now in your employ. You must keep things a hundred percent professional."

He shut his suitcase, grabbed his briefcase and phone then headed out the door to the airport, taking a big chance that he was going to be successful in wooing his old prep school mate, Mick Worthington.

As he sat in the airport terminal, he placed the call to Johns

Hopkins and asked for Dr. Worthington. He was transferred to a receptionist who answered, "Johns Hopkins Department of Geriatrics and Gerontology. How may I help you?"

Trevor put on his most distinguished voice and replied, "Yes. This is Mr. Trevor Harding, Avon Old Farms class of 1995. I'm an old classmate of Dr. Worthington. Is he in?"

Sounding a bit confused, the receptionist responded, "Just a minute and I'll check. Please hold."

Trevor was listening to a recording lauding all of the developments, research and breakthrough medicines that were being conducted at Johns Hopkins when the tape cut off, and there was a slightly squeaky voice that said, "Well, Trevor Harding. Long time, no see, no talk, no write. Haven't seen you since prep school graduation but heard through the grapevine that you're some big deal developer in Florida."

Trevor quickly ran a number of replies over in his head, but decided to get straight to the point saying, "Yes, Mick. Can I still call you that?"

"I never liked that nickname back then, and I don't ever use it now," Michael answered somewhat abruptly.

Trevor was quite impressed with the gumption that Michael had apparently acquired and said, "I'm very sorry, Michael. I know your time is just as valuable as mine, so I'm going to get right to the reason for the call."

"Yes, please do," Michael said in a cold voice.

Undaunted, Trevor continued on saying, "I'm embarking on a groundbreaking development in Naples, Florida, that will totally transform senior living and healthcare. Being a very successful developer, I have the living part of the equation handled, but I want you to head up the healthcare side."

Michael audibly inhaled and said, "Well, to say that this is completely out of the blue is a huge understatement. Look Trevor …"

Trevor couldn't lose him, so he interrupted by confidently saying, "Listen Michael, I did my homework, and you are the best at what you do. I'd like to think that I'm the best at what I do. We could do so much real good together for our seniors."

Before Michael could reply, Trevor pushed all his chips in and continued saying, "Michael, I'm going to be in Baltimore in three hours. Can we at least have dinner so that we can discuss and I can explain it all to you? What do you have to lose?"

Michael's interest was piqued by Trevor's idea, and he was persuaded by his unbridled enthusiasm, so he sighed and replied, "I'm sure your extensive research has also shown that I am usually a very busy man. However, if I remember correctly, you always had uncanny luck. It just so happens that I'm free tonight. Where and when?"

Trevor did a fist pump and excitedly replied, "Excellent Michael. Believe me, the one thing I can't stand is someone wasting my time, so I promise to not waste yours. How about the Ocean Breeze Seafood Room at 6:30?"

"All right," Michael conceded. "I'll see you there at 6:30." Then he hung up the phone and said to himself, "This should be interesting. Odd, but interesting. Let's see what old smooth-talking Trevor has up his sleeve."

Trevor put his phone down and said, "I had better make a Perry Mason ironclad case that my jury of one, Michael B. Worthington, will not only buy into but commit to whole-heartedly."

Then he looked at this briefcase that was bulging with

Excelsior materials—brochures, floor plans, and all the rest—but the most important document was one he had never shared with anyone: his own personal mission statement on why he felt this project was unlike any other; his true passion to provide nothing but the best to the elderly as a testament to the never-ending faith that his mother had in him. This drive was also powered by the guilt that he always felt because of his helplessness when it came to her fight against cancer and her ultimate death. He paused for a moment. *Come join me Michael, and we will build a magnificent legacy to Elaine Margaret Whitehead-Harding.*

Trevor's plane touched down at Baltimore/Washington International Airport at 2:52, and his car dropped him at the Four Seasons at 3:30, where he checked in, got to his room, and promptly took a nap.

Trevor was a huge proponent of a power nap, every day if possible, but always mandatory if he had an evening function. Just twenty to twenty-five minutes, no more. He was firm in his belief that it served to recharge one's energy and reset the mind to accomplish more later in the day and evening.

At 4:20, he awoke, got up and went to the desk in his room. He took his time reviewing the notes he'd written on the plane, often interrupting his thoughts with mutterings like, "Gotta make this a slam dunk. Am I providing enough motivation and incentive for him to sign on? Will he see how much we can accomplish? We'll be setting a new bar for the health and well-being of our older population. He has to want to be a part of that. What doctor in his shoes wouldn't?"

After an hour, he stopped, looked up and said, "Please Mom, let him see the need. Please let him feel my true passion for this project. Please help convince him that he is the man to partner with me to see that this dream becomes a reality in honor of you."

Trevor closed the lid of his laptop, put it back in his briefcase, and went into the bathroom to shower, shave and dress for one of the most pivotable meetings of his career.

At 6:25, Trevor looked across the entryway of the restaurant and recognized an older version of the shrimpy kid he had known at Avon. More put together and adult, but still with an air of awkwardness that made others not want to include him. Trevor pushed those memories aside and confidently walked toward the now-renowned doctor, Michael B. Worthington, who was one of the world's preeminent authorities on geriatrics and the elderly.

Extending his hand, Trevor warmly greeted him saying, "Michael, it's Trevor. I'm so appreciative that you've been kind enough to take the time to meet with me."

Michael accepted his hand and replied, "Trevor Harding, not in a million years did I think, you, of all people, would be calling me for a meeting."

Trevor was afraid he was alluding to how standoffish he was to Michael when they were young but decided to just continue smiling and said, "Well, I trust by the end of this evening, it will be the first of many meetings. Let's get to our table and I'll share my thoughts."

Two and a half hours later, the two very different men shook hands again with Trevor saying, "I can't tell you how exceedingly happy it makes me to have you on board. I promise, we will be making a real difference."

Michael responded, "I will tell you that I would have lost a lot of money if I had bet that I'd leave my position at JHU and move to Florida to lead up a private healthcare facility."

Trevor laughed and said, "Well Michael, let's both be glad you're not a gambling man."

Michael laughed too and added, "You know it will take a good three months to wrap up things here."

"Of course, of course," Trevor nodded. "That actually fits the timeline perfectly. Let's leave the details for the next time we talk. I'm just honored to be your partner. I assure you I will live up to it."

They said goodbye and Trevor returned to the Four Seasons. Instead of going up to his room, he stopped at the bar for a nightcap and to reflect on the monumental achievement he had just accomplished. Then he thought of Jackie and what he had said to her earlier in the day. *None of this 'what we may do or think we can do or could possibly do.' Instead, 'this is what we are going to do, and this is how we are going to do it.'*

He raised his glass and said, "Jackie, Michael, Alan, Pete and especially Mom—let's do this!"

Chapter Twenty-Four

Even though she was exhausted, Jackie still walked the beach that evening, as it was a sacred rite that she would not forego. However, instead of her normal brisk pace, tonight Jackie meandered down the beach and really took her time to breathe and take in all that was around her.

It's all so amazingly beautiful. From the sea oats to the myriad shells, driftwood and seaweed that's washed up on shore.

The birds were always her favorite. The prehistoric look of pelicans flying overhead. The sandpipers doing their continual dance down to the water then scurrying back. The snowy egret patiently watching the water and walking step by step as if to sneak up on the guppies below. Her favorite bird of all was the osprey, which was a perfect combination of grace, speed, beauty and efficiency. All manner of birds there for her to watch in wonderment. No zoo necessary. No entrance fee required. "Just amazing," she uttered as she looked all around.

Because she was walking so slowly, Jackie had only made it down three-quarters of the beach she normally covered. She realized that she had to turn around and get moving the other way to get home in time to relieve Maria.

"Yikes!" she cried out loud as she remembered what would come next. "I have to suffer through an evening of overpriced games, crappy food and screaming kids. The things we do for our children."

Just before she did an about face, she looked down the sand and eyed "The House" that was still a ways down the beach. *So, whoever you are in your big fancy house, I want you to know that Mr. Trevor Harding thought my presentation was, and I quote, 'very well done.' So, put that in your diamond-encrusted pipe and smoke it.*

Then she swiftly turned on her heel and picked up the pace to get home on time.

Jackie took the last bite of her sadly mediocre salad, while Emily finished off her final chicken nugget.

"Yummmm!" Emily exclaimed as ketchup dripped down her chin. Jackie reached over and dabbed it off as she wondered what it was about this awful food that made kids go crazy for it. She looked around, and there were tables packed with antsy kids munching on everything from breadsticks to pizza to French fries to the most popular—rainbow churros that came in all different colors.

"Yeah," Jackie said out loud. "I'm sure there's absolutely nothing artificial in those. It's got to be a rainbow of dyes numbered one through ten."

Emily interrupted Jackie's rant asking, "What Mommy?"

"Oh, nothing sweetie. I'm glad you're having fun, but it's getting late, so we're going to have to leave soon. You've played pretty much every game here."

Emily frowned, stuck out her lip and said, "But Mommy, we haven't seen Charlie yet. Please, Mommy, please!"

Jackie hated the asinine character, but, just like everything else there, the kids went gaga over the mouse. She sighed. *I am way too tired to get into a back and forth with a three-year-old about seeing a ridiculous mouse.* So, she looked at Emily and was about to put her foot down, when the overhead speaker came on and someone in a bad version of a ring announcer's voice said, "Do you know what time it is?"

With that, Emily jumped up and exclaimed in unison with the other children, "It's Charlie Cheese Time!!"

"Oh Lord," Jackie muttered as the announcer then asked everyone to help with the countdown. Emily jumped up and down with each descending number yelling, "5, 4, 3, 2, 1—It's Charlie! Yaaaaaay!!"

Emily looked up at her mom, and Jackie realized that she had met her match against what was probably some flunky high school kid under the goofy costume and said, "Go on Em, go show Charlie how to dance."

Emily tore away as fast as her little feet could carry her and over to the gathering of half-crazed kids crowding around the star of the show. Then she started dancing, jumping and twirling to the super-loud, god-awful music.

Although Jackie hated everything this place stood for, she had to admit that she loved seeing her daughter so happy and couldn't help but laugh and smile at her precious little girl.

When the singing and dancing was over, Charlie handed each child a lollypop, and then Emily skipped back over to her mom with a gigantic grin on her face saying, "Look what Charlie gave me, Mommy."

"That's very nice Em. You can eat it in the car on the way home because I am super tired now and we need to go."

Jackie looked Emily in the eyes for any sign of a pushback coming, but Emily bobbed her head up and down and said, "OK Mommy, we can go now. I'm tired too."

Jackie took Emily's little hand and walked out hoping to never have to come there again, or at least she would have a very long break from that goddamn rodent.

Chapter Twenty-Five

The next afternoon, Trevor's plane landed at 12:30 in Fort Myers. As it taxied down the runway, Trevor looked out the window as the palm trees and scrub bushes passed by and thought, *Hello, my land of sunshine and profit. Now let's add good works to the mix.*

He retrieved his car from the parking lot and headed home. Between the meeting at the law firm, the phone call with Michael, flying to Baltimore, dinner and the flight back, even the indefatigable Trevor Harding was wiped out.

As he pulled into his garage, he made a pact with himself to take a breather just for the afternoon and then it would be right back to work in the morning. He recalled one of his mother's favorite sayings: *If you run yourself down into the ground, it will take ten times longer to get back up. Don't be stubborn. Just give yourself a rest.*

Trevor looked skyward and said, "Yes, Mom. Oh, and Mom, thanks for being there last night. We really did it." He turned off the car, grabbed his suitcase, but left the rest of the work-related things in the car.

"Welcome home, Mr. Harding," Andre said as Trevor walked into the house.

"Glad to be back, Andre. It's been quite a day and a half. Exhausting, but exceedingly successful. Don't be shocked, but I've decided to take the rest of the day off."

Andre hid his astonishment, as he had never known Trevor to take any time off, and said, "A very good idea indeed. Any requests for dinner or should I come up with something?"

"I'll leave it to your expertise, Andre, but just know that I had some marvelous Maryland crab cakes last night so please stay away from anything similar."

"Of course, sir. I'll create a dish that will certainly go in a different direction."

Then Trevor stopped, turned around and said, "On second thought, I will choose. Please make rack of lamb with whatever you feel best to accompany it. It was my mother's favorite."

"Will do, Mr. Harding" Andre replied and added, "May I get you anything now?"

Trevor never drank during the day because he always had to remain focused and able to concentrate, but this afternoon was different, so he nodded his head and said, "As a matter of fact Andre, yes please. Make me a Dark and Stormy with extra lime and a splash of seltzer. I'll meet you by the pool in ten minutes."

Andre smiled and concurred, "A splendid choice, sir, and if I may be so bold, you very much deserve an afternoon to relax and unwind."

"Thanks Andre. I'll see you in a few minutes." With that, Trevor picked up his bag and went to his bedroom. He took his bathing suit out of a drawer and went into the bathroom to change. When he saw his image in the mirror, it made him stop and say out loud, "Jeez Trevor, you look a mess. Let's chill, decompress and put some life back into those baby blues."

After changing, he walked out to the pool and dove in. He always kept the water at a cool 77 degrees so it would refresh him when he was tired like today and so he wouldn't get too hot when doing his workout.

"Boy, does that feel good," he said out loud as he came up from a long glide under water.

"I bet it does," Andre commented as he held Trevor's Dark and Stormy in hand.

"Just set it on the table please. I'm going to soak a bit, no laps, but a good long float about. I think I'm even going to sit in the spa. I can't remember the last time I did that."

Andre set down the drink and said, "Good for you, Mr. Harding, but don't let this drink go to waste. If you would like another or need anything else, just let me know."

"Thanks very much, Andre. I really do appreciate it."

Andre left and Trevor was alone in his palatial pool. He slowly floated through the tunnel of thick foliage and then pushed himself up into the spa. Unlike the pool, it was kept at a very warm 101 degrees. It took a bit for Trevor's body to adjust, but when it did, he could feel his muscles relaxing and the stress that he always carried in his shoulders release. He looked around at the beautiful array of orchids and muttered, "My God, this is exquisite. Why in the world have I ignored this? I know the answer good and well. My world is so crammed with meetings, planning and work, I get total tunnel vision. That's what has always led to my success."

He sank farther down into the water and recalled the events

of the last day and a half. *Not that I'm complaining, but that whirlwind was a lot, even for me.* He laughed and continued, *I mean, out of the blue, I meet the woman I've been admiring for months, and I get one of the most respected authorities on geriatrics to come on board my project. Seriously, who does that.*

The next morning, Trevor slept in longer than he had in years, and when he awakened, he picked up his phone to see that it was 8:52. He pushed himself up on the pillows and talked to himself in the third person saying, "Holy smokes, Trevor, you must have been super tired, but there has been a lot going on, so I'm going to give you a pass, just this once."

He laughed, got up, put on his robe and made his way to the kitchen where coffee was waiting for him. He poured a cup, took a sip and realized it was cold. "Of course, it is," he said while dumping the rest down the drain. "The timer is set to brew at 6:45. It's been off for more than an hour."

Not used to making his own coffee, he fumbled around the cabinets and found the coffee filters. "Step one," he said. Then he took the tops off the canisters and discovered the coffee beans. He scooped out the dark brown Arabica beans while making a mental note to tell Andre that they should be in the container directly next to the maker, not the third one away. He pressed the switch on the grinder and enjoyed the wonderfully rich smell that helped to wake him up further. Then he put the fresh grinds in the awaiting filter, added water and hit the "On" button.

While waiting for it to brew, Trevor perused the headlines. Nothing terribly interesting, just the normal politics, economic news, and a fair amount of fluff. The Naples paper had a giant spread about the annual wine festival, praising the participants and going on and on about how much money was raised to help the underprivileged—all while decked out in tuxes and gowns, carted around in stretch limos, and bidding on extravagant trips, wines, cars and experiences.

Trevor threw the paper on the table and scoffed, "Why do I feel like I'm the only one who sees the self-centered hypocrisy in this? Do you really need to have some spectacle of wealth to raise money and do good for the community? Just absurd!"

The coffee was done, so he poured himself a cup and made his way out to the balcony. He took a sip and said, "Much better," as he looked out over the sand. He glanced to his right and scanned all the women who were walking the beach, then immediately shook his head and admonished himself. *Now you know good and well that she won't be here today, or tomorrow for that matter. Her schedule is like clockwork and you know it— Tuesday, Thursday and Friday evenings, that's it. Get over it!*

He took another sip. *Part of me sort of wishes I could get over it. I have so much on my plate already. Yes, now I know who she is, but there are far too many important matters that I cannot, and will not, let this crazy admiration—OK minor obsession—get in the way of.*

He looked at his watch. *Oh Lord, it's 10 o'clock already! Enough daydreaming and taking it easy. Time to get back to work and prepare for tomorrow's agenda, especially my follow-up with Alan. And I need to start fleshing out the initial details of the medical center.*

Chapter Twenty-Six

Jackie also spent Saturday and Sunday in a well-deserved chill mode. Saturday, she and Emily slept late and spent the rest of the morning at the park.

Jackie loved watching Emily master new skills every time they went. She used to have to stand behind her as she climbed the stairs to the slide and hold on to her as they glided down together. Now, Em could race up the steps all on her own. She would wave to Jackie as if she were on top of a mountain and shout, "Watch me Mommy!" and then slide down. Once she got the bottom, she would pop up, run around to the back, and do it all over again and again.

She had also graduated from the baby swing to what she called "The Big Girl Swing." She was still in the process of learning how to pump her legs to get it going, so Jackie stood behind giving her pushes.

"Wheeee!" exclaimed Emily. "Push me higher, Mommy!"

As much as Jackie loved the daredevil in Emily, it was balanced by the worrywart mom mentality, so she replied, "OK

Em. I'll push you a little bit higher, but make sure you hold on super tight."

After an hour of playground fun, they both were hot and sweaty. Jackie opened the cooler and gave Emily a juice box, and she took a long drink out of her water bottle.

"Boy, it's hot and it's not even summer yet," Jackie said to herself. Then she turned to Emily and said, "What do you say we go cool off at the splash park over there?'

"Yay! Yay! Yay!" Emily squealed as she started taking off her shirt.

"Wait a second, little one. Let's walk over there and find a place to put our things before you start peeling like a banana."

They both laughed and Emily said, "OK, Mommy. Let's go," as she broke out into a half run, half skip.

"Wait for me," Jackie chuckled as she gathered up the cooler, her purse and tote bag.

They got to the splash park, and Emily took off her top, shorts and sneakers, throwing them to Jackie as she went, until she was only in her pink bathing suit with rainbows across the front.

"Can I go now, Mommy?" she asked.

Jackie smiled widely at her and said, "Go for it, my darling Em. Have a blast!"

Emily ran into the sprinklers first and shrieked with glee, running from one to the other. Then she pranced over to her favorite spot where you step on a circle and a fountain shoots up.

While Jackie watched her daughter frolic about, all she could think of was how much she loved her precious girl. So many people might think that she was missing out by being a single mom, but she could think of nowhere else she'd rather be right now than at this very spot with the love of her life.

After another half hour of splashing about, Jackie wrapped Emily up in a big fluffy towel, picked her up and said, "Time to go home and take a lovely nap."

Emily snuggled into her mother's arms and quietly replied, "Yes, Mommy. I'm very sleepy."

Sunday, they slept late again and lazily laid around the house all morning. Jackie usually didn't let Em watch a lot of TV or videos, but today she sat next to her on the couch as they watched Finding Nemo and Frozen back to back and enjoyed every minute. They ate peanut butter and jelly sandwiches, had popcorn, and just enjoyed vegging in each other's company.

"I like this, Mommy," Emily said as she laid her head on Jackie's lap. "I wish we could do this every day."

Jackie stroked her daughter's soft brown curls and gently said, "Yes Em, but if we did it every day, then it wouldn't be so special, right?"

Emily stretched and replied, "I guess so."

"Plus, my little one, Mommy has to go to work so we can have all of the special times like we've had this weekend."

"OK," Emily nodded. "But let's do it again soon, OK?"

"You've got a deal," Jackie said as she gave Emily a little tickle and then got up to clean the kitchen.

Yes, work, Jackie thought to herself as she washed the dishes. *I had better get myself prepared for the next part of this whole deal. Just because we got the account doesn't mean things are going to be any less demanding or stressful. Mr. Harding was a lot more normal than I thought he'd be, but you can tell that he has a certain way he likes things done. I had better not let my foot off the pedal one bit.*

Chapter Twenty-Seven

Trevor arrived at 7 o'clock Monday morning and took his usual drive around the property to assess the progress being made before anyone else got there. Just since Friday, the models were much further along. Pete's report had noted that midweek would be the projected timeline for framing and roofing, but Trevor was quite pleased to see that all the models were actually very close to finishing this phase.

The wood subsurface was on all the roofs and the sheathing was also finished. Each unit had stacks of tiles waiting on the ground in front of the buildings to be installed to complete the roofs.

"Good job, Pete," Trevor said out loud as he slowly drove by.

As he got to the middle of model row, he stopped the Tesla, reached in the back for his hard hat, and got out to inspect the interiors of two of the units. As with the roofs, the framing had also progressed further than Pete's report led him to believe. Wood beams had been erected in each structure to the point where Trevor could see and feel each floor plan starting to come to life.

"It's really happening. Excelsior is beginning to take shape," he said to himself, as he took his phone out of his pocket and dialed Pete's number.

"Good morning, Mr. Harding," answered Pete.

"Good morning, Pete," Trevor replied. "Hey, I'm down here at the models and I want you to know how impressed I am with how quickly you're getting these online. It really helps to accelerate our whole timeline."

"Thanks a lot, Mr. Harding," Pete replied trying to hide the excitement in his voice. "We lucked out and scored a couple extra crews who helped us bust it out. I know how important getting these models up and running is to you and the project."

"Well Pete, yes, it is very important, and I appreciate it. I'm coming to the office now, so let's sit down and discuss where we are with the rest."

"All right, Mr. Harding. I'll see you in a few minutes."

Trevor hung up and clapped his hands together as he stomped the dirt off his shoes. He got in his car, tossed the hard hat in the back, and sped off to the construction trailer.

Once there, he swung open the door, grabbed a cup of coffee while greeting the receptionist, and then went to his office and sat behind his always crowded desk.

"Pete!" he shouted. "Come on, let's get going. I've got a lot on my plate today."

Pete hurried in and sat down saying, "Yes, sir."

Trevor took a sip of coffee and began the briefing. "So, again, the models are looking great. Please give me an update on the others—condos, clubhouse and medical facility."

As he had done thousands of times, Pete consulted his notes and began his report.

"As you noted, no need to discuss the models anymore. We finally got the permits for the condos, and the foundations were poured on Friday. They'll need at least three weeks to cure, and then we'll be off and running."

Trevor was surprised and looked up from his desk saying, "I thought you said midweek for the concrete? How did you pull this off on top of all of the progress made on the models?"

"Well, Mr. Harding," Pete grinned. "It's nice to have friends, but it's also very nice to have a boss who's not stingy and is willing to drop a few to get the job done."

"OK Pete." Trevor smiled back. "I understand, but we still have a budget to adhere to."

"I know, boss. But, as you always say, 'The sooner we build it, the sooner they can buy it.'"

Trevor nodded and replied, "Truer words have never been spoken. All right, but don't get carried away. Now, what about the clubhouse and medical building?"

Pete answered "Both are on schedule. We're going to do both simultaneously to save some money. See, I do have your bottom line in mind."

They both laughed and Pete continued, "The areas have been filled and leveled. Then they'll be framed and the footings filled. After that, the real work begins."

"Yes, it does," Trevor replied. "Thanks again, Pete, and please thank your crews for me, too."

"Will do, Mr. Harding. Have a good day," Pete said as he gathered his things and headed out the door.

Trevor sat at his desk and thought about what to do next.

He was about call to Alan to follow up and finalize things and then a thought hit him. *I should show Alan and Jackie around Excelsior personally. I know they're on board, but they need to see this project in person so they can see and feel what it is that we're doing here and become a hundred percent invested.*

He picked up his phone and dialed Alan, who answered on the second ring.

Trevor greeted him saying, "Well good morning, Alan. I trust you had a pleasant weekend?"

Alan was a bit surprised by the call, but replied, "Good morning, Trevor. Why, yes, I did and you the same?"

"Yes, yes, thanks," Trevor answered and then got to the point saying, "So, Alan, I've been thinking and I really feel it's critically important for you and Ms. Summerville to come out to Excelsior to get a firsthand appreciation for all we're doing out here and to keep your fingers on the pulse of its progress."

Still taken aback, Alan managed to sound enthusiastic and replied, "Yes, Trevor. I think that's a wonderful idea. It would certainly allow us to get a feel for the development. When did you have in mind?"

"This morning," Trevor shot back.

Knowing how jam-packed his workday already was, Alan coughed and replied, "Well, I can't see why that wouldn't work. I'm expecting Jackie to come in any minute, but I'm certain that she's available to accompany me."

Trevor grinned and said, "Splendid! Let's say we meet in my office in the construction trailer at 9:30 and I'll personally give you a tour."

"All right. Sounds good. We will see you then."

"See you then. Goodbye," Trevor said as he pushed the

end call button. Leaning back in his chair he smiled. *Good business? Yes. A way to see Jackie again? Absolutely! Sometimes I am downright brilliant!*

Chapter Twenty-Eight

Jackie woke up on Monday morning feeling a little less stressed and harried than she had during the days leading up to last Friday's meeting, but still amped up to get to work and make some progress on the actual project that was Excelsior instead of the massive amount of prep work she had been consumed with just to get to this spot.

I hope we get all the existing contracts in this morning so I can get started, she thought as she sipped her coffee. *I need to reach out to the salespeople so they can get to know me and have confidence in me. Not that they would ever question the judgement of Mr. Harding, but it's important that each of them feels comfortable working with me.*

She walked to her bedroom, opened her closet and decided to wear a black and white striped dress with a black cropped jacket. Not as formal as the outfit she wore to Friday's meeting, but still well-tailored.

She put on her makeup and was just finishing up with a reddish rose lipstick when she felt a tug on her sleeve. Emily smiled shyly and said, "Good morning, Mommy. You look pretty."

Jackie looked down at her daughter and said, "Oh Emily, I didn't even hear you come in. Good morning to you. How's my little girl doing today?"

Emily yawned and replied, "I'm good, but still a little sleepy."

Jackie held out her arms for Emily to give her a hug and said, "Come here." She picked her up and started walking to her room while saying, "My sweet Em. Why don't you get a little bit more sleep so Miss Maria doesn't have a cranky girl on her hands."

Jackie laid her down on the bed, pulled up the comforter, gave Emily her favorite stuffed bunny to snuggle, and then kissed her on the forehead whispering, "Mommy loves you." Then she tiptoed out of the room.

By the time she reached the kitchen, Jackie heard Maria's key in the lock and the door opening. She put her finger to her mouth and softly said, "Shhh, I think I just bought you an hour of peace and quiet."

"Gracias," Maria softly replied. "Did you have a nice weekend?"

Jackie jokingly moaned and replied, "Well, I barely survived Charlie Cheese, but the rest was really, really nice. We went to the park, watched movies, and just enjoyed each other's company. How about you?"

Maria smiled widely and said, "We also had some very nice family time. My younger two children came home from college for the weekend, so we had a big family dinner yesterday. Everyone is well, thank God."

Jackie returned her smile and said, "They should be thanking

God for having such a wonderful mother." She gave Maria a kiss on the cheek and said, "Look at the time. I've got to go." She picked up her purse and briefcase and whisked out the door.

"Have a good day!" Maria shouted after her.

Once at the office, Jackie stepped off the elevator, and the receptionist immediately told her that Mr. Wright wanted to see her. Jackie said "OK," turned and started walking toward Mr. Wright's office as her thoughts went haywire.

What in the world can he want this early? See, this is what happens when you start to relax even a little bit.

Then the other voice chimed in. *Oh, Jackie, calm down. He probably just wants to go over something from Friday. I'm sure it's nothing serious. We haven't even received any contracts yet.*

She got to his door, took a deep breath and knocked.

"Come in," Mr. Wright responded, so she pushed open the door. He was sitting behind his desk and, as usual, it was hard to read what kind of mood he was in, so she moved closer while saying, "You wanted to see me, sir?"

"Yes Jackie," he answered. "It seems we are going on a little field trip this morning to tour the Excelsior site."

Although quite surprised, Jackie nodded and said, "I see. I hope I'm dressed appropriately enough."

Mr. Wright smiled a bit and continued, "Yes, I'm not exactly dressed for a construction zone either, but Mr. Harding called me earlier today and wants to personally give us a guided tour of his project. It's certainly not something you can say no to."

"Of course not," Jackie agreed. "What time are we going?"

"He wants us there at 9:30, which means we leave here at 9 o'clock. We'll take my car. I'll see you in the lobby then. Thank you."

He put his head down and started reading whatever was on his desk, which was the sign that the conversation was over and time for Jackie to leave. She turned, walked out of his office and headed down the hall to see what she could accomplish in the forty-five minutes she had remaining. She plopped down in her chair, and her thoughts turned to Mr. Harding. *Wow, a personal tour. I wonder what he wears when he's on site? Will he show a bit more of his personality or still be all buttoned up and formal? I wonder what he drives?*

Then she shook her head and said out loud, "Snap out of it, damn it, and get some work done!"

Jackie and Mr. Wright pulled up to the construction trailer at 9:25, got out of the car, walked up the somewhat wobbly steps and entered.

A young lady greeted them and said, "You must be from the law firm. Let me tell Mr. Harding you're here."

As she was about to call him, a door opened and out he stepped. He held out his hand and said, "So glad you could come on such short notice."

Mr. Wright shook Trevor's hand and replied, "Of course, this outing will only add to our complete understanding of your vision."

While they were exchanging pleasantries, Jackie was observing as many details about Trevor as possible. Khaki pants and white perfectly tailored button-down with sleeves rolled up to just below the elbows. He had on a brown belt and work boots that didn't have a speck of dirt on them.

Trevor interrupted her inspections by saying, "I'm very pleased that you were able to join us as well, Ms. Summerville," and held out his hand to shake.

Jackie looked into his crystal-blue eyes, took his well-manicured hand in hers and replied, "Thank you, Mr. Harding, for taking time to show us around. This is very exciting and, please, call me Jackie."

Trevor held onto her hand a bit longer while noticing how well put together she was. Lovely dress with a modest jacket. Makeup very natural and highlighting her beautiful features. Even though he was making every effort to act professionally, inside he was thrilled to finally see her up close again, instead of from a balcony. His heart jumped a beat when she said to use her first name.

Not wanting it to get too awkward, he let her hand go and announced, "Well, let's get out there so I can show you my Excelsior. I hope your nice clothes and shoes don't get too dirty."

"We'll be just fine," Mr. Wright responded, as he looked down at the very expensive dress shoes his wife had bought for him for Christmas.

They left the trailer, got into an oversized golf cart and sped off as fast as it would go. Mr. Wright was alongside Trevor in the front and Jackie sat in back.

"We're going to the sales center first so I can introduce you to our agents whom you'll be working closely with, Ms. Summer … I mean Jackie."

"Excellent," Jackie answered and then added, "Would it be too much trouble to get copies of all of the existing contracts while we're here? It would save time and a courier."

Trevor turned around for a second, smiled at Jackie, and then turned back to watch the road while replying, "I like the way you think. I'll request that they put it all together while we're on our tour and then we can swing back around and get it."

Jackie was glad she was sitting behind Trevor because she could feel the warmth of an obvious blush in her cheeks as she said, "Thank you."

They pulled into the sales center parking lot, and Trevor stopped the cart next to others that were used to drive prospects around the property. Everyone got out and marched up the steps with Trevor leading the way. Instead of going in first, however, he held the door for Mr. Wright and Jackie saying, "After you, and welcome to my dream that is on its way to becoming my long-desired reality." Realizing his unintended, but hopefully accurate, double entendre, Trevor let out a quiet laugh.

Jackie looked around at all of Excelsior's different communities, the scale models and mockups of units and photos of other Prestigious Properties' developments. All were perfectly laid out, displayed and lighted.

Trevor interrupted her scanning by saying, "Alan, Jackie, I'd like you to meet our broker, Ted Sullivan." With that, he knocked on an office door and called out, "Ted, do you have a minute?"

The door opened almost immediately, and a tall, thin, red haired man came out saying, "My goodness, Mr. Harding. I'm so sorry, but I didn't know you were coming. What a pleasant surprise. What can I do for you?"

Trevor shook Ted's hand and replied, "I want to personally introduce you to our new closing attorney. This is Alan Wright, and this is his assistant, Jackie Summerville. They gave me quite the convincing presentation on Friday, and they certainly know our product and vision extraordinarily well. I know you'll work together seamlessly."

Ted shook their hands and said, "Words of such praise do

not come out of Mr. Harding's mouth unless they are warranted, so that's more than enough to convince me that we're going to be a great team. Let me introduce you to our sales associates."

After meeting the four agents and making the rounds through the office and examining all the sales tools, Trevor clapped his hands and said, "OK, now that you've seen the paper products, let's go get our feet dirty and see the real deal."

Ted said, "Thanks for stopping in and, again, I really look forward to teaming with you. Enjoy the rest of your visit."

They were about to leave when Jackie caught Trevor's eye. Trevor understood what she meant and said, "Oh, right. Ted, please have copies of all the existing contracts put together and we'll be back to get them. Ms. Summerville wants to get right to work on them. Oh, and I'm also borrowing three hard hats."

"Of course, Mr. Harding," Ted obediently replied. "Since you gave us the green light to start marketing last week, we've had some nice activity."

"Good," Trevor said as he started walking out the door. "We'll be back." Jackie and Alan followed him, and the three of them got back into the golf cart and sped off to the model section of Excelsior.

Pulling up to the first home, Trevor put on his hard hat, handed one to each of them, and got out of the cart while saying, "These are our six models. There are three single-family homes complete with a small yard for those who still enjoy that type of activity. There are also three villas with much smaller and scaled-down yards where the maintenance is provided to the owner."

Jackie and Mr. Wright both felt a little ridiculous but put on their hats and listened to Trevor as if they were hearing a church sermon, even though they already knew everything he was talking about—Jackie especially.

She decided to be bold and make a comment saying, "Yes, Mr. Harding, I'm so impressed with how your floor plans, cabinetry, and even color selections are so thoughtful and senior friendly. I find the psychology of colors especially fascinating."

Trevor smiled a bit and said, "Again Jackie, you've done your homework. If we're really going to change how older people transition from one phase of their lives to the next, we have to be especially mindful of their needs. Too many are living in situations where little, if any, thought has gone into this."

Wanting to be included in the conversation, Mr. Wright added, "Yes, Trevor. It'll make a considerable difference in their everyday enjoyment of life."

Trevor nodded sincerely and said, "Thank you, Alan. Don't get me wrong, I do think it will be highly marketable and therefore highly profitable, but I do truly have the motivation to assist our ever-expanding elderly population. Let's go inside."

Trevor, Mr. Wright and Jackie stepped toward the three-bedroom home where workers were busy sawing and hammering, so Trevor had to shout.

"This is our largest model. Some might think it's too big for our market, but think about—you're older and living in Florida and your kids live elsewhere. When they come to visit, do you really want them in a hotel or sleeping on air mattresses? Of course not. This model gives your relatives their own separate wing. They can do their own thing and not feel like they're putting their parents out. Then the time they do spend together is by choice and not just because they can't get out of each other's way. It benefits everyone, and the visit becomes much more enjoyable and special."

As he was talking, he became more and more excited and animated and then looked at Alan and Jackie and asked, "Do you get it?" To which they both nodded vigorously.

Trevor continued on saying, "All of the single-family homes are scaled down but have ample lawns and landscaping for those who still like mowing the grass or gardening. Of course, each owner has the option to contract the work out as well."

As if he hit the end of a script, Trevor quickly turned around and said, "Let's go over to the villas now."

Jackie and Mr. Wright followed Trevor like two little ducklings until he stopped in front of a model that was on a considerably smaller lot.

Talking loudly again, he narrated, "As you can see, this is aimed more toward an owner who no longer wants a large yard. There will still be beautiful landscaping, but it'll be maintained by a company who will take care of the grass, tree and bush trimming and the rest but will still allow the owner to plant a garden if he or she so desires."

Mr. Wright interjected, "Very thoughtful."

Trevor continued, "We mirror the same three-bedroom, two plus den, and two-bedroom idea as the single-family homes, and all will have the same design elements that Jackie so aptly referred to."

Jackie had been watching Trevor intently as he gave the tour and was amazed how a man with his money, power and success could almost seem like an excited child when talking about Excelsior. She found this quite endearing.

Just then, Trevor stopped his lecture again, hopped into the cart while waving his arms for them to join him saying, "Come on, there's more to see. Off we go to the condos."

Jackie and Mr. Wright hurriedly got in, and Trevor swung the cart around and headed down the street until they came up to four large concrete slabs that were going to be the foundations for Excelsior's condominiums. As Jackie had noted when first studying the various products, there were four square areas that had been staked off in each slab. She surmised that these would be the locations for the buildings' elevators. She decided to be brave again and commented, "Mr. Harding, providing so many elevators for your residents is such a wonderful service to them. What an outstanding idea!"

Trevor looked at her, smiled and said, "Well Jackie, I'm paid to have outstanding ideas."

Mr. Wright looked at both of them and said, "I seem to be in the dark here. Elevators?"

Trevor answered, "Yes, Alan. Because we're dealing with seniors who are still somewhat self-sufficient yet not as vital as they used to be, I decided that all the condos will have four elevators. This way, the walk to their door is shorter and a lot more manageable. Did it cost me a lot more money? Absolutely, but I'm confident that we'll recoup it in sales."

Alan nodded in agreement and said, "I'm sure you will."

Trevor was on the move again and headed back to the cart, which was their clue to get going. They all got in, and Trevor floored it again.

"Now we're going to the sites for the clubhouse and nearby medical facility. Not much has been done yet, just some clearing, but that's about to change once the permits are issued."

They pulled up to a very large vacant piece of land that adjoined another somewhat smaller parcel. There was no sign of activity, just dirt-filled areas that had the promise of something being built.

Trevor continued being the tour guide saying, "As you can see, we need to play catch-up with these two phases of Excelsior, but the land you see to your left is where the finest geriatric care facility will sit, and directly in front of you will stand our expansive clubhouse. This will not just be a place for lunch, dinner and bridge, but will offer a full complement of activities and classes to keep our residents both challenged and engaged."

Mr. Wright commented, "Alan, just like everything we've seen today, it certainly is impressive and so well thought out."

Jackie was surveying the land before her and trying to imagine what the completed structures would look like, when her eye caught some movement on the clubhouse lot. She blinked and tried to focus on the area where she saw it. Again, she saw something move right where a small mound of dirt was. She scanned the ground to the right and left of the mound and saw more. Curiosity got the best of her, so she asked, "Excuse me Mr. Harding, but what are those mounds over there?"

Trevor looked puzzled and replied, "Mounds, what mounds. What are you referring to, Jackie?"

She knew that she was taking a chance by prolonging this conversation but continued saying, "I don't mean to take up more of your time, sir, but just look." Then she pointed and said, "There's something over there, and there, and there."

Trevor trained his eye to where Jackie was pointing and agreed saying, "You're right. I do see something." Then he took his phone out and dialed Pete.

"Yes, sir," Pete answered.

Trevor quickly replied, "Pete, my guests and I are just leaving the clubhouse property and we've noticed something odd on the site. I need you to come out here and check it out and report to me ASAP."

"I'll get right on it," Pete answered.

Trevor hung up the phone, turned to Jackie and Mr. Wright and said, "I'll have a report from my construction manager shortly. Thank you for pointing it out, Jackie. Now let's go back to the sales center so we can pick up those contracts and let you go back to doing what you do best."

They all got in the cart again and drove to the sales center where Jackie volunteered to go inside to return the hard hats and pick up the package. While she went up the steps, Trevor couldn't help but notice her well-shaped legs, one of the first things that attracted him to her. He then turned to Mr. Wright and said, "Alan, you have quite a fine assistant in Jackie."

Mr. Wright smiled a bit and replied, "Yes, Trevor, I know, so don't try to steal her away from me." To which they both laughed.

They returned to the construction office, and Jackie and Mr. Wright once again extended their thanks to Trevor, said goodbye and headed back to their office to first clean their shoes and then get back to work.

Fifteen long minutes later, Trevor's phone rang. He looked at the caller ID, and when he saw that it was Pete, he immediately answered it. "Yes, Pete. What have you found out?"

Pete swallowed hard and replied, "Well, Mr. Harding. It seems we have a problem."

Trevor quickly shot back, "Problem? What kind of problem can a bunch of dirt have?"

Pete braced himself again and continued, "I went out and inspected the property like you asked, and you were right. There's definitely some activity on the lot."

Trevor could feel his anger rise and his patience dwindle so he demanded in a louder voice, "Pete, tell me what the hell is the problem!"

Pete gave him the shortest answer he could think of and said, "Burrowing owls."

Trevor repeated him, "Burrowing owls!" and then loudly added, "What in God's name does that mean?"

Pete used the most calming voice he could and replied, "Mr. Harding, burrowing owls love to nest on vacant land, and we have a number of them on the clubhouse lot."

Trevor was further annoyed and shot back, "OK, so we get rid of them. Move them or something."

Pete was still trying to stay calm and answered, "I wish it was that easy."

Trevor had had enough and said in a very curt manner, "OK Pete, now you listen to me very carefully. I need you in my office for a full briefing on this at 12 noon today. Oh, and bring that environmental engineer guy that we paid a pretty penny to. Some good that did us!"

"Ron Wilkes," Pete replied and continued, "Yes sir. We'll be there at noon."

Trevor added, "And check the medical site ASAP. If it's clear of owls, get it covered immediately!" Trevor then hung up without saying goodbye, quickly turned to his computer and googled burrowing owls.

Ten minutes and a lot of cursing later, Trevor leaned back in his chair, sighed and muttered, "Seventy-four days. I do not have seventy-four days to wait for these pain-in-the-ass birds to hatch and grow. I've got to figure something out."

He then started his own back and forth saying, "We absolutely need this clubhouse built, but these owls are a god-damned protected species. I have always prided myself on being an environmentally responsible developer, but this is asking way too much. How about a relocation? Trevor, you know good and well that will not fly with the Wildlife Commission. What the hell to do? Am I going to be stymied by a little yellow-eyed bird? Cute, yes sort of, but not at the expense of my Excelsior!"

He buried his head in his hands and tried to force himself to think and be the outstanding problem solver he could always count on. At noon sharp, there was a knock on the door. "Come in," shouted Trevor.

Pete and the environmental engineer, Ron Wilkes, stepped very gingerly into the office. Trevor pointed to two chairs and said, "Sit and let's get to it. What is going on and what can we do about it?"

Pete started, "The good news, Mr. Harding, is that the owls are only nesting on the clubhouse lot and only on the middle portion. The medical site has no signs of activity, and I have a team covering all of the unaffected areas as we speak, so these little critters don't get any ideas."

Trevor nodded and responded, "Well, I guess that's some good news."

Even though his research since this morning informed Trevor of the answers, he still asked both Pete and Ron, "OK, now give me the bad news. What does this invasion do to our timeline?"

Ron took the lead now and replied, "Mr. Harding, as you are

aware, we have a number of burrowing owl colonies on the land that was set aside for the clubhouse."

Trevor lost his patience again and loudly said, "Don't waste my time telling me things I already know!"

Ron coughed, swallowed and continued on, "My apologies. The facts are that these birds are on the state's threatened species list and are also protected under the Federal Migratory Bird Treaty Act, so they cannot …"

Trevor interrupted again saying, "Yes, Ron. I get it. Enough about the problem. What I want to know is what can be done about it?"

Ron looked at his notes while trying to steel himself for Trevor's next outburst. He then replied, "We could apply for a permit to what we call take the birds. It's basically a relocation."

Trevor brightened and said, "Great! Let's proceed with that."

Ron found his courage, put his hand up and said, "Mr. Harding, I'm afraid it's not a quick enough fix. As you are well aware, everything that has to do with the government is long and drawn-out, and this process is no exception. There are permits to apply for, applications and mitigation forms to file. Quite honestly, it's a nightmare."

Trevor hit the top of his desk with both hands and got up shouting, "No, this is a verifiable nightmare! I've heard enough. Not a word about this to anyone."

Pete and Ron both nodded vigorously, quickly got up and left. Without saying a word of goodbye, Trevor sat down again and whispered, "There has to be a better solution. Come on Trevor, think."

Chapter Twenty-Nine

Jackie sat down at her desk and was about to open the envelope containing the contracts, but instead allowed herself to reflect on the morning while talking to herself.

"Well, that was certainly unexpected, yet remarkably pleasant. He's so ... I don't know ... real. Not at all like the pompous arrogant jackass that I originally thought he might be. Driven, yes that's obvious, but not the typical tyrannical developer type who feels like yelling and threatening is the only way to get things done. Yes, I do believe I'm going to like working for Mr. Trevor Harding. And he's not bad to look at either!"

Then she chided herself saying, "OK enough with the girly stuff. You've got work to do." She picked up the envelope, pulled out the contents and started sorting through the papers when she was interrupted by Ryan and Karen who were standing in her doorway.

Ryan piped up first saying, "So, I hear you had a morning rendezvous with Mr. Rich, Powerful and Handsome."

Jackie stared him down and said, "First of all Mr. National

Enquirer reporter, it wasn't anywhere near a rendezvous. If you would check your facts, you'd know that it was a tour of the Excelsior project—with Mr. Wright, might I add."

Karen got involved in the conversation saying, "I'm sure it was all aboveboard Jackie, but now you've spent a fair amount of time with him on two separate occasions. What's he like, other than super good looking?"

Jackie smiled and replied, "He's actually very nice. You can feel the command that he has of what he does, but he's also down to earth. More importantly, you can see and feel that this project means more to him than your ordinary development."

Ryan scoffed and said, "Yeah, probably because he'll make more dough than usual."

Jackie waved her hand to dismiss Ryan's sarcasm and retorted, "No, no, he truly is invested in creating something unheard of and very special. You can just tell by the way he talks about Excelsior."

Karen chimed in and said, "From the little I've heard about it, it sounds really amazing."

Ryan shook his head and said, "My, my, aren't you two something. Jackie, you can be president and Karen you're vice president."

Jackie was growing impatient, so she played along with Ryan in hopes of putting an end to his childish remarks and asked, "OK, I'll bite. President of what?"

Ryan laughed out loud and announced, "The Trevor Harding Fan Club, of course!"

Jackie let out an exasperated sigh and then put up both hands saying loudly, "Enough! I've already missed half the day, and I've got contracts to review. And last I checked, you both still work here, too. Accent on 'work'!"

"OK Pres, and even though I didn't hear him speak, I'm guessing he's not from Australia," Ryan quipped and then they both left Jackie to finally get to her work.

Jackie realized that she had gotten caught in her previous white lie about Trevor, but dismissed it as Ryan was just being his normal pain-in-the-ass self, so she picked up the first contract and read the name aloud, "Mr. and Mrs. Swartz, Stanley and Rose. Buying a two-bedroom villa home for $429,000. Don't I wish I had that kind of money!"

Then she opened a file on her computer and input all the pertinent information and dates that would now be flagged. Next was Mr. Williams, Robert, and, again, Jackie talked to herself, "Hmmm, a two-bedroom condo on the first floor. Preconstruction pricing of $329,000. Such a deal," she laughed out loud to herself.

She went through the same process with each of the remaining ten contracts and when she was done, she commented, "Wow, twelve contracts, and they've only been at this a week. I'd better be ready for a total onslaught. I'm so glad that I went ahead and set up all these programs, even though it would have been a total waste of time if we hadn't gotten the project."

Then she admonished herself, *Jackie, but now you're wasting time thinking about what isn't. You've got the blasted project, now focus all your energy on busting your butt to help Excelsior soar.*

Just then, Jackie's intercom buzzed, and it was Mr. Wright. "Jackie, I just got a message that Mr. Harding wants to talk with us on a conference call at 2 o'clock."

Jackie was taken aback and quickly said, "Didn't we just see him this morning?"

Mr. Wright somewhat sternly replied, "It doesn't matter if we just saw him five minutes ago. He wants to talk, so we talk."

Jackie realized that she had been rash and apologized, "I'm sorry Mr. Wright. You're a hundred percent correct. I'll be in your office at 1:55."

The line went dead, and Jackie couldn't help but wonder what Mr. Harding wanted to talk about. They had gone over everything she could think of, and the tour showed them the entire development. *What does he want? I hope everything is OK with him.*

She immediately realized she had just crossed that threshold again where she started to care about her client and found herself invested in their well-being. She firmly instructed herself. *Stop going there! You are only supposed to do what the job calls for—get contracts closed efficiently and on time.*

Then she retorted her argument. *But Mr. Harding cares so much about Excelsior, shouldn't I too? If he succeeds, so do we. Plus, he really seems like a good man.*

She flipped back again. *Jackie, you are a legal assistant in the firm that he has hired to get a job done. Nothing more! Now, go to Mr. Wright's office and leave your emotionally codependent self at the door.*

She got up from her desk, tried to smooth her dress that had seen too much in and out of a golf cart to keep its crisp line, and then walked down to Mr. Wright's office.

He was at his desk and waved at Jackie to sit down in one of the chairs facing him and said, "Jackie, no matter what it is that Mr. Harding wants, I will take the lead in responding, and we'll be conciliatory yet confident in our demeanor."

Jackie nodded and responded, "Of course, Mr. Wright."

Just then, Mr. Wright's phone buzzed, and the receptionist announced that Mr. Harding was on line three. Mr. Wright smoothed his tie, pushed the button and greeted him saying, "Hello Trevor. I have you on speaker as Ms. Summerville is also here as you requested. What may we do for you?"

Trevor inhaled deeply and answered, "Hello Alan and Jackie. I know we've spent quite some time together over these last few days, but something has come up that must be disclosed and then addressed."

Jackie and Mr. Wright exchanged looks, and then Mr. Wright said, "All right Trevor. You know that anything we discuss will be kept in the utmost confidence."

"I know," Trevor replied. "That's why I'm talking with you and not some blabbermouthed broker or construction guy. What we discuss must stay totally between us."

Jackie and Mr. Wright now exchanged a look of concern and then he answered Trevor in his most lawyerly tone, "Trevor, you have my word. What is it you would like to discuss?"

Trevor hesitated a few seconds and then answered, "Jackie, remember the mysterious activity that you spotted on the club-house parcel?"

Having been asked a direct question, Jackie had to enter the conversation, so she confidently replied, "Yes, sir."

"Well, it seems we have some uninvited visitors in the form of burrowing owls, and it has created a colossal mess!"

Mr. Wright interjected saying, "My goodness, Trevor. I've never had a client who had to deal with this issue, but I know it can be quite problematic."

"Problematic is putting it mildly, Alan" Trevor retorted. "I've already met with my environmental engineer, and he briefed me on the consequences of this—none of which are good. If we can't figure out a solution, this is going to delay work on the clubhouse for four months. Just think of the impact it will have on sales!"

Jackie raised her hand, and Mr. Wright nodded signaling that she could speak, so she said, "Mr. Harding, I'm certainly not an expert on burrowing owls, but I'm sure there has to be a way to deal with them."

Trevor sounded exasperated and replied, "Believe me, I've been wracking my brain since I received the news. Every possible remedy takes much too long—absent going there in the dark of night and eliminating the problem."

Jackie put her hand to her mouth, gasped, and couldn't restrain herself from blurting out, "You can't do that!"

"Jackie," Mr. Wright admonished her.

Trevor laughed loudly and said, "Alan, it's quite all right. I wasn't being serious Jackie. I would never do such a thing."

Jackie calmed down and said, "I'm so sorry, Mr. Harding. Just the thought of those poor little birds … I mean, of course you wouldn't do that. Sometimes, I get a bit too involved."

Then she looked at Mr. Wright and mouthed "I'm sorry" to him.

Trevor laughed again saying, "I like involved and, plus, your little outburst gave me the first lighthearted moment I've had since we landed in bird land. There hasn't been a lot of laughing going on around here."

Mr. Wright took the lead again saying, "Trevor, we'll keep moving forward with contracts and closings. Business as usual unless and until you tell us otherwise."

"Yes, Alan," Trevor replied. "Let's give this matter a day or so and let me continue to brainstorm for a solution that will keep us on track."

"Sounds good," Mr. Wright answered.

Trevor then said, "Oh, and Jackie, you keep staying involved. Who knows, maybe you'll come up with the magic bullet. Mind you, not to shoot the owls, just one to figure this mess out."

He let out another chuckle and added, "I've got a million other things to attend to, so goodbye for now."

"Goodbye," both Mr. Wright and Jackie said in unison. The phone went silent and Mr. Wright looked at Jackie with a frown that morphed into a grin. He said, "Well Jackie, that could have ended very badly, but fortunately our Mr. Harding is a very ethical man and apparently likes your quote-unquote involvement."

"Yes sir," Jackie responded. "Again, I'm very sorry, but I was imagining those little owls being …"

Mr. Wright quickly interrupted her and said, "Yes, yes, enough already. I have work to do, as I'm very certain you do, too."

With that, Mr. Wright looked down at the papers on his desk which, as always, was the sign to go. Jackie said "Yes, sir," while getting up. She then left, swiftly returned to her office and got back to work.

Chapter Thirty

As usual, Jackie had just finished turning her key when Emily came bounding out of the door shouting, "Mommy, Mommy, Mommy!"

With a huge smile, Jackie picked her up and said, "Oh my goodness Em, you are getting so big. Pretty soon, I won't be able to lift you."

Emily snuggled into Jackie's neck as she was carried inside where Maria was waiting. "So, how did your first official day working for Mr. Bigshot go?" Maria asked.

"Well, Maria," Jackie replied. "It certainly wasn't your run-of-the-mill day." Then she gave an abbreviated account of the day's events.

"Dios mio!" Maria exclaimed. "That was a very hectic day. I never imagined all of that, but I did think that you'd be tired, so there's a chicken and rice casserole in the fridge. Just heat it up for thirty minutes at 350 degrees."

Jackie put Emily down and reached out to give Maria a hug saying, "Thank you so, so much. I know I say it all the time, but I truly don't know what Emily and I would do without you."

Maria hugged her back and said, "It's the least I can do. I know how hard you work."

She gave Jackie a tender kiss on the cheek, turned to Emily and kissed her on the forehead saying, "You two take care of each other. Have a good night and I'll see you in the morning." Then she picked up her purse and went out the door.

Jackie wiped away the tear that had started rolling down her cheek and turned her attention to Emily asking, "So my big girl, what did you do today?"

Emily smiled her sweet smile and replied, "I painted you a picture, Mommy. Do you want to see it?"

"You did! Of course, I do," Jackie answered as Emily was already pulling her by the hand down the hallway to her room.

In the corner, there was a child-sized table that Emily loved to sit at and do all sorts of activities, from playing with her stuffed animals and looking at picture books to doing puzzles. On it was a piece of drawing paper that had been filled with a painting that included every color in her paint kit.

Jackie looked at it lovingly and said, "My goodness Em, this is beautiful. Can you tell me about it?"

"Course I can, Mommy," Emily proudly answered and proceeded to point out various shapes saying, "This is your big building, this is a pelican, and this is our house."

Jackie could barely make out the images, but rubbed Emily's back saying, "How lovely. Look at all the colors you used make it so pretty. Should we put it on the fridge?"

Emily looked up at Jackie and replied, "No Mommy. I made it special. Just for you."

Jackie gave her a kiss and said, "Why thank you, Em. Where

would you like me to put it then?"

Emily picked up her picture and grabbed Jackie's hand again. She led her to her own bedroom and pointed to Jackie's dressing mirror saying, "Let's put it there. That way when you're getting ready for work, you can smile."

Even though the paper would cover a good portion of the mirror, Jackie clapped her hands and said, "What a great idea! I'll go get some tape and we'll put it right up. You are such a special girl, my Em."

Jackie went into the kitchen, opened the junk drawer, found the tape and went back to her room to find Emily twirling in front of the mirror singing, "I am the Pelican Princess and I'm going to get Mommy a really big house someday."

Jackie paused and watched her beautiful daughter while thinking, "No matter how nice a big house would be, I treasure nothing more than magical, unforgettable moments like these."

"OK my Pelican Princess," Jackie said with a chuckle, "Where do you want your masterpiece to be hung?"

Jackie did her best attempt at motherly coaxing and persuaded Emily to tape the picture on the lower part of the mirror, so she still had enough uncovered to see her reflection. "See Em, now it's at the perfect height for you to look at it too," Jackie said convincingly.

"Yes, Mommy. It's perfect," Emily happily agreed and then immediately switched gears and announced, "I'm hungry!"

"Me too," Jackie said. "Let's put that delicious casserole in the oven, I'll make a quick salad and we'll be eating in no time."

Emily smiled up at her mother and asked, "Can I help?"

"Of course, my best assistant ever. Let's do this!"

After dinner and some stories, Jackie put Emily to bed.

Then she poured herself a glass of wine and started to reflect on the day's events. *What a first day,* she thought as she reviewed the unexpected tour and the really unexpected phone call about the owls.

She turned her thoughts to Trevor. *For as much of a tough businessman as I'm sure he is, he is still so passionate and seems to have a really strong moral compass.*

Then she let out a soft laugh and said out loud, "I can't believe I yelled at him. Even more, I really cannot believe that he thought it was funny. I thought I was going to get canned right then and there."

Then the owls came into her mind, so she grabbed her phone and googled burrowing owls. Seeing the first picture of them she said, "Ohhhh my, they are the cutest things ever! We have to come up with an answer for both the owls and Mr. Harding." She sat for an hour looking at the pictures and reading up on their habitats and behaviors, but no ideas came to mind other than the increased pressure to somehow find a solution. "Come on, think Jackie, think," she said out loud, but then decided that it would be best to sleep on it, so she clicked off her phone and went to her room.

Jackie woke up with a start. She looked at her phone, and it read 4:52 in the morning. She rubbed her eyes and said out loud, "I think I've got it! An aviary, of course! We can't get rid of the owls, so let's include them in the clubhouse plans. Plus, old people love to bird watch. It's a total win-win!"

She got out of bed, grabbed her laptop and a legal pad out of her briefcase and went to the kitchen table. She went to the Excelsior website, clicked on amenities, then the clubhouse icon. Up popped some marketing verbiage and then she saw the existing floor plan. As she homed in on the layout, she thought, *Let's see, there has to be an area that can be amended to include our aviary. Where did they say the owls were located? Oh crap, he didn't. This is a waste of time until we can superimpose the floor plan over the lot so we can see exactly what portion of the clubhouse is impacted.*

She closed the laptop. *Now how in the world am I going to pitch this idea? Obviously, I have to pass it by Mr. Wright first and hope he can think outside of his normal 'work within the parameters of your job description' box and allow me to get more involved. Mr. Harding did say he liked it.* She giggled a little, and knowing that she was definitely not going back to sleep, she hit the ON button for the coffeemaker, got up from the table and went to take a shower.

Trevor had a fitful night's sleep, tossing and turning all night with the owl problem always at the forefront of his waking thoughts.

There has to be an answer, was the thought that immediately popped into his head when he woke up at 12:33. Finally falling back to sleep at 1:47 without a viable idea, he slept until 3:25 but woke up again. *Maybe I can call in a favor and get the process fast-tracked.*

As soon as he finished, he rebutted himself. *Trevor, you have never, ever operated in the good ole boy system of you scratch my back and I'll scratch yours. Are you really going to start now?*

He rolled over and used a relaxation technique that usually worked like magic. He started counting backwards from 714 to preoccupy and ease his mind. Most nights, it didn't take very long at all, maybe 50 numbers max, but this time he finally drifted off again when he had reached 527.

He managed to get another hour and a half of sleep until

he opened his eyes and his mind came awake again. He stared at the ceiling. *Of all the hurdles I've overcome, all the problems I've solved, all the roadblocks and bumps that I've managed with ease, are you really telling me that this is going to be the one to beat me? Come on, I can persuade the top doctor to leave Johns Hopkins and his practice to come here, but I am at the mercy of a little winged enemy?*

He chuckled at his choice of words and added, *OK, maybe enemy is too strong a word. For God's sake, they don't know what they're doing. Nonetheless, we've got to come up with a viable plan. There has to be a way, but I am totally striking out.*

It was now 5:30 in the morning, and Trevor knew he was not going back to sleep, so he threw off the covers, got up and went to take a shower.

Chapter Thirty-One

Jackie got to the office at 8:15 and waited in her office for Mr. Wright's secretary to arrive at 9. In the meantime, she printed out a copy of the clubhouse floor plan and searched out a copy of the survey for the lot, so she would be ready to present her idea. She looked at both plans. *I just know this aviary can work, but I also know Mr. Wright, and I have to be a hundred percent practical and businesslike. If I get even the slightest bit excited or emotional, he will shut me down and tell me that it's not part of my job to be worried about Mr. Harding's owl problem.*

She looked at the floor plan more closely. *I don't know exactly where the owls are, and I'm far from a construction expert, but I don't see one thing on here that can't be moved or adjusted. Just think, Excelsior's own aviary, not just for burrowing owls, but all kinds of species of birds. Who knows, maybe we can partner with the Florida Wildlife Commission or, better yet, The Audubon Society.*

Then she stopped and verbally reprimanded herself again saying, "See, there you go again, carrying on and on. Just focus on what you're going to say to Mr. Wright."

By then it was 9 o'clock, so she buzzed Mr. Wright's secretary and asked, "Good morning, Amanda. Could you please tell me if Mr. Wright has any available time this morning?"

Amanda answered, "Let me check, Jackie, but he did say when he was leaving yesterday that he had lost almost an entire day of work because of the unexpected Harding issues."

Jackie pressed her hands together as if to pray and said, "Yes, I know, Amanda, but my needing to see him does relate to those issues, so it's pretty important."

Amanda replied, "OK Jackie. It looks like he has a half-hour window right now. I'll advise him that you'll be here momentarily, but I caution you to be super concise with whatever it is and definitely do not—I repeat do not—waste his time."

"Of course, Amanda," Jackie replied as she silently fist pumped and got up from her chair. "Thank you so much."

Jackie threw on her blazer to appear more businesslike, grabbed both plans, and quickly headed down the hallway to Mr. Wright's office. When she got there, he looked up from his readings, peered over his glasses and said, "Jackie, I know whatever this is has to be critical for you to interrupt my workday before it even has a chance to start."

Jackie sheepishly replied, "Yes sir. It does rise to that level." She tried to sound confident and continued, "If I can ask you to come over to the meeting table, I have something I'd like to show you."

Mr. Wright decided to indulge her request, so he got up and followed her to the table while saying, "All right, Jackie. What is it?"

Jackie smoothed both papers on the table and put some nearby books on the corners of each. Then she took a hard swallow and started her explanation saying, "Mr. Wright, as you can see, here we have the floor plan for the clubhouse and the other is the survey of the lot."

"Yes, Jackie," Mr. Wright said with an edge in his voice, "I've seen enough of these in my career to know what I'm looking at."

Jackie didn't respond and continued, "Well, I was thinking that our owl problem could be solved if we just incorporated them into the layout of the clubhouse."

With even more sternness in his voice Mr. Wright shot back, "What on earth are you thinking about? We do not decide nor influence what our client wants to include as an amenity. Further, why in God's name are you spending your time and energy on this? That is not your job! It's not our owl problem, it's Mr. Harding's."

Jackie steeled herself and continued on by replying, "But Mr. Wright, Mr. Harding did ask for our help in finding an answer to the owl dilemma, and I'm certain that an in-house aviary would keep the timeline pretty much intact. Don't get rid of the owls, but instead build an aviary to house them and other birds. It would also be an excellent attraction for the residents. This amenity featured at Excelsior would be uniquely superior to anything remotely offered at any other development."

Mr. Wright was now looking from the floor plan to the survey and back again.

Jackie liked that he seemed at least somewhat interested, so she went on saying, "I was going to draw where the owls are as it relates to the floor plan in order to see what is impacted, but Mr. Harding never specified where they're located, so I'm at a dead end right now."

Mr. Wright looked at Jackie and said, "In all my years of

practicing law, I never thought I would be discussing owls, aviaries and amending floor plans, but I do have a duty to assist our client in any way we can, especially this odd predicament he's found himself in. I also believe it's my further duty to at least present the idea to him."

Jackie gave another little fist pump under the table as Mr. Wright picked up the phone and dialed Trevor's number. While it was ringing, he quickly told Jackie to let him start the conversation and not to enter it until he said to. Jackie nodded in agreement.

"Good morning, Trevor," Mr. Wright said assuredly.

"Good morning, Alan," Trevor replied and added, "I wasn't expecting to hear from you."

Mr. Wright answered, "Yes, I know Trevor, but Ms. Summerville has come up with a somewhat unorthodox idea that I feel we at least have to propose to you. I'm going to put you on speaker now, if that's all right."

Trevor's curiosity was piqued, so he said, "Yes. That's fine. Good morning, Jackie."

Mr. Wright nodded to Jackie and she answered, "Good morning, Mr. Harding. I've been giving this whole owl situation a lot of thought."

Trevor said, "That makes two of us. I've come up with nothing viable. How about you?"

Jackie summoned up her courage once again and began, "Well, Mr. Harding, after you went over all of the hardships that you and Excelsior would suffer if you went down the normal avenues to deal with the owls, I had an idea to go down a different path."

She paused a few seconds and Trevor said, "Go on."

She knew this was the make-or-break moment, so she took a deep breath and said, "Instead of removing them or delaying construction, why not incorporate the owls into the first of its kind in-house aviary?"

She paused again to allow him to respond, but all he calmly said was, "Continue."

"I have copies of the clubhouse floor plan and the lot survey. Once it's determined exactly where the owls are on the survey in relation to the clubhouse, the floor plan can then be amended to include the owls in an aviary that will be built in that location. Other birds can be added too, and plants and foliage."

Then she got a bit bold and asked, "Mr. Harding, don't you think the residents would absolutely love watching all the birds? It would add such a wonderful pastime for them and could even be educational."

Trevor was floored by the genius of her plan. It was a win-win plan, just like the kind he usually devised. He let out a laugh and replied, "Why, yes, Jackie, I believe they certainly would enjoy and benefit from a feature like that. How in the world did you come up with this idea?"

Jackie was so relieved by his answer that she allowed herself a smile and replied, "Believe it or not, it just popped into my head while I was sleeping. It woke me up out of a deep sleep."

Trevor was also smiling and responded, "I do believe that's called inspiration, or maybe divine intervention. Regardless, it is a fantastic idea. Creative, smart, and should be very doable."

His voice got excited as he continued on, "I'll immediately get the surveyor to add the location of the owl area to the survey and have the blueprint company lay the floor plan over it, and then we'll see exactly what we're dealing with. Obviously, I'll put a critical rush on all of it and expect it to be done by the end of the day. Can we meet in the morning to go over the findings?"

Mr. Wright had been sitting back listening to the two of them converse, but then joined in saying, "Trevor, with all due respect, this is way out of my realm of expertise, so I'm going to decline. However, if you'd like to go over this with Jackie, by all means, I'll make her available."

"I fully understand, Alan. I got a bit carried away. Jackie, would you like to continue to be involved with this?"

Jackie couldn't believe her ears. She looked at Mr. Wright who nodded his approval and then replied, "Yes, Mr. Harding. I would like nothing more than to see the findings. If you'd like, I could come to your office at 8:30 tomorrow morning?"

Trevor smiled widely and answered, "Excellent. I'll see you then."

Mr. Wright then said, "Have a good rest of your day, Trevor."

Trevor replied, "It has already been much better than I could have possibly wished for. Thank you both very much. Goodbye."

The phone went silent and Trevor leaned back in his chair and said, "Wow, beauty and brains, too. I know I have to keep this professional, but I so very much want to get to know the complete picture of Ms. Jackie Summerville."

Then it occurred to him that he didn't have to wait until tomorrow to see her again because she would be taking her beach walk this evening. "Dare I?" Trevor questioned himself. He was very tempted, but concluded, "Best not. At least not yet." Then he picked up the phone again and dialed his surveyor.

Chapter Thirty-Two

Jackie really had to force herself to concentrate but managed to make progress on all the files throughout the day. She sent out introductory emails and hard copies to the twelve existing buyers and sent a similar letter to all the outside real estate agents who had brought a buyer into Excelsior. For those who were obtaining financing, she sent a letter to each bank or mortgage company informing them that Wright, Stewart & Blake would serve as the closing agent and that she was the contact person for the firm.

All this type of work she had repeated thousands of times, so she went about it easily with her routine down pat. New construction like Excelsior can have a more fluid timeline based on the progress being made. The closing date was always tied to the certificate of occupancy issued by the county, so there was no finite date, but she knew once that happened, all hell broke loose. Everyone would start vying to close as soon as possible, with the developer pushing even harder for everything to close yesterday so the money would start flowing his way instead of the other way around. Time, as they say in the legal field, is of the utmost essence.

"The developer in this case being one Trevor Harding," Jackie said aloud and continued, "With whom I'm going to meet one on one tomorrow morning. Go figure! We will see if my idea can be a reality or just some half-baked pipedream. Oh God, please don't let that happen. I'd be soooo mortified."

Thinking about this made her turn her attention back to the clubhouse floor plan and survey again. She tried to match them up together in her head while muttering, "I'm no architect or builder, but I really don't see why this space can't be altered to accommodate our little feathered friends. So, you lose a card room or two. What's the big deal?"

Then she reined in her thoughts saying, "Stick with your initial thought, Jackie. You definitely do not know the first thing about building, and you absolutely don't know a damn thing about building an aviary, so stop being so flippant!"

She looked up from the plans and noticed it was 5:13. "Oh Lord," she exclaimed. "I've got to get going. My sanity walks are going to be that much more important as things really start ramping up around here."

She snatched her things, rushed out the door, hit the elevator button, and off she went to her car and her beloved beach.

As she felt the sand sink beneath her feet, Jackie also felt her stress level fall. It was a beautiful sunny and calm evening, and the gulf looked like one long lake extending to the horizon and beyond. Jackie gazed at the water. *I'm very glad they don't use it in interior decorating anymore, but seafoam green water like this is incredibly beautiful.*

She giggled and started leisurely strolling down the beach.

This evening, the gulls were particularly active, swooping over-head and cackling until they were out over the water. Then they would turn downward and divebomb with their wings tucked in and pierce the water's surface like a torpedo. They'd submerge for a split second and hope to retrieve a nice-sized fish. Over and over, they continued.

Jackie stopped and smiled as she watched this aerial dance. *It's pretty much like people's luck with fishing. Sometimes you hit it big, but a lot of times it's a bust. Those birds look pretty plump though, so the fishing must be good.*

She continued and looked to the dunes that divided the beach from the mega-mansions she had started to pass. Instead of the normal beige sand mixed with woodsy sea oats, she spotted the most gorgeous purplish pink flowers blooming out of a deep green leafy vine. She looked at them in wonderment. *I can't even keep a plant alive with potting soil and fertilizer, and these beauties just grow out of the sand. I'm telling you, Mother Nature is just amazing!*

Then she looked up at "The House" and addressed the imaginary owner, "Well, I'm not exactly friends with someone as rich as you, but I do have a personal meeting with Trevor Harding tomorrow. Not so bad for a struggling single mom. I wonder if you know each other?"

She allowed herself to fantasize for a moment and visual-ized herself sitting down at a well-set table in the luxury of the same dining room that she had imagined many times before, but this time there was only herself and another. They were enjoying a delicious meal and exquisite wine. Unlike all the other fantasies, this time when she looked across the table, the image was no longer blurred and fuzzy. It was crystal clear, and she was staring at Trevor.

She immediately shook her head to snap out of it. *That's enough of this foolishness. Yes, he's charming and smart and handsome and seems to be a good person, but he is so out of your league. Plus, he happens to be your client. Enough being a dizzy-headed schoolgirl. You know better!*

She turned and started back the other way, but no matter how hard she tried, she couldn't shake the image of Trevor smiling at her across the table. Little did she know, Trevor was in his usual spot on the balcony with his binoculars trained on her every move and imagining pretty much the same scene— just the two of them sharing a lovely dinner together.

Chapter Thirty-Three

Trevor decided it was best to have Pete sit in on the meeting with Jackie. He would contribute both expertise and an added buffer to Trevor's growing desire to let Jackie know his true feelings for her.

At 8:20, Jackie pulled her eight-year-old Honda Civic into the parking lot of the construction trailer, checked herself out in the mirror and applied a last bit of lipstick. She got out and scanned the parking lot and noticed a big heavy-duty truck and a sleek steel-gray Tesla sports car.

That's got to be his, she thought as she walked across the gravel. She climbed the three wobbly steps leading up to the door, held her breath for a few seconds, let out a long cleansing breath and then turned the knob.

Instead of being in his office, Trevor was waiting right behind the door dressed in crisp gray pants and a light blue button-down, which again had the sleeves rolled up right below his elbows. He wasn't wearing boots today, but instead coal-black loafers. She resisted the urge to examine him more and said, "Good morning, Mr. Harding."

"Good morning, Jackie," he smiled and replied as he quickly took in as much of her as possible—a business-like yet very feminine light green and navy print dress, nicely paired with a navy jacket.

He continued, "I've asked my construction manager to be part of our discussion." He then pointed to Pete and said, "Ms. Jackie Summerville, this is Pete Williams."

"Nice to meet you," Pete said while also appreciating her lovely appearance.

Trevor led them both to his office where a big sheet of blueprint had been laid out on a conference table. He pointed at it and said, "The print company was backed up with other jobs yesterday, so even though they were doing me a big favor, this just got here five minutes ago. Let's take a look."

Trevor, Jackie and Pete took places around the table and looked down at the drawing that showed the clubhouse overlaying the lot, and specifically the owl habitat. Both Jackie and Pete knew to be quiet and let Trevor examine and digest what he was looking at. A few minutes passed and Trevor stood up straight saying, "This might very well be doable, quite doable in fact. So we'll have to rearrange the meeting spaces and shift the main dining room to a different side of the building, but all in all, not too big of an obstacle."

Jackie felt like it was OK to join in the conversation, so she said, "Yes, Mr. Harding. I'm far from an expert, but from what I can see, it doesn't look like the owl area, or should I say aviary, impacts anything too major. If I'm reading this right, the kitchens can all stay where they were originally planned."

Pete then interjected saying, "Yes, Mr. Harding. We're lucky that all the engineering demands, load-bearing walls, etcetera will not be affected at all. It's all just interior walls and space that, as you know, isn't a big deal to change."

Trevor took a hard look at the blueprint again and then raised his eyes to meet those of Jackie and Pete. Then he clapped his hands and shouted, "We are back in business my friends!" He excitedly went on, "I'll get with the architect and make the necessary changes ASAP. We will then launch Excelsior's new groundbreaking clubhouse aviary as soon as the materials can be printed."

He turned to Jackie, put out his hand and said, "Jackie, I can't thank you enough for your inspiration, intervention, involvement or whatever you want to call it." Then he politely asked, "May I give you a hug?"

Having already taken his handshake, Jackie was startled by his request, but she too was overjoyed that her idea had made such an impact on both the project and Trevor, so she accepted his embrace and returned it willingly.

Pete interrupted them by saying, "Yes, Jackie, you had one hell of an idea. Plus, it's going to save us a ton of time and money."

Jackie backed away from Trevor to an acceptable distance and said, "Thank you both. To be honest, sometimes I don't know where these thoughts come from. They just occur. May I be bold and mention another one?"

Trevor smiled and answered, "Well, you haven't steered me wrong so far, so what is it?"

Jackie pointed to a different rendering that showed various views of the clubhouse space and pointed, "If the aviary is going to be located here, why not make it circular with glass all around so residents can walk around it and take in all the sights?"

Then she pointed to the overhead view of the roof and continued, "This area will be directly over the aviary. I really think it would add to the authentic outside atmosphere if it was made of glass."

Trevor looked at the plans and then to Pete asking, "Can this be done?"

Pete walked back over to the table and looked down at the renderings for a few minutes and then nodded saying, "It'll add some major dollars back to the cost, but I can't see why it can't happen."

Trevor turned to Jackie and said, "Even with the added expense, this glass feature will certainly add to our residents' experience. It'll be something no other senior community has—or any kind of community for that matter. If Excelsior is truly meant to be the most superior in its class, then I think it's a marvelous idea."

Upon hearing his approval, Jackie relaxed and replied, "Thank you, Mr. Harding."

Trevor added, "I mentioned to Mr. Wright that he had quite an assistant in you Jackie, but God knows, I never expected this."

Jackie blushed and said, "Thank you again" and then added, "However, I really do have to get to the office. I'll stop by the sales center on my way out and pick up any new contracts."

"Yes, yes," Trevor replied. "Pete and I also have a lot to get to." He put out his hand again, looked Jackie in the eyes and said, "I am truly indebted. You've saved me and Excelsior from a very serious calamity."

Jackie took his hand gently and held it a little longer than usual saying, "You don't owe me anything. It really is my pleasure. I'm just happy that I could help."

They held each other's eyes for a moment longer and then let go. Jackie said goodbye to Pete, turned around and left the office.

Once she had gone, Pete looked at Trevor and said, "If you don't mind my saying, she's really something special and quite a beauty, too."

Trevor nodded his head saying, "I know, Pete, I know."

They exchanged goodbyes, with Trevor instructing him to keep the pressure on the construction guys to continue making progress saying, "Remember, we don't start making money until the buyers start giving us money at the closings. Now, the architect and I have to figure out how to install a lot of expensive glass."

Pete smiled and said, "Yes, boss," and then left.

Jackie went to the sales office where there were six more contracts to pick up. She saw Ted and said, "Wow, can you imagine what's going to happen when we have actual models for prospects to see and walk through?"

Ted smiled broadly and replied, "I can hardly wait."

She picked up the envelope with the documents inside saying, "Believe me, Ted, Excelsior is going to be like nothing else before," and quickly left before he could respond.

When she got into her car, Jackie decided to take a drive around the development to get even more familiar with its layout and experience its overall feel.

She passed by the models where the crews were working feverously. *Excellent! The sooner they get these babies finished, the more the prospects can see, feel and touch their senior living dreams.*

Then she drove past the condo site and continued. *Most of Excelsior's buyers will be interested in one of these. No lawn or landscaping. No pool or roof to worry about. These same buyers are probably ones who want to see exactly what they're getting. They're most likely very cautious with their spending. There should be some kind of model for these condos, too.*

Then she realized what she had just thought and admonished herself saying, "Jackie, you really need to stop! It was one thing with the owls because he asked you to help, but the rest of this project is for him to figure out. He has done this once or twice before, ya know."

She laughed at her foolishness and decided to forego the rest of her drive and head back to the office. As she drove, she kept thinking back to the meeting this morning. She was still somewhat in awe that her idea had worked, and that he liked it. Then she thought about that hug. Of course, it was totally just congratulatory, but the feel of him holding her was not only comforting, but exhilarating. His scent was a combination of the freshness of just coming out of the shower with a hint of a peppery cologne. She allowed herself to relish in the memory and then reminded herself that he said that he was indebted to her.

How many pompous, egotistical developers would ever even utter those words? Yes, I do believe he is different.

Chapter Thirty-Four

Trevor stood over the plans again and started reshaping the clubhouse in his brain. *If we are really going to do this right, the aviary should be the focal point of the entire clubhouse and not just located where the owls are now. I know we can't move the birds, but who says we can't redesign the entire space to have everything revolve around a central aviary? The rooms will be almost like spokes coming off an aviary wheel—dining rooms, fitness center, card and lecture rooms and then a large section where those who just want to sit and view the activity will have ample room.*

Then he said out loud, "I like it! By God, Jackie can't be the only one to be inspired around here!"

He laughed a bit. *What am I going to do about this Jackie thing. I can't wait forever to let her know how I feel, and it's not like it just came upon me when she started working for me. That would be a different set of circumstances. I've been attracted to her for a very long time, and now that my attraction is not just some weird fantasy but grounded in sincere admiration, affection and who knows ...*

Then he reflected on the hug they shared. *Yes, I was excited that her idea rescued us from a gigantic mess, so it was a bit impulsive, but it also seemed so natural. Nothing forced and so comfortable. I wonder if she felt the same?*

He snapped out of his musings and reminded himself that the architect must get to work on the redesign of what would be Excelsior's exquisite clubhouse. He picked up his phone and dialed.

After a long conversation in which Trevor had to explain what had happened with the owls, the aviary idea, and the changes he wanted made, he finally got his somewhat shocked and confused architect to understand what he wanted. He finished the conversation by saying sternly, "Yes, do whatever you need to do to make the aviary the main feature. Do it well and do it fast."

He hung up the phone and then finally turned his attention to the call that he had scheduled tomorrow with Michael Worthington. "Jesus Christ," he said loudly. "With all this owl nonsense going on, I've dropped the ball on preparing for that call. I had better get to it, and now."

He took the medical center plans out of their file and scanned over them. Residents' rooms, plus physical, occupational and mental therapy rooms all laid out before him. He was pleased with what he saw, but then it occurred to him that he was not an expert on what these people needed. Yes, he thought he had good ideas and surmised what was needed, but he was a real estate developer. He looked down at the plans again and said, "What the hell do I know? Just like with Jackie and the owls, maybe another perspective would create a better product for our residents. I'm not going to present this to Michael as a fait accompli but instead more of a blank slate for him to give input, design and make his own. He is the expert, Trevor, not you."

Trevor rolled up the plan and called his very surprised architect yet again and directed him to get him plans of each floor of the medical center, but just showing the shell of the space. Then he instructed him to overnight a copy of the old plan and the new shell to Michael and messenger one to him. He finished the call by saying, "I need both delivered by 10 o'clock tomorrow morning, and then I'll have the changes to the original plan, hopefully, by the end of tomorrow, but it may take longer. I'll keep you posted."

He hung up and said to himself, "Looks like this inspiration stuff is contagious. I'm on a roll. I can only imagine what all these change fees are going to cost me, but if Excelsior is going to live up to its name, it must be the best, hands down. I refuse to spare any expense, and I know for certain it will all be worth it."

Having decided to wait until his conversation with Michael to address the needs of the medical center, Trevor turned his attention back to the aviary. He had the general idea of it being the central focal point of the clubhouse, but he again acknowledged his own ignorance by saying, "OK, we're going to have an aviary. That much is a given, but what in God's name does that even entail?"

He sat in front of his computer and googled various aviary-related terms and kept getting sites that sold freestanding aviaries for personal use, sites that sold birds for aviaries and aviary supplies. He let out a sigh and said, "No, no, no. That's not what I want." Then he typed in aviary experts and, finally, up popped The National Aviary.

"That's it!" he said excitedly. When he saw that it was in Pittsburgh, and he saw another trip in his future. *Hmmm, Director of Animal Programs, Director of Buildings and Grounds. I should probably talk to both of them.* Then he saw the name of The Aviary's veterinarian and noted, *Yup, we'll need to have a vet on retainer, too.*

He continued going through the website commenting, "This place is huge and quite impressive. Ours should be a piece of cake for these guys to act as consultants for us."

His eye then caught the "Please Donate" icon. He laughed and said, "I'm very sure that a generous donation will assist in our collaborating as well."

He picked up the phone, dialed the number and was greeted by a computerized message system "hours, press one; tickets, press two." Trevor sighed heavily and pressed zero hoping that a real person would answer. It rang three times, and finally there was a woman's voice on the other end who said, "National Aviary, how may I help you?"

Sounding authoritative, Trevor replied, "Mr. Matthew Shields, please."

To his pleasant surprise, she responded saying, "One moment, please."

While on hold, Trevor thought, *Wow, that was way easier than I anticipated. Let's hope the rest of the conversation goes as well.*

Then, the line came alive and a deep voice said, "Matt Shields, Director of Animal Programming."

Trevor put on his salesman's voice and said, "Hello, Mr. Shields, my name is Trevor Harding. I know you don't know me, but I'm intending to build a large aviary, and I want advice from the best source possible, and I'm confident that you are just that source."

Although not in his job description, Matt Shields did experience people reaching out to him for his opinion and expertise from time to time, so he told Trevor to continue. Trevor briefly explained the circumstances that had created the aviary idea and his vision for what he wanted to create. He finished off his pitch by saying, "I, however, am a real estate developer and definitely not an expert on birds. That's where you come in."

Mr. Shields coughed a bit and said, "Mr. Harding, I love your idea, as we all know the benefits that birdwatching can provide, especially for older people, but I'm in Pittsburgh and you're in Naples, Florida. That is quite a logistical dilemma, wouldn't you say?"

Trevor knew it was time to pounce, so he replied, "Believe me, Mr. Shields, that hurdle can be overcome. I just need you to agree to assist me, then I'll take care of the rest."

Without giving Mr. Shields a moment to say no, Trevor continued saying, "Why don't I come to you first. I can be in Pittsburgh by tomorrow afternoon and we can meet on Friday morning, if that works. Of course, please feel free to include whomever you would like to sit in on our meeting."

Then he dropped the deal clincher by saying, "It's also imperative for you and the rest of your team to know that I always generously support causes that are important to me, and this is extremely important indeed."

Mr. Shields was quite taken aback by Trevor's boldness, but couldn't really come up with any reason to object. *He's got what sounds like a great project in mind, he's willing to come here, and apparently he's loaded.* So, he agreed by saying, "All right, Mr. Harding, we will meet and discuss this further on Friday. Come to the main gate at 10 a.m. and I'll meet you there."

Trevor grinned widely, pumped his fist and replied, "Fantastic! I look forward to creating a long-lasting relationship. I'll see you Friday."

They both hung up, and Trevor immediately called his architect one more time and told him that he now needed the revisions to the clubhouse no later than noon tomorrow. Although, completely exasperated, the architect knew better than to say no to Trevor Harding.

Trevor dialed his phone again and instructed his travel agent to get him on a late afternoon flight to Pittsburgh tomorrow. He hung up and then realized that he wouldn't be here to watch Jackie on her Thursday evening walk. "Damn," he said. "She never walks on Wednesdays. Am I really going to have to wait until Friday to see her?"

Then he remembered telling her that he was indebted to her. *What better way to start paying off my debt to her than taking her out to a working lunch? After all, shouldn't she be the first person I share the new floor plan with? It's only the right thing to do, right? Right. Plus, I can also let her know about our potential partnership with The National Aviary.*

Then he stopped and asked himself, "Did I just say 'our'? Hmmm, I've never used the word 'our' in relationship to any of my projects before. I do believe that it's a good omen."

He picked up his phone again and dialed the law firm. Lindsey, the receptionist answered, "Wright, Stewart & Blake. How may I help you?"

Trevor replied, "Yes, this is Trevor Harding."

Lindsey quickly said, "Yes, Mr. Harding, I'll ring through to Mr. Wright immediately."

Trevor interrupted her and said, "Wait, please. I'd like to speak with Ms. Summerville."

Caught off guard, Lindsey replied, "Oh, I see. I'll see if she's in her office. May I put you on a short hold?"

"Of course," Trevor responded.

She buzzed through to Jackie's office, and Jackie picked up saying, "Yes?"

Lindsey couldn't contain her excitement and burst out saying, "Jackie, Mr. Harding is on line four, and he's not calling for Mr. Wright but asked to speak with you instead."

Jackie was shocked and blurted out, "What?"

"I'm telling you," Lindsey answered. "He asked specifically for you, and he's been on hold, so you'd better pick up fast."

"OK Lindsey. Thank you," Jackie replied. Then she took two deep breaths, swallowed hard and pushed the button for line four.

"Jackie Summerville," she said in as professional a voice as she could muster.

"Hello Jackie. It's Trevor Harding. I know we just saw each other this morning, and I really hope that I'm not taking up too much of your time."

Jackie interjected, "No, of course not, Mr. Harding. What can I do for you?"

Feeling like a schoolboy asking for a first date, Trevor felt nervous but continued on saying, "Well, Jackie, after you left, I continued making changes for our aviary. It's now going to be right in the middle of the building, so all the other rooms can enjoy the view."

Jackie smiled when she heard him say "our" and then said,

"Why, that's a wonderful idea, Mr. Harding."

Trevor also smiled wide when he heard her approval and then went on saying, "I'm so very glad you like it. I'm having my architect make the changes as we speak. They'll be done by noon tomorrow, and I was hoping that I could show them to you."

Jackie blushed a bit and answered, "I would love to see them. I'm sure this new plan will be spectacular."

Trevor was excited at the thought of seeing her again and quickly added, "Outstanding! And as I said, I do owe you one. I'd really like to treat you to lunch as a payback. We can go over the plans at the same time."

Jackie was dumbfounded, but managed to answer, "Mr. Harding, that's certainly not necessary."

Even though she couldn't see him, Trevor held up his hand and said, "I didn't say anything about necessary. I said I'd like to."

They both laughed nervously and then Jackie said, "I'd like that too."

Trevor sat up a little taller in his chair and replied, "Great. I'll meet you at the Capital Room at 12:15. Does that work for you?"

"Yes, yes," Jackie responded excitedly. "That will work just fine."

With a big smile, Trevor said, "I'll see you then. And Jackie, I also have some other exciting news to share with you, but I know I'm keeping you from your work, so that can wait until tomorrow."

Jackie was quite stunned by his wanting to share this news with her and curious about what it could be but put those thoughts aside and said, "I understand, Mr. Harding. I look forward to tomorrow."

Trevor felt a rush, but calmed himself and replied, "As do I. Goodbye, Jackie."

"Goodbye, Mr. Harding," Jackie said softly and put the receiver down. She exhaled and said, "Holy crap! What just happened?"

She looked up, and Lindsey, Karen and Ryan were peeking around the door. As usual, Ryan took the lead in the inquisition asking, "Exactly, Jackie. What did just happen?"

Jackie settled herself and retorted with, "Since when do you have to know everything about my life?"

Ryan laughed and replied, "To be quite honest, there hasn't really been anything interesting to know about until now. So, what's going on?"

Knowing that it was best to just answer the question than to let the rumor mill go crazy, she responded saying, "It's not that big of a deal. Mr. Harding is having the clubhouse plans redrawn to include the aviary that I suggested, and he just wants me to see them. That's all."

All three at the door clamored for a moment and then Karen said, "For real Jackie? You suggested a change of plans to probably the most successful developer in Florida? Talk about nerve!"

Jackie got defensive and shot back saying, "Look, he had a major problem, he asked for help, and I had an idea. Just doing my job."

Ryan scoffed and said, "Let me take one second to check your job description. Ah, yes, absolutely nowhere does it say to advise one of the most powerful businessmen in the country."

Jackie grinned and replied, "All right, thank you for your oh-so-predictable sarcasm, but he did ask, and Mr. Wright is A-OK with it."

All three exchanged shocked glances, and Ryan continued

saying, "Just when you think you know someone. Old play-by-the-book, define-your-role-and-stick-to-it Mr. Wright has evolved!"

Now it was Jackie's turn to scoff, and she looked sternly at Ryan saying, "We've had this discussion before, Ryan. You will not say one derogatory thing about Mr. Wright!"

Ryan held up his hands and said, "Whoa, I was actually throwing him a compliment."

Jackie backed off but said, "Sometimes it's not easy to even understand what you've just said."

Lindsey brought the conversation back to Trevor by asking, "So when are you meeting with him?" and then added, "Again."

Jackie couldn't help but feel excited but didn't want them to see it, so she calmly replied, "Well, we're having lunch tomorrow to go over the new plans."

Again, the three of them looked at each other and Ryan said, "Ah, the famous working lunch" as he did air quotes with his fingers.

Jackie was now mildly miffed, raised her voice and said, "Stop being such an ass, Ryan!"

Ryan laughed again and said, "Well Jackie, it looks like you are no longer president of the fan club, but now you are on the team."

Jackie threw a pen at him and shouted, "All of you out, right now! And Ryan, I will kill you some day. Mark my words!"

They all quickly fled the doorway with Ryan yelling "I love you too, Jackie" as he left.

Jackie was finally alone again and repeated her initial question to herself, *What the hell just happened?* She then added, *And what in God's name should I wear?*

She also allowed herself another thought. *What could this news be that he wants to tell me and where might it lead?*

Chapter Thirty-Five

Jackie got home and Maria could tell that something was up. "Que pasa, my Jackie?" she asked as Jackie set her things down and was hugging Emily.

Jackie knew better than to try to disguise or hide anything from Maria, so she decided to just get it out there saying, "Oh Maria, I had the most incredible meeting with Mr. Harding today. I told him my ideas and instead of being dismissive as many men with his power would be, he actually listened and agreed with me."

Maria grabbed Jackie's hands and said, "I have a few extra minutes before I have to go. Come sit and tell me more."

Emily could also see that her mother was excited, so she added, "Yes, Mommy, tell us."

All three sat at the small table in the kitchen, and Jackie recounted the events of the morning and then said, "I couldn't believe it when he said that he was indebted to me."

Maria laughed and said, "Well he is, isn't he?"

Jackie blushed and replied, "Well, I guess he is, but for

someone like him to admit it and not take credit for everything is, I don't know … refreshing."

Maria nodded knowingly saying, "Yes, it is unusual for most men to accept the wisdom of us women and to actually give credit—this sounds like a very special man."

As much as Jackie tried to feign indifference, it was a lost cause, so she nodded her head while saying, "Yes, Maria, I truly believe that he is special."

Maria patted Jackie's hands and rose to leave when Jackie stopped her by saying, "Wait that's not all."

"Dios mio, Jackie," Maria responded. "What do you mean that's not all?"

Maria sat down again, and Jackie explained, "Maria, he called me this afternoon and asked me to go over the new plans with him tomorrow while we have lunch."

"Aye-yai!" Maria exclaimed. "This is now a totally different tale you are telling me!"

Jackie blushed again and said, "It's not like that. He said that he owes me for helping him and wants to repay his debt."

Maria snickered and said, "I don't care what excuse he uses, this man wants to share time with you and has feelings for you."

Now it was Jackie's turn to hold Maria's hands while Emily sat on her lap taking it all in. Jackie swallowed and asked, "Oh Maria, do you really think so?"

Maria looked at her lovingly and answered, "My dear Jackie. Trust me, I know a love story in the making when I see one."

Jackie got scared and squeezed Maria's hands saying, "Oh my." Then she added, "Now let's not get carried away. It really is just a lunch."

Maria squeezed softly back and replied, "If you say so." She laughed lightly and said, "Now, I really do have to get going."

She got up and kissed both Jackie and Emily tenderly on their foreheads and whispered to Emily, "Thank you for being such a good listener to your momma's story."

Emily smiled and said, "It's fun seeing Mommy all excited."

Maria nodded her head saying, "Yes, it certainly is. I'll see you both tomorrow. Buenas noches, my darlings."

Both Jackie and Emily replied in unison, "Buenas noches, Maria," and added a combined "We love you!"

Maria closed the door as she replied, "I love you too."

Jackie sat quietly for a minute and then was brought back when Emily asked, "Mommy, what are we having for dinner?"

Jackie shook her head slightly and answered, "Well, my little Em, let's see what we've got in the fridge."

Chapter Thirty-Six

Morning came quickly as if it almost knew how much Trevor had on his plate today and needed to get there fast. It was 6 o'clock, and Trevor was at the table eating his bagel and yogurt while going over his itinerary. *First, tour the worksites as usual to make sure all is on schedule and moving forward. Then, assess the clubhouse site and affirm that the owls are contained, yet healthy. The medical parcel is owl-free, so let's get the foundation poured ASAP—even with Michael's changes, the footprint remains the same.*

After that, I need to inform the bankers of these changes. Even though I hate the fact that I've involved them and can't abide their meddling checks and balances, they should be advised. I know they'll get all nervous and ruffled, but I've played this game once or twice before and they never risk more than I do anyway, so I'll talk them down off their imaginary ledge.

Next up is my first follow-up call with Mick, I mean Michael. I do hope he appreciates my openness in allowing him to take the lead on the medical center design. After all, he does know a lot more about this than I do.

Trevor took a moment to reflect, and then said out loud, "My God, I do believe I'm learning to rely on others. Evolving … maybe."

Then he turned his attention to his lunch date with Jackie and realized that he had made a big mistake. *Capital Room? Did I really choose that restaurant? It's so stuffy and formal. You'd think I was closing a business deal. Bad choice, my man. I should change it. It might seem odd to her, but I think she'd much rather be in a lighter, more casual atmosphere. The Dolphin Club. Yes, that's it. We can be outside and eat by the beach that brought us together, even though she doesn't know that part yet.*

He chuckled and then set a reminder on his phone to call the restaurant for a 12:15 reservation, cancel the one at Capital Room, and make another to call Jackie to let her know of the change, although he was sure that no reminder was necessary for that.

I really hope she likes the changes I've made to the aviary and clubhouse. It is her idea after all, but I do have a considerable edge on her when it comes to design and building.

He laughed slightly and then went back to the day's events. *Flight out at 3:34, land in Pittsburgh at 6:28, arrive at the Renaissance Pittsburgh Hotel by 7:30. Get a good night's sleep and then meet with Shields on Friday at 10. Flight back to Fort Myers at 2:43.*

He chewed his last bite of bagel. *Even by my standards, that is a full docket, but at least I'll be back in time to see her on the sand.*

Jackie picked out her favorite dress from the closet. It was still appropriate for work but had a bit more flow to it than her normal tailored look. It was a soft pinkish color with a muted floral design. Sleeveless, with a cinched waistline and small pleats all around the skirt portion. It was originally bought at White House Black Market by some unknown rich person, but Jackie found it at a consignment shop for $40. Still a major expenditure for her, but she fell in love with it and it's still her best go-to outfit. Of course, she made it more businesslike by wearing a light beige blazer over it. She complemented the outfit with buff-colored pumps, some gold earrings and a bangle bracelet.

After applying her makeup, she looked at her reflection in the part of the mirror that wasn't covered by Emily's painting, and she was pleased with what she saw.

Then she looked harder at her image. *This just feels right. I was so incredibly nervous before our first meeting but don't have many butterflies today. After talking with Maria, I've felt very much at ease. Am I attracted to him? Yes, so that gives me a flutter, but am I scared? No. I really feel like I can trust him. Plus, it is just lunch. Don't you start letting your imagination run away with you.*

Just then, she got a tap on her arm and turned around to see Emily standing behind her in her cute princess pajamas.

"Good morning, Mommy," Emily said as she yawned.

"Good morning, my sweet Em," Jackie replied as she held out her arms.

Emily snuggled into Jackie's embrace saying, "You look very pretty today, Mommy. That's my favorite dress."

Jackie hugged her tight, kissed the top of her head and said, "Why thank you. It's my favorite, too."

She let Emily go and said, "Maria should be here any minute. Let's go get some coffee for me and some breakfast for you."

She took Emily's hand and they walked into the kitchen. "How about some waffles?" Jackie asked while pouring herself a to-go cup of coffee.

Emily clapped and replied, "That's sounds yummy."

Jackie popped two frozen organic waffles into the toaster and took down the bottle of pure maple syrup from the shelf while saying, "Two delicious waffles coming right up for the best girl in the world."

Jackie was about to pour Emily some apple juice when Maria opened the door saying, "Buenos Dias, mis queridas ninas."

"Good morning," both Jackie and Emily responded.

Maria looked at Jackie and nodded saying, "I dare Mr. Harding not to find you attractive today. Impossible."

Jackie waved her hand and said, "I've worn this dress a hundred times."

Maria laughed and said, "Not with that special look, you haven't," and gave Jackie a wink.

Jackie blushed a little, waved her hand again and said, "I've got to go. Emily's waffles should pop any second."

She leaned down and gave Emily a kiss saying, "I know you'll be a good girl for Maria. Mommy loves you."

Emily looked up and said, "I love you the mostest Mommy."

Jackie grabbed her coffee and things, gave Maria a peck on the cheek and said, "I can hardly wait to tell you how it goes."

Maria kissed her back saying, "Just be your lovely self and it will all be wonderful."

Jackie got to her office and saw that her voicemail light was blinking. She sat down, pulled out a legal pad and said, "OK, here we go. People have probably received their introductory letters and are full of questions."

She pressed the button and, indeed, she had ten messages. The first two were from buyers with questions that had easy answers. The next three were from Excelsior sales agents with file updates. Another from an outside agent, three more from buyers, and then there was a now familiar voice saying, "Yes, hello Jackie. This is Trevor Harding. I hope you don't mind, but I'm thinking that our lunch would be much more pleasant at the Dolphin Club where we can be outside and enjoy the view. I hope the change works for you. If I don't hear from you otherwise, I'll see you at the Dolphin Club at 12:15. Have a good morning."

Jackie leaned back in her chair. *Holy crap. I've always dreamed of going there. It seems like such a lovely place to have lunch.*

Then she shook her head and said aloud, "Come on, Jackie. Don't think about that now. You have a lot to do before noon. Buckle down!"

She pulled the first buyer's name up on her computer and reviewed the specifics of the contract. She tried to anticipate possible questions or concerns and then picked up her phone to start her morning rounds of calls and paperwork.

Chapter Thirty-Seven

Trevor was waiting for Jackie at the hostess stand and immediately opened the door for her when she arrived. He was dressed smartly in black pants with a short-sleeved gray polo, black belt and black loafers. A more casual look than usual, but Jackie liked it. Especially, because she was able to see his well-toned arms under which he carried what appeared to be a rolled-up plan.

The hostess led them to a table right next to the beach and asked Trevor if it would do. Trevor looked at Jackie and she nodded quietly. He pulled out a chair for her sit, but before doing so, Jackie took off her jacket. Trevor held out his hands to take it from her and then realized how absolutely stunning she was. He tried to remain calm and draped the jacket over an extra chair. Then he held Jackie's chair again and she sat down.

While he was walking over to the other side of the table, he thought, *God, she is more beautiful than ever, and this all just feels so right.*

He sat and broke the ice by saying, "I trust that my switching lunch spots meets with your approval."

Jackie smiled widely and replied, "Of course. How can you not love this?" She stretched out her arms to the beach that spread out in front of them.

Trevor took in the shape of her lovely arms, smiled back and said, "I'm so glad you like it. It is much better than the stuffy atmosphere at The Capital Room."

"Yes," Jackie agreed. "I love being outdoors, especially the beach."

Trevor nodded and added, "Me too. I'm on the beach pretty much every day." Not wanting to get too specific, he changed the subject by saying, "Well, before we eat, why don't we take a look at our new clubhouse?"

Jackie noted that he used "our" again and enthusiastically replied, "I can hardly wait."

Trevor had already instructed the staff to not bother them until they saw the paper put away, so he started to unroll the plan. He tried to anchor the corners with butter plates but missed a corner. When it started to roll back, Jackie and he reached to stop it at the same time, and their hands brushed up against each other's which made both of them tingle. As Trevor held down the paper, Jackie snatched the plate and put it securely over the bothersome corner saying, "Got it."

They both laughed and then Trevor looked at her more seriously and said, "We really do make a good team, you know."

Jackie blushed slightly and remained silent as they both turned their attention to the drawing in front of them. Neither said a word for quite a few minutes while they took in all that they were seeing. It was magnificent! The circular aviary in the center of it all with windows soaring from the floor to a thirty-foot-high ceiling and then tapering to a peak. It was all topped off with a stunning paned-glass cupola.

Jackie looked at Trevor and could see the pride that was emanating from every pore. She put her hands to her face and softly said, "Oh Mr. Harding, this is absolutely amazing."

He held her glance for a moment and then started talking excitedly, "Jackie, look here!" He pointed to the long expanse of glass that fronted the main dining room. "Every diner will have a view. Same with those in these exercise rooms over here and card rooms over there."

Jackie leaned over the plans and pointed to an area that looked like a small amphitheater asking, "What is this space?"

Trevor smiled widely and answered, "Another slight change. I decided that we shouldn't just have a few chairs in the viewing area, so I came up with a room that I'm calling The Observatory. Think of it as a movie theater with reclining seats, a spot for your drink, and even a small fold-out table for note taking. Instead of a screen, you look at this beautiful bird sanctuary. This way our residents will be more comfortable and want to stay longer."

Jackie gazed at Trevor and sincerely said, "Mr. Harding, it seems like you're the one with the inspiration now. This is truly phenomenal! You should be very proud."

Trevor engaged Jackie's eyes and seriously said, "I'm so very glad you like it and, yes, your inspiration is apparently contagious. But remember, the original idea was all yours. How about we both share in its success?"

Jackie had never felt so valued in her adult life. She got a little emotional, but managed to say, "That's very nice of you, Mr. Harding."

Trevor smiled and said, "I didn't say it to be nice. You totally earned it. Now, what do you say we do away with the Mr. Harding stuff and you call me Trevor?"

Jackie was visibly startled and started to say that it wouldn't be appropriate when Trevor cut her off saying, "OK, Mr. Harding when we're in the business world and Trevor when we're not. Deal?"

Jackie was thrilled to think they might meet outside of the business world again, so she nodded and said, "Deal."

Trevor rolled up the plan and almost immediately a server appeared and handed them menus. She asked if they'd like something to drink, to which they both answered, "Iced tea, please." They started to peruse the menu when Trevor looked up and asked, "Have you been here before?"

Jackie smiled and replied, "No, but I've walked by a million times and have always wanted to try it, so thank you."

Trevor dismissed the thanks and said, "Everything here is good, but if you like salmon, I highly recommend the almond-encrusted salmon salad. The fish is excellent, and you get lots of delicious berries."

Jackie read the description and said, "Yes, that does look very good."

Trevor looked at her again and couldn't believe this was really happening. The woman he had admired from his balcony all this time was sitting across from him and sharing lunch. Better yet, what he had learned about her so far only made his attraction grow. He decided to take a risk and ask a more personal question saying, "So Jackie, other than working for Mr. Wright and providing me with outstanding ideas, what do you like to do?"

Jackie was a bit taken aback by the question and quickly

debated in her mind on how to answer. She finally decided to just be honest and responded by saying, "Well, Mr. ... I mean, Trevor, I really don't have much free time."

Trevor nodded in understanding and said, "I know the feeling. I work way too much too."

Jackie took a sip of her tea and explained, "Yes, there's always that, but I also have a three-year-old little girl who pretty much takes up the rest of my time."

It took a moment for Trevor to digest this news, but then he looked at Jackie and said, "I'm sure you're a great mom."

Jackie let out a little laugh and said, "Well, it's not exactly what I had planned to be doing at this point in my life, but now I can't see myself doing anything else. My little Emily is the center of my universe."

Trevor was very taken by the love that was so evident as she spoke of her daughter and was about to continue the conversation when the server came to the table and asked, "Have you decided what you would like?"

Trevor held out his arm for Jackie to order and she responded, "Yes, I'd like the almond-encrusted salmon salad, please."

Trevor nodded his approval and added, "I'd like the yellow-tail snapper grilled with the beurre blanc sauce on the side, please."

They gave the server their menus, and Trevor turned his attention back to Jackie and restarted their conversation saying, "Jackie, if I'm being totally honest, I think you're lucky to have a child. I always thought I'd be a father by now, but with my career and its demands, I never settled into the family man life."

Jackie took another sip of her tea and replied, "Yes, I'm sure it must be difficult with your schedule."

Trevor decided to take another even bigger risk. He looked Jackie in the eyes and said, "It is, but I also never found the right person."

Jackie suddenly got nervous, but also felt an exhilaration she had never experienced. Not knowing what to say, she instead pointed to the gulf and blurted out, "The water is such a beautiful color today."

Trevor turned toward the surf and agreed, "Yes, it's almost like it can't decide if it wants to be green or blue."

Jackie smiled and said, "Exactly." Then she added, "That's what I love about the beach. It's never the same. Every time I come here, I see something new and have a different experience. It really is almost magical."

Trevor seized on the opportunity to have her open up about her walks asking, "So, do you get to come to the beach often with your daughter?"

She nodded her head slightly and replied, "We do come from time to time, but mostly I come after work just to get in some 'me' time."

Trevor was intrigued to learn the reason behind the walks and said, "Yes, I'm sure you need that time alone."

Jackie giggled and said, "To be truthful, I actually call them my sanity walks. They put a pinch in my childcare budget, but I don't know how I'd survive without them."

Trevor gently laughed and said, "Maybe I should take them up myself. God knows, I could do with a little more sanity too."

They both laughed and Jackie reflected on how amazingly natural this all felt. She loved how he was so confirming of her. He didn't even miss a beat when she told him about Emily.

Not the slightest hint of disapproval, and she may have even detected a bit of envy, but in a positive way.

The lunch continued while they easily conversed about Excelsior and its progress. They were so caught up in their chat when suddenly Trevor realized he had forgotten to tell her the news about the potential partnering with The National Aviary. He held up his hand and said, "Oh my goodness! I'm so sorry. I completely forgot to tell you the other news I have."

Jackie hadn't forgotten but didn't want to be presumptuous so she hadn't said anything earlier, but after his confession she said, "I knew you'd come around to it."

"Well, Jackie," Trevor said lightly, "I think we both can agree that we were quite inspired with our aviary idea and design, but in reality, neither of us knows a damn thing about how to set one up and run it."

Jackie smirked and said, "A fair enough statement."

Trevor got excited and continued saying, "So, here's the news. This afternoon, I'm flying to Pittsburgh where tomorrow I have a meeting with the experts who operate The National Aviary. They've pretty much already agreed to act as consultants for us. They'll make sure the aviary is set up and managed correctly. I'm just going there to meet with them and seal the deal."

Jackie was blown away by his genius yet again and asked, "Wow, Trevor! That's such a great idea, but how in the world did you get them to agree?"

Trevor waved his hand and replied, "Oh you have no idea of how convincing I can be." Then he added, "Plus, a promise of a considerable donation tends to make people much more willing to assist."

They both laughed then Trevor looked at his watch saying,

"As much as I'd really love for us to spend more time together, I have a 3:34 plane to catch and I haven't even packed."

Jackie looked at her phone, which read 1:28, and immediately put her napkin on the table, got up and said, "Oh my! Yes, I'm also running quite late. Thank you so much for a lovely lunch, but I was supposed to be back at the office almost fifteen minutes ago."

Trevor stood up, smiled and replied, "I'll write a late slip to Mr. Wright if you'd like."

Jackie got nervous and exclaimed, "Oh God, no! That's the last thing I need. I'd have to explain and he'd ... "

Trevor reached out and held both of her hands, saying softly, "Jackie, I was only kidding."

She looked into his eyes and instantly felt calm. "I know. I'm sorry. I overreacted. It's just ... "

Trevor squeezed her hands and gently said, "I know, and I feel the same way. Now, we both have things to get to, but please know how much I enjoyed our time together and, if I can be so bold, I'd like to do it again."

Jackie peered into his blue eyes and nodded, "I'd like that very much." Then she took her hands from his, put her jacket over her arm while saying, "Safe travels, Trevor," and started to leave.

He replied, "Thanks, Jackie. I'll let you know how it goes." He stood silently as he watched her beautiful figure walk gracefully over the sand and out of view. *Oh God, I do believe she likes me. What now, Trevor? What now?*

He snapped himself out of it, paid the bill, and then headed to his house to pack and get to the airport.

Chapter Thirty-Eight

Trevor woke up in his hotel room at 6:30 and reflected on his conversation with Dr. Michael Worthington. *I'm very happy I decided to ditch my floor plan and defer to his expertise. He seemed genuinely impressed and almost appreciative of my letting him take the lead in designing the space. Just during our conversation, it was absolutely apparent that he knows the needs of these residents inside and out and what services we should provide to meet them. It worked so well, I'm going to use the same strategy with my aviary friends.*

He let out a little laugh, got out of bed, showered, dressed and went to the hotel café for breakfast. While sipping his coffee and munching on a bagel, he read his emails. The one he always read first was Pete's daily update. Pete wrote that, as he had requested, the medical site slab had been poured without any bothersome birds getting in the way.

Then he stopped himself. *How in the world can I still call them bothersome when they helped us transform our somewhat run-of-the-mill clubhouse into the magnificent centerpiece that it will be now? Also, those little feathered friends gave me the opportunity to get closer to Jackie. I should be thanking them profusely.*

He smiled and continued reading. Next was the daily sales report from Ted Sullivan, which noted that the marketing they ramped up was starting to show results. "Very impressive," he said, as he checked each product's numbers. "Five new single-family homes, seven villas and ten condos. I bet Ted is one happy camper."

His thoughts then turned to Jackie and the impact that this windfall would have on her. *Wow, twenty-two new contracts in addition to the ones she already has. I hope she can keep up.*

Realizing how ridiculous this concern was, he chided himself. *Twenty-two contracts is a walk in the park for her. I bet she already has them input and introductory letters sent out.*

He sat back in his chair, took a sip of his coffee and acknowledged to himself that he was worried, albeit needlessly, about her. He hadn't truly been concerned about someone else's welfare since his mother passed away, and she was the only exception before that awful day.

"Jackie Summerville," he said pensively. *I knew it the first moment I saw you walking. I knew you were different. So different from your typical Naples fashion plate who thinks more about her hair, nails and clothes than anything of substance. You live in a real world, with a real job, a real brain, real concerns and a real kid. Hmmm.*

He stopped for a moment and pondered, *What must that be like? Working full time and trying to raise a three-year-old? Again, so different from the Naples high-society mode, yet again, so real.*"

He finished his yogurt, paid his bill, and went back up to his room. He had an hour and a half before his meeting, so he used the time to prep himself on The National Aviary that he was about to visit.

In his readings, he was impressed to learn that over 500 birds representing 150 species were housed there, including many that are rare and endangered. He was also very pleased to learn that they were quite the experts on owls, having had two species breed in captivity and hatch owlets.

"They aren't burrowing owls," Trevor said to himself, "but I'm sure they're all cousins."

He continued reading and noted that The Aviary was founded in 1952 as a small conservatory and had expanded immensely since. He connected this to the fundraising and monetary needs that always go hand in hand with growth. *Yes, I will definitely play that card for my interests, but the more I learn, the more I really think this is a worthy cause and not just a means to Excelsior's end.*

Then he clicked on the gallery icon and was amazed by all the remarkable birds that came in every size, shape and color. Clicking from one to another, he said, "Yes, I'm sold."

He freshened up, picked up his briefcase and decided to walk to The Aviary, as it was less than a mile away and it was a beautiful late spring day in Pittsburgh. He arrived at the entry gate at 9:53, so he sat on a wall and watched the visitors as they went in. They all seemed excited and expectant about what their visit would entail. He heard a young girl shout that she could hardly wait to see the penguins, and it made him smile.

Just then, a young man in his mid-thirties walked across the entrance area. He had on army green pants and a khaki shirt that displayed a name tag. He also had a lanyard around his neck with his ID and barcode attached. Trevor hopped off the wall and walked toward him asking, "Dr. Shields?"

Matt reached out his hand and said, "Yes, and you must be Trevor Harding."

"I am," Trevor said while grasping Matt's hand in a firm shake. "I certainly appreciate your taking time to meet with me. Did you get the copy of the plans that I had sent?"

"Yes, I did. It's quite an undertaking you're proposing."

Trevor didn't let the slight negativity affect him as he continued on saying, "Well, Dr. Shields, that's precisely why I'm here. I want to hear and learn from the best so we can make that amazing space we've designed come to life."

"All right, Mr. Harding. We might as well get to it then. Please follow me, and we'll sit down and start exploring your options and possibilities."

"Excellent!" Trevor said excitedly as he walked side by side with Matt. "Again, I'm just the money guy. I'll look to you for your expertise and guidance. You and your team will be taking the lead on this a hundred percent."

Matt stopped, looked at Trevor seriously and said, "Well, I must say, that is quite a refreshing attitude. Most quote-unquote money guys think their resources can sway what we know to be best."

Trevor engaged his look and replied, "That's not my style. I'm not going to ask you to help me develop a piece of real estate, because that's what I do exceedingly well. In the same light, you excel at housing birds in an environment they'll thrive in. I definitely won't try to pretend I know how to do that."

They both looked each other squarely in the eyes and nodded. Then they came to a door that led into a conference room. The table had the plan spread out on it, which prompted Trevor to inquire, "So, Dr. Shields, what do you think of the design?"

Matt didn't answer the question but instead said, "First, let's dispense with the formalities, OK? I'm Matt and I hope you don't mind me calling you Trevor?"

Trevor liked the assured way he conducted himself and replied, "Of course, I don't mind."

Matt pointed at the plans and said, "Well, Trevor, this design is very ambitious and, quite honestly, something I've never come across before. Please explain to me again how this whole thing came about."

An hour and a half later, Trevor and Matt were shaking hands with Trevor saying, "Thank you so much for everything, Matt. This is going to be a great partnership."

Matt responded saying, "Not at all. I've always wanted to build a large-scale aviary from the ground up. In the meantime, make sure you put that enhanced barrier around those owls as soon as possible and be extremely careful with your construction."

Trevor nodded enthusiastically and said, "Absolutely, we can't let anything happen to the main stars of our show. With the extra care that this process mandates, I expect the space to take at least four months to be completed."

Matt smiled and said, "It's a good thing I have another job then, isn't it?"

Trevor laughed lightly and replied, "True. In the meantime, please assemble a list of birds that you recommend we have and the costs that come with acquiring them."

Matt answered saying, "I'll get right on it. Trevor, you have so many outstanding species in Florida. I can hardly wait to explore all the possibilities."

Trevor smiled and jokingly said, "Yes, I'm looking forward

to the birds, but not necessarily the bill that comes with all of those bills."

"Oh, come on Trevor," Matt retorted. "You're making history. A groundbreaking advancement in the senior citizen life experience."

Trevor looked at Matt quizzically and said, "All right Dr. Shields, you don't have to butter me up anymore. I'm already committed to this project with both my heart and my wallet. You agreed to partner with me, and I'll live up to my end of the bargain. Here's my first installment."

Trevor reached into his jacket pocket and pulled out a check made out to The National Aviary for $10,000 and handed it to Matt. Matt looked at the check and then looked at Trevor saying, "You have no idea how much we appreciate this."

Trevor waved his hand saying, "A deal is a deal. Ten thousand more when the structure is completed and the last $10,000 when the aviary is up and running. Of course, you'll also receive your personal consulting fee. Now, I do believe that takes care of everything. I have a 2:15 flight, so I've got to get back to the hotel and be on my way."

They shook hands again and said their goodbyes. Both walked away from each other feeling very pleased and confident in the promise of their partnership.

* * *

Trevor had to race home to get there just in time to catch Jackie making her way down the beach. As usual, her easy gait and the way she swung her arms as she walked had Trevor mesmerized. *Is this the right moment to go say hello?*

Then he immediately thought better of it. *No, not yet. I don't want to blow all the positive energy from the other day by popping up out of nowhere. She'd probably think I'm stalking her and that is definitely not the vibe I want. Plus, she told me these are her sanity walks. I'm sure she needs the time just to be alone and decompress before she has to go from one highly demanding job to the even more demanding job of being a mom.*

So even though it took a lot of resolve to stay put, he stood in his normal spot on the balcony with his binoculars trained on Jackie's every move. She was facing out to the gulf watching two seagulls swoop around each other as if they were playing a game of tag. Then she bent down and picked up a sand dollar, walked to the water and gingerly placed it back in the gulf so it would live.

Trevor smiled at the tenderness he had just witnessed. *See, that's why she's so special. She only has a little bit of time to herself but is willing to stop and save a little sand dollar.*

Jackie let the sand dollar out of her hands saying, "There ya go little buddy. You have a lot more life to live."

She wiped her hands on her shorts to get the sand off and began walking again. The last day and a half had been a mix of a ton of work and the same amount of thinking, and then forcing herself not to think about Trevor. She tried to immerse herself in her surroundings as she walked while watching gulls, sandpipers, and a squadron of pelicans flying in formation down the coastline. Her thoughts then went to the aviary. *I'm not sure if these magnificent creatures are going to be included, but just think of how beautiful it will be. It's going to be so spectacular. I so hope Trevor's meeting went well. I can't believe he said he would let me know when he gets back. It's as if he not only wants to include me in his dream but also truly wants to share it with me.*

Then she was there, at "The House." She looked up and said, "OK Mr. Whoever You Are. Usually, I'm jealous of you, wanting to know why you have all of that and I'm working my ass off to just make ends meet. But today I'm completely content just to be me. I have my Em, I have my job, and, maybe, just maybe, I have a kindred spirit in Mr. Trevor Harding. So I may have wanted to be your friend all this time, but no longer. For the first time in a very long time, I do not wish for anything more than what I have."

She laughed gently and added, "OK, that's a lie. I am happy with everything, but I can't ignore the fact that I would really, really like to get even closer to Trevor. Likely? No. But everything that's happened so far is so incredibly unlikely. What's one more?"

She took one last look at "The House," brushed her hands against each other to get rid of any remaining sand, turned around and headed away from Trevor, who was watching her every move. He was endlessly intrigued by her outward interest in his house. *There are at least fifteen other houses she could focus on, but it's always been mine, and she always seems to be having some sort of conversation while looking up. Fate? I never believed in it, but maybe, just maybe. I do know that I'd love to know what she's saying and thinking.*

Suddenly, it occurred to him that it was Friday, and he would not have the opportunity to see her again until Tuesday. "Oh God!" he said. "That's way too long." Then he remembered that he promised her he would let her know how the meeting with The Aviary people went. He clapped his hands together and decided to leave her a voicemail, hoping she'd check over the weekend. *From what I've seen and learned about Jackie, I'd bet a fair amount of money that she will check her messages. She's conscientious to a tee.*

He dialed the law firm's number, waited for the recording to get Jackie's extension number, and then punched it in. As her voice went through the usual voicemail greeting, he pondered what to say. The beep came and Trevor started recording, "Hi Jackie, this is Trevor Harding. I know it's after hours but wanted to check in as promised. First, thanks again for a wonderful time at lunch yesterday. Secondly, I want to let you know that my meeting with The National Aviary people was very successful. Instead of filling your entire voicemail with the details, I'd love to update you in person. If you get this before Monday, maybe we could meet over the weekend. If not, I'll wait to hear from you on Monday. I can hardly wait to let you know what lies ahead. OK, bye for now."

He hit the end button, hoped that he didn't sound like an idiot, and prayed that her strong sense of responsibility would work to his favor and she would be calling soon.

Chapter Thirty-Nine

Jackie was sitting at the table on Saturday morning watching Emily spoon scrambled eggs into her mouth. She took a sip of her coffee. *It's amazing how watching such an ordinary thing fills me with such love and pride.* Then she got a bit melancholy. *My little girl is becoming so self-sufficient lately. The next thing you know, she'll be going off to school and then what?*

Emily noticed her mom looking at her and asked, "Do you want some of my eggs, Mommy?"

Jackie chuckled and replied, "No sweetie. You enjoy them. I'm going to make myself a bagel."

"OK, Mommy," Emily said and went back to eating.

Jackie got up, pulled an organic whole-grain bagel from its bag and put it in the toaster. While waiting for it to toast, Jackie decided to check her work voicemails. She always checked in at least once a day anyway, but she had left some messages of her own to others, so she wanted to see if there were replies. She put in her code and started listening.

The first was from an agent who answered Jackie's questions

by replying that her clients' mortgage application was, indeed, on track and once approved the second deposit would follow. "Good to hear," said Jackie.

The second was a client who asked if he needed to get his own survey or was that something she did. Jackie rolled her eyes saying, "I am still amazed at some of the goofiest questions people ask." She made a note to call him on Monday.

The third message was Trevor's, and as soon as she heard his voice, her heart skipped a beat and she had to sit down. Listening, she heard that excited sound in his voice she had grown to love. She paused, realizing she had just used the word love in relation to Trevor. *I really want to hear about his trip and, let's be honest, to see him. He said he could get together this weekend. Wouldn't that be better than Monday, because it would be outside of work?*

Just then, she looked up and saw Emily putting her plate in the sink. *Now Jackie, how in the world can you meet Trevor over the weekend when you have Emily to take care of?*

She put the phone down and said, "Em, let's go pick out what you want to wear today."

Emily looked at her mother and asked, "Mommy, can I pick it out on my own like a big girl, please?"

Jackie gave her a kiss and replied saying, "My big girl. Yes, you go on and pick out something nice."

Emily started skipping away while saying, "Don't worry, Mommy. I will."

Once Emily left, Jackie listened to Trevor's message again. She really didn't want to wait until Monday, so she decided to take a risk and suggest that they meet with Emily in tow. *But where? Even though she's usually very well behaved, she's still a three-year-old.* Her office wouldn't work because she had already used that card on Emily and now the novelty was gone. A restaurant could work, but it's still too much of a hands-on proposition to make sense—especially for the first time Trevor meets Emily.

Jackie wracked her brain and then a lightbulb answer came to her. *Why, of course, I'll suggest that we meet at the beach. He said himself that he's there all the time. Emily can occupy herself by playing in the sand, and Trevor and I can discuss the aviary. As Trevor would say—inspiration!*

She started putting cream cheese on her bagel, took a bite and started doubting herself. She began her usual back-and-forth debate. *You're out of your mind, Jackie! Why in the world would he want to hang out on the beach with you and a three-year-old?*

Then she switched. *Well, he might just enjoy some regular-world people time.*

Back again. *But Jackie, he is not a regular-world person. He's Trevor Harding for God's sake!*

She finally decided there was no harm in proposing the idea. *The worst that can happen is that he says no. No big deal, right?*

Then Emily came walking back into the kitchen with her favorite pink polka-dot shirt on and purple shorts with flowers all over. Not exactly what Jackie would have selected, but she looked at her precious daughter, smiled widely and said, "Why Em, you look so pretty. What a big girl you're getting to be."

Emily twirled and proudly said, "I know Mommy. I did it all by myself!"

"Yes, you did," Jackie said while smoothing Emily's hair. "Why don't you watch a little bit of Paw Patrol while I figure out what we're going to do today?"

"Yay!" Emily exclaimed. "I love that show. I want to be just like Katie and take care of all of the dogs and cats."

Jackie smiled and said, "What a nice idea." Then she ended the conversation quickly before the "Mommy can we have a pet?" questions started.

Emily settled onto the couch with her favorite blanket, and Jackie went into her bedroom to call Trevor. She nervously dialed the number he had left for her and waited through three rings before she heard him somewhat sternly say, "Trevor Harding."

She swallowed hard and said, "Hi, Trevor, this is Jackie."

He quickly replied in a much softer tone, "Oh goodness Jackie, I'm sorry I was so formal. I just didn't recognize the number."

Jackie liked how he had warmed once he knew it was her and said, "I totally understand. You're probably not used to getting calls from unknown numbers on Saturday mornings."

Trevor laughed a bit and said, "Yes, that is very true." He then added, "I hope this is in response to my message."

Jackie replied, "Yes, it is. I'd love to hear how your Pittsburgh visit went."

She was about to continue, but he interjected saying, "Jackie, we have them on board. Isn't that great? I'd really like to tell you all about it in person."

Jackie smiled at his use of "we" again and answered, "That is fantastic news!" She braced herself and continued, "Well, you know I have my daughter to take care of, so I know this might sound crazy, but if you're OK with it, I thought we could meet at the beach."

He didn't respond, so Jackie nervously went on saying, "That way, Emily can play in the sand and you and I can talk." Still nothing, so she panicked a bit and added, "But, if that's not good for you, I totally understand. I know a kid on a beach isn't exactly an ideal setting, but, quite honestly, it's the best I've got."

Then she heard Trevor let out a big laugh and say, "Jackie, you really do have some outside-the-box ideas, but somehow they all end up being outstanding. How about I meet you in front of the boardwalk at 10 o'clock?"

Jackie was thrilled. She looked at her watch, and it read 8:47. She decided that was doable, so replied, "OK great! We'll get ready and see you then."

Trevor was also excited and told her, "You have enough to do, so don't worry about drinks or snacks. I'll pack a cooler and will also bring chairs. I don't have any sand toys, however, so that's all on you."

Jackie giggled and said, "You have yourself a deal. I'll see you soon. Bye, Trevor."

"Goodbye, Jackie," Trevor said as he hung up the phone. Then he felt a panic that he had never felt before.

"Oh God," He said loudly. "My mother told me to never lie, and I just told a bunch."

Looking at his watch, he saw that it was 8:50. He got up and admonished himself for being so nervous. *Now Trevor, you are the owner of a major company and have handled much bigger issues than this with ease. Just go to Walmart—no Target, I hear they have higher quality things—and buy some beach chairs, a cooler and maybe an umbrella. Do you think an umbrella is a good idea? Yes, of course it is. Emily is three and the sun is brutal. What else?* He questioned himself trying to do a rundown of things necessary for the beach. *Yes, sunblock and water and snacks. What in God's name does a three-year-old even like?*

It was now 9 o'clock and Trevor knew he had to go and get this done pronto if he was ever going to make it back in time, so he got in his car and raced to Target.

Jackie was in the middle of her own mild panic attack. Since being caught unprepared last time, she now had the beach routine down pat and already had everything but towels in her trunk. Her main concern was what to wear and how to explain to Emily why she was meeting a stranger at the beach. Emily was still engrossed in her show, so Jackie decided to tackle her wardrobe question first.

She didn't have a lot of bathing suits, but she chose her favorite black tankini and a black and gray patterned scoop-neck coverup and simple black flip-flops. After she was dressed, she walked into the living room and tapped Emily on the shoulder. Emily looked up at her, jumped off the couch and yelled, "Yay! Mommy, are we going to the beach?"

Jackie loved her daughter's unbridled enthusiasm and answered, "Yes, Em. We are going to the beach. I know you just got dressed, but can you change into your bathing suit really fast for Mommy?"

"Yes Mommy," Emily replied. "I'll be super-duper quick," and ran into her room.

Moments later, Jackie opened Emily's door to find her dressed in her pink and rainbow suit with her previous clothes in a pile on the floor. Normally, Jackie would make Emily pick them up, but they didn't have time, so she said, "You can clean those up when we get home." She took Emily's pink terrycloth coverup out of the drawer, told her to raise her hands and slipped it over Emily's head saying, "Way to be super-duper fast. Now, let's get some towels and head to the beach."

"Yay!" Emily shouted.

During the drive over, Jackie explained to Emily that they would be meeting a friend. Emily just said, "OK, Mommy." Jackie continued saying, "Em, this friend is a man and we'll be talking, so I need you to play nicely in the sand."

Again, Emily responded with "OK, Mommy," and Jackie realized that her Emily couldn't care less about what was going on in her adult world—she just wanted to have fun at the beach.

Trevor was busy clipping price tags off his newly acquired beach paraphernalia—three chairs (two adult sized and a little one for Emily), an umbrella, and a cooler on wheels. Then he began to hurriedly fill the cooler with water, juice boxes, a tub of fruit salad, and some turkey and ham pinwheel sandwiches. He topped it all off with ice saying, "OK, I think that's enough."

He left the kitchen, went to his room, and changed into a navy, white and gray striped bathing suit. He put on a white T-shirt that had a navy collar and slid into some navy and white sandals.

Even though the beach was right outside his house, he had way too much to carry to walk, so instead he loaded the trunk of his car, got in and started out of the garage, when he realized that he didn't have a towel. "Damn it!" he said loudly as he slammed the car into park. He ran inside and out to the pool where he grabbed the first towel in the cabinet and ran back to the car.

He got to the parking garage and realized that he didn't have a parking sticker. As he fished through his wallet for the $8 fee, he thought, *I can't believe I'm paying to go to the beach that is literally my backyard.* Then he looked at his watch and realized that he was five minutes late, rolled up the window and said,

"Goddamn it. Come on Trevor. Find a spot!"

He finally found one on the second floor and quickly pulled in. He jumped out and unloaded, putting the chairs, umbrella and towel under one arm and then pulling the cooler with the other. He tried to hurry as best he could while juggling it all.

Jackie was standing at the front of the boardwalk holding Emily's hand. She looked at her phone and it was 10:12. *This is not like him at all.* Then she looked down the sidewalk and saw Trevor schlepping along with his arms full. She giggled at how ridiculous he looked, pointed and said, "Emily, that's my friend. Come on, let's go help him."

"OK, Mommy. He looks silly," Emily said.

Jackie put down her bag, and they both walked quickly down the sidewalk to where Trevor was trying to navigate his way. Jackie reached out and said, "Here, let me take these chairs."

Trevor happily relinquished them saying, "Thanks."

Emily piped up asking, "What can I carry?"

Jackie stopped and made the introduction, saying, "Mr. Harding, this is my daughter Emily. Emily, this is Mr. Harding."

Trevor held out his now freed hand and said, "Well, Emily, it is very nice to meet you and, please, call me Trevor."

They shook hands and Emily asked again, "What can I carry?"

Trevor looked at what he still had and replied, "Will you be nice enough to carry my favorite towel? It seems I've dropped it."

"Sure," Emily answered and picked up the towel from the ground.

"Thanks a lot," Trevor said. "I'm much better now. Let's go."

They walked to the boardwalk, picked up Jackie's bag and then searched for a nice spot to set up camp. Trevor had never installed a beach umbrella before but used his common sense and corkscrewed it into the sand until it was sturdy. They set up the chairs with Jackie commenting, "Somehow I don't think you had a child's beach chair just lying around, so thank you."

Trevor blushed a little as he realized that he had been caught in his white lie, but just waved his hand signaling that it was no big deal. They met each other's eyes and smiled while taking in each other's figures now that they were in their swimsuits.

Jackie broke the trance and picked up her bag. She opened it and poured all the toys for Emily out on the sand.

"Yay!" shouted Emily as she started dancing around the pile of toys. Jackie picked up Emily's hat that had fallen out too, put it on her head and said, "Have fun, but make sure this stays on." She gave her a kiss on the top of her head for emphasis and then turned back to Trevor, who was watching them intently.

She sat in her chair and he commented, "That was so sweet."

Jackie replied, "Yes, she's a good girl and the light of my life." Then she laughed and added, "However, there is a time limit to her ability to self-occupy, so please tell me about your trip."

Trevor recounted his visit with Matt and excitedly told her how Matt really liked the aviary design and was going to start assembling a list of birds to be featured. Jackie listened to his every word as if he was telling a great fairy tale and then finally broke in by asking, "Did he really call it groundbreaking?"

Trevor nodded and then added, "But, he may have been trying to schmooze me."

Jackie laughed and said, "Maybe so, but come on, Trevor, it is pretty amazing. A breathtaking showcase of all kinds of birds, right in the middle of Excelsior."

Trevor smiled and looked at Jackie more seriously saying, "As usual, you're right. It's going to be fantastic. If we do say so ourselves!"

Jackie smiled and felt warmed, not by the sun, but because he was speaking about the two of them as if they were a team. Just then, Emily looked up from the sand and asked, "Can you come play with me?"

Jackie giggled, looked at Trevor and said, "Do I know my daughter, or what?"

She started to get up when he asked, "Do you mind if I join you?"

Jackie looked into his eyes again and could tell how sincere he was, so she replied, "Of course I don't mind. What's a day at the beach without a sandcastle or two?"

They all played in the sand building a make-believe kingdom with shells and sticks for decorations and even a seagull feather on top of the tallest castle. Emily was in all her glory acting as the designer and boss of the sand construction project, which prompted Trevor to say to Jackie, "Hey, it looks like someone is out to take my job!"

Jackie laughed and said, "Yes, she does have many an idea. Sorta like her mom, but don't worry, no one could ever take your place."

He smiled and continued digging a trench in the sand just as Emily had ordered. As he dug, he tried to remember if he had ever built a sandcastle when he was young. He couldn't pull up a memory, and he definitely knew there was no way his parents would get on their hands and knees in the sand with him.

After their kingdom was finished, Emily stood up and clapped her hands saying, "Yay! We did a super-duper job!"

Jackie brushed her hands together to get the sand off and replied, "Yes, it's magnificent! Now, let's go in the water to cool off and get this sand off us."

Emily immediately started running down to the water as Jackie and Trevor quickly got to their feet to catch up with her. Once by her side, Jackie grabbed one of her hands while Trevor held the other, and all three of them walked into the surf together. Emily squealed with delight as the soft waves hit her in the belly. Trevor and Jackie couldn't help but look at each other with big smiles.

Again, Trevor was trying to remember a similar scene from his own childhood but drew another blank. Then, Jackie interrupted his thoughts saying, "Isn't it a glorious day? That lovely breeze makes all the difference, doesn't it?"

Trevor glanced all around him—the beautiful aqua water, the almost cloudless sky, the soft white sand—and then looked at Jackie and Emily and replied, "I can't imagine anything better" as he looked deeply into Jackie's eyes.

Jackie held his gaze and softly said, "Neither can I."

They both stayed engaged in each other until Emily tugged on Jackie's hand and announced, "I'm hungry!"

Trevor shifted his attention from Jackie to Emily and said, "Well, Miss Emily, I just so happen to have just the thing to fix that."

They all walked out of the water and back to the chairs. Jackie wrapped Emily in a towel and after drying off a bit, Trevor offered her a juice box. "Thank you, Mr. Trevor," Emily said as she pulled the straw from the box.

Trevor smiled at his new name and then took out the fruit and pinwheels and suddenly realized that he hadn't bought any plates or napkins. He decided to fess up saying, "Well, ladies, to be honest, I'm not very experienced at this picnic stuff. I blew it and forgot to bring plates and napkins."

Jackie smiled at his humble candor, touched his arm and said, "Not to worry, we're very good at winging it. Aren't we, Em?"

Emily nodded and promptly snatched a big piece of watermelon out of the tub and munched down on it so the juice streamed down her cheeks. Trevor and Jackie laughed and dug into the fruit and sandwiches, too.

After lunch, Emily still seemed to have a fair amount of energy, but Jackie knew that she would hit the wall soon, so she said, "Hey, why don't we take a walk and work off some of that lunch?"

Trevor got a little excited, yet apprehensive, as he knew they'd be heading toward his house. He still loved the idea of finally getting to walk with Jackie, so he replied, "A fine idea," as he jumped up from his chair. He looked at Emily and said, "If you start feeling tired, just say the word and Mr. Trevor will give you a lift."

Emily smiled widely and the three of them started down the beach. They were quiet as they walked with each caught up in their own thoughts. Trevor was reflecting on how wonderful this day was and why he never got to experience anything so naturally joyful when he was a boy.

Jackie was also absorbing how perfect the day was. Nothing seemed awkward or forced. It was such a natural, calming, and even comforting feeling. She was also blown away at how he immediately gravitated to Emily. She could tell he was totally different from the few other men that she had dated. Trevor wasn't trying to impress her with his parenting skills or put on some fake affection for Emily. He genuinely seemed to like getting down in the sand and playing with her.

They continued walking in silence until Emily pointed up to the sky and exclaimed, "Pelicans! My favorite!"

Trevor and Jackie looked skyward and there were eight pelicans flying in formation right above them. "Very cool, Emily," Trevor said. "See how they fly like a vee? That's so they can go through the air better."

"Wow. I just like them 'cause they're fun to look at."

Trevor replied, "Yes, Miss Emily. You're right. They are fun to look at." He turned to Jackie and said, "Did you know that their bill can hold three gallons of water?"

Jackie looked up at them again and replied, "No, I never knew that."

Trevor continued, "Yup, it gets filled when they scoop up the fish and then they dump the water and the fish goes down the hatch."

Jackie looked at him coyly, smiled and said, "Mr. Trevor, my, you are a wealth of information."

Trevor smiled back and replied, "Oh, you have no idea all of the trivial yet fascinating things I know."

By then, they had started to pass the beachfront mansions, and Trevor was debating on whether to say anything, but just then Emily pulled on his hand saying, "Mr. Trevor, I'm really tired now."

Trevor looked down at her sweet face and asked, "Shoulders or arms?"

Although she was very worn out, she clapped her hands and said, "Shoulders, please. Mommy says I'm too big for her to do that anymore."

Trevor glanced at Jackie who just shrugged, and then he lifted Emily up and over his head and told her to hang on tight. They turned around on the sand and started back to their spot. Once they got there, Trevor asked Jackie, "How's she doing up there?"

Jackie put her hands together and mimicked laying her head down, so Trevor whispered, "Just grab your stuff and we'll get her to your car."

Jackie looked surprised and softly said, "But what about all of this?"

Trevor started walking and replied, "Don't worry about it. I'll come back and get it. Emily needs to get home. It's been a very long day for a three-year-old."

Jackie nodded, gathered her things, and caught up with Trevor. When they got to Jackie's car, Trevor stooped down and Jackie leaned over to pull Emily off his shoulders. In doing so, they came face to face with only a few inches separating them. For a second, they looked, and each saw true caring in the other's eyes. Emily stirred a little, so Jackie took her and buckled her in the car seat. Trevor put his head in the car, gave Emily a soft kiss on the forehead and shut the door.

They were standing next to Jackie's car and Trevor said, "Jackie, this has been one of the best days I've had in a very long time. Thank you for sharing it, and Emily, with me."

Jackie looked at him and smiled saying, "You took the words right out of my mouth. It was absolutely wonderful, and thank you for being so kind to Emily."

Trevor smiled back and said, "It was my pleasure and, you're right, she's a very special girl."

"Thank you," Jackie replied.

Trevor reached out and held both of Jackie's hands like he had done at the Dolphin Club and said, "Just like her mom."

Then he pulled Jackie closer and gave her a kiss that extended and turned into a long embrace. Both felt like they could stay that way forever, but Jackie stepped back and said, "Mommy duty calls."

Trevor was still holding her hands and gave them a gentle squeeze while saying, "Of course." He held the door for her as Jackie climbed into her car, started it and drove off.

Both Jackie and Trevor were elated about their shared kiss but also quite stunned, with each asking the same question, "Oh my God. Did that really happen?"

Jackie got home, put Emily gently in her bed and took a shower. While rinsing the conditioner from her hair she thought, *What in God's name do I do now? I've never, ever felt this way about someone, but I'm still working for the firm that he employs, and I'm horrible at hiding my feelings. Especially ones that I really don't want to hide. I want to feel that moment forever.*

She finished her shower and wrapped herself in a towel. Looking in the mirror, she saw a happiness in her image that had been missing for a very long time. "Well," she said out loud. "If having a relationship with Trevor is going to make me feel and look like this, I'd be a fool to deny it."

Trevor was also just toweling off from a shower when it occurred to him that he forgot to get Jackie's personal number. "Damn," he said as he folded the towel over its bar. *Leaving voicemails on her work phone is not exactly the most romantic way of communicating.*

Then he also thought about their kiss and embrace. *Nothing had felt so right in a very long time, if ever. She's beautiful, smart, funny, a great mom and a fantastic kisser.*

He started to ponder. *How and when can I figure out a way to see her again. Tomorrow would be too soon—she'll think I'm obsessed. I know she doesn't walk on Mondays, so maybe I can ask her out then. Except she told me that she goes home right after work to relieve her babysitter. Wait, I know, I'll see if she wants me to bring a pizza over and we can just chill and hang out with Emily. It's worth a shot.*

Then it suddenly occurred to him that he hadn't thought about work all day. He laughed. *Now that's really a major miracle. See what the company of a beautiful woman does to a man.*

He took out his phone and checked his emails. There were seventeen from all sorts of people needing his attention, including Pete, the architect, Michael and Matt. He opened the first one and started to read saying, "As Jackie says, duty calls."

He got himself into work mode and addressed all his business concerns, but there was always the thought of Jackie in the back of his mind.

She was also trying to get back to normal. Emily had awakened from her nap, and Jackie was giving her a bath when Emily looked up and said, "I really like Mr. Trevor. He's nice."

Jackie smiled and replied, "Well, my little Em, he likes you very much, too."

While washing Emily's hair, Jackie got lost in her thoughts again. *Yes, he truly did seem to like Emily. My momma bear antenna was up very high, and every interaction between them seemed genuine and real. At times, it looked like he was enjoying himself just as much as she was. It was almost as if playing in the sand was all brand new to him.*

Meanwhile, Trevor leaned back in his chair and thought

about the three of them building the sand kingdom. *How much fun was that? I can't believe I have no memory of ever having done that. Yes, there were days at the country club pool with whichever nanny happened to be working for us, but no real family memories of shared fun times together. Mother was probably playing bridge and, God knows, Father would never give up his precious work or time on the golf course courting his clients to take a day off for something so trivial as spending time with his son on the beach.*

He sighed. *Maybe I've become too much like him. All this time, I've strived to break out of his mold, but if I'm being totally honest, even though it's not stocks and bonds, I've still become a slave to my work. Yes, I am still inspired and love what I'm creating and developing, but the harsh truth is I live directly on the beach and today was the first day I've gone out there and enjoyed myself.*

He closed his eyes and pictured the three of them in the water with Emily squealing with glee as the waves hit her. He relished how incredibly gorgeous Jackie was, even with her hair tousled and her legs covered in sand.

"I have to make this work," he said to himself as he picked up his phone and dialed the law firm's number. He listened to her voicemail message again, but now that her voice had so much familiarity to it, he laughed at her attempt to sound formal and businesslike.

After hearing the beep, he said, "Hi Jackie, I'm so sorry to leave you yet another message on your work voicemail, but I totally forgot to get your personal number. Not like me to miss a step, but I was preoccupied with the outstanding company and wonderful day we shared together. I know I accuse you all the time of thinking outside the box, so I'm going to give it a try. Please give me a call when you can. Thanks." Then, he hung up and hoped that his message didn't sound ridiculous or trite.

Jackie was in the middle of making spaghetti and meatballs with Emily. She instructed her by saying, "Remember to roll and roll them, so they look like little balls."

"Yes, Mommy," Emily answered as she maneuvered the meat concoction around in her little hands. "How's this?" she asked as she showed Jackie a somewhat oblong one.

Jackie smiled and replied, "That's perfect. Here, put it on the plate. We've got lots more to do."

Once the meatballs were all made, Jackie supervised as Emily thoroughly washed her hands and then told her to go watch some TV while she cooked. While Jackie watched the meatballs brown, she reflected again on the incredible day she'd experienced. *If I had read this story, I probably would have put it down for being way too farfetched, but this is not some silly romance novel. This is actually happening to me. Who in the world would ever have thought?*

She flipped the meatballs. *Let's get more real, Jackie. Can a relationship with a man of his means and power be possible?*

She decided to leave that thought alone and committed herself just to live in the present, see what happens next, and be incredibly grateful for the amazing day that they had shared.

Chapter Forty

Both Jackie and Emily slept in late on Sunday, with Emily lazily creeping into Jackie's bed at 8 o'clock for another hour of peaceful, comforting sleep with each other. Jackie opened her eyes first and saw the angel-like face of her beloved daughter. She softly whispered, "Oh, Em, I love you so much."

Emily stirred and reached out to her mom. They snuggled together for another twenty minutes, and then Emily rolled over and said, "Mommy, I'm ready to get up now, OK?"

"Yes, of course, my Em. Let's go get some breakfast and figure out what we want to do today."

As Emily was busy eating her favorite waffles, Jackie sipped her coffee and decided to check her work messages. Again, there were those with mundane questions and some giving her updates, but certainly nothing that couldn't wait until tomorrow. Then, she was startled to hear Trevor's now familiar voice talking about something "out of the box." Jackie giggled and felt excited. *Mr. Buttoned Up Harding is starting to think outside the box, go figure! Maybe I'm rubbing off on him.*

She checked the time and it was 10:22. She decided that it was late enough to call on a Sunday morning. She dialed his number and heard him answer, "Trevor Harding."

She laughed and said, "Haven't we been down this road before?"

Trevor gasped and replied, "Oh my God, Jackie. I'm so, so sorry. How could I be so stupid? If I'd just created a contact the last time you called, I wouldn't have had to leave another idiotic voicemail and answer your call like you're some intruder."

Unlike a lot of men, Jackie really appreciated his willingness to be self-critical and admit making mistakes, but she didn't think it was that big a deal for him to be so harsh, so she gently said, "Trevor, believe me, it's really nothing. You have a lot on your mind, and I honestly thought the message was quite charming."

Trevor's voice relaxed as he said, "Thanks, Jackie. Yes, there's certainly been a lot going on lately, but the one thing that I can't get off my mind is you."

Jackie blushed and responded, "Yes, I know the feeling. You mentioned you had an outside-the-box idea—what do you have in mind?"

Trevor knew that it was his turn to go out on a limb, so he swallowed hard and replied, "Well, you see … damn it, Jackie. I just really want to see you again, but I know how busy you are with work and Emily."

Jackie's curiosity was piqued, but all she said was, "Yes … "

Trevor continued, "Well, I thought that we could spend some time together by … uh, I mean, if it's OK with you … "

Jackie was touched by how this man who was usually in full control was stumbling over his words, so she calmly said,

"Trevor, what is it that you want to ask me?"

He was feeling like a shy boy asking a girl for the first time to dance, so he swallowed again and blurted out, "How about I come by tomorrow night with a pizza and you and Emily and I can eat and watch a movie or something?"

At first, Jackie panicked at the thought of Trevor seeing her bare-bones existence and cramped apartment, but then decided that if this relationship was going to go anywhere, she had to be honest and he had to be a part of all that she was and experience her world, no matter how uncomfortable. She was about to speak when she heard him somewhat urgently ask, "Jackie, are you there?"

She shook her head to clear her thoughts and replied, "Yes, yes, Trevor. That would be very nice."

"Excellent," Trevor said as he did his familiar fist pump. "Now, before I go being a knucklehead again, I will immediately create a contact for you. Please text me your address when we hang up, and I'll see you on Monday. How does six sound?"

Jackie was still panicked but thrilled all at the same time and replied, "Six is great."

"Fantastic! I'll see you then. I'm guessing just a plain cheese pizza would be best considering Emily is so young?"

Again, Jackie was touched. This time for how remarkably considerate he was and answered, "Thanks for thinking of her. Cheese is perfect. And Trevor, Emily likes you already, but she's really going to like you when you bring her pizza."

Trevor laughed and said, "Yes, my diabolical plan exactly." Then he added, "I'm very much hoping her mom will feel the same. I'll see you tomorrow, Jackie. Take care."

Jackie managed to say, "You, too" as the call ended. Then she sat down while trying to digest, yet again, what was going on and if it was real.

Trevor also sat down. *She's willing to let me into her personal space. Such a promising sign, but I better not screw it up. No matter what, Trevor, make sure you leave your preconceived ideas at the door and just accept and enjoy being with her ... um ... them.*

Chapter Forty-One

Both Jackie and Trevor had very normal and nondescript Mondays. She plowed through all her work, while he went about all his inspections and was quite pleased with the progress. However, regardless of this normality, the thought of each other was always hovering over whatever they were doing. Before she left for work, Jackie told Maria all that had happened at the beach. Maria smiled, laughed lightly and said, "You see, Maria knows."

Jackie smiled back and said, "Yes Maria. I'm sorry I doubted you." Then she told her that Trevor was coming over tonight.

Maria feigned shock and then said, "How exciting! I'll make sure the house is perfectamente and Miss Emily is all ready."

"That would be so nice," Jackie replied and then added, "But I want Trevor's visit to be a surprise for Emily. He's bringing pizza."

Maria laughed and said, "I'll keep it a secret, but, boy, does he know how to win a three-year-old's heart—and I think he might just be winning her mom's heart, too."

Jackie got serious and looked at Maria with trusting eyes, saying, "Oh Maria, I really do think he might be the one that's worth climbing out of my shell for. You should have seen him on the beach playing with Em. He was like a little boy himself."

Maria gave Jackie a hug and reassured her saying, "Yes Jackie, my dear, he does sound special, but never forget how special you are too, and, of course, Emily."

Jackie hugged her back and said, "As always, you are so wise."

Jackie sat at her desk while reflecting on the morning and what a wonderful gift Maria was to both her and Emily. Then she looked at her phone and realized that the workday had ended. She tidied up her desk and packed her things to go home. *I had better buy some beer or maybe wine to go with the pizza. Oh hell, I'll buy both just to be safe.*

After stopping at the liquor store, she walked into her small, cramped, yet immaculate apartment. "Oh Maria," Jackie exclaimed as she picked up Emily. "This all looks sooo amazing! Thank you so much!"

"De nada," Maria replied. "And our Emily was a very good helper. I'm so very happy for you. I hope you have a wonderful evening. Buenas noches."

Jackie put Emily down, gave Maria a big kiss on the cheek and said, "Fingers crossed."

Maria laughed a bit and said, "Jackie, my dear, you don't need luck when you have love." She then gathered her things and left.

Jackie turned around and noticed that Emily was dressed in her favorite pink with white polka-dot dress and had two pink bows in her hair. She took in the beautiful image of her daughter and said, "Oh Em. You look so pretty, and thank you for helping Miss Maria today."

Emily did a twirl while saying, "Thank you, Mommy. Yes, I helped, but why was Miss Maria cleaning so much today?"

Jackie smiled at Emily's inquisitiveness, which reminded her so much of herself, and then replied, "Well, my darling Em, we are going to have a special guest tonight who's nice enough to bring us dinner."

Emily clapped her hands and shouted, "Who, Mommy, who?"

Just as Jackie was trying to think of an answer to stall, there was a knock on the door. Jackie felt her nerves jump and started to panic a bit but reminded herself that this was where she and Emily lived and there was nothing to be ashamed of. She walked over to the door with Emily hiding right behind her left leg. She opened it, and there stood Trevor with a pizza box in one hand and a bag with beer and wine in the other. Emily exclaimed, "Yay, it's Mr. Trevor!"

Trevor put the pizza and bag on the counter, looked at Emily and said, "Yes, Miss Emily, I thought I'd come by and say hi to my two most favorite girls. Do you like pizza?"

"Pizza, pizza, Mommy! I loooove pizza!" Emily shouted in a singsong voice.

Jackie glanced at Trevor and mouthed, "I told you." She turned to Emily and said, "Yes, isn't this very nice of Mr. Trevor to treat us to one of your favorites?"

"Yes, Mommy," Emily replied as she held out her arms to give Trevor a hug. He picked her up and she said, "Thank you, Mr. Trevor," and squeezed him in a big hug.

Trevor hugged her back and said, "It's my pleasure, but what do you say we stop talking and start eating?" He opened the box while Jackie got some plates from the cabinet. As she reached up, he noticed her exquisite figure and had to stop himself from going over and embracing her. Instead, he said, "I didn't know what you like, so I bought both beer and wine."

She put the plates down on the counter as she took in his physique and then smiled and said, "Funny, I had the same dilemma, so I bought both as well."

Trevor touched her hand, laughed and said, "Well, we definitely won't go thirsty then, will we?"

Emily had grown impatient and loudly said, "I'm hungry!" which broke the moment between them. Trevor bent down, picked her up and said, "OK, Miss Em, you get the honor of picking the first slice."

Emily saw one that had a big bubble on it, so she pointed and said, "That one please. I love the bubbles."

As Jackie picked up Emily's piece and put it on her plate, Trevor set her down while saying, "A fine choice. I love the ones with bubbles, too."

Jackie brought Emily to the table and said, "Now, please be patient Em and wait until we're all seated before starting. Plus, you know we have to say grace."

Emily wasn't thrilled at the delay in eating her special slice but nodded reluctantly saying, "OK, Mommy."

Jackie went back to the counter and Trevor asked, "So, beer or wine?"

Jackie turned, smiled and said, "I follow the pizza-and-beer school of thinking. You?"

Trevor smiled widely and agreed saying, "Absolutely! Other Italian red sauce dishes are wine meals, but pizza is absolutely meant for beer."

"Exactly," Jackie concurred as she put a slice on her plate and opened a beer. They made their way to the table and sat down when Jackie realized that here they were all sitting at her very small table in her extremely confined apartment. She looked at Trevor and said, "Welcome to my world. It's not much, but it's filled with love."

Trevor hadn't even noticed his surroundings as he was so caught up with trying to engage Jackie and Emily. He looked around and saw a bare-bones existence, but everything seemed to have importance and had been put in its own particular place with such evident care. He also could almost physically feel the love that Jackie had just mentioned. He looked at Jackie sincerely and said, "It's perfect, and I definitely can see and feel how much love is present."

Just then, Emily pulled on Jackie's sleeve and Jackie knew her patience was over, so she said, "Thank you for waiting so nicely, Emily. Can you show Mr. Trevor what we do before we eat?"

"Sure, Mommy," Emily said proudly and continued, "First, we put our napkins on our laps and then we hold hands and say our blessing."

Emily put out her hands for Trevor and Jackie to take, and then she and Jackie said in unison, "Thank you God for this day, thank you God for this meal, and, especially, thank you God for each other. Amen!"

Trevor watched them go through their ritual that was so grounded in reality and love. Such a far cry from the stoic graces that were muttered at his family dinners. When they were done, he gave both of their hands a little squeeze and said, "That was just lovely."

As soon as her hand was released, Emily picked up her long-awaited pizza and took a big chomp. Trevor and Jackie looked at each other, laughed and began to eat as well. He reflected more on Jackie's small yet cozy home. *Everything in my house was picked out by some hired decorator who doesn't even know me. Here, Jackie and Emily have their personal imprint on everything that's around us. What does some fancy designer stuff matter if it has no meaning?*

Jackie noticed that Trevor had become pensive and asked, "Is everything OK?"

Trevor broke out of his thoughts and answered, "Oh goodness, I'm sorry. I was just thinking about how wonderful it is to be in a true home. My bachelor pad is so sterile and staged."

Jackie was surprised by his response, since she thought he had everything most people could wish for, but didn't want to press the issue, so she just said, "We're so happy that you're here." They met each other's eyes, and both knew that they were falling hard for each other.

Just then, Emily smacked her hands together and said, "That was soooo good! Thank you, Mr. Trevor. What do you want to do now?"

Jackie switched into mom mode and said, "Well, first my little one, you need to be a good hostess and ask Mr. Trevor if he'd like another piece, and then you need to clean up your plate."

"Yes, Mommy," Emily replied and then turned her attention to Trevor saying, "Mr. Trevor, would you like another piece of pizza? It's really, really good."

Trevor smiled and answered, "Why thank you for asking and you're right, it is very good, but why don't you bring in your plate and I'll help myself. It might be just a little too high for you to get."

"OK," Emily agreed, but followed up with, "So, what do you want to do after you're done eating?"

Trevor had no idea how to respond because, other than the other day at the beach, he had never been around a three-year-old before. All he knew was that he wanted to be near Jackie, but he was at a total loss about the rest.

Jackie was watching their interaction and purposely didn't intervene as she wanted to see where their exchange would lead, but once she saw Trevor obviously struggling with an answer, she stepped in and said, "Hey Emily, would you like to show Mr. Trevor your favorite movie?"

Before they knew it, all three of them were sitting on the couch while Frozen played for the umpteenth time. Trevor reached for Jackie's hand, which she readily gave him, and they pulled themselves closer. Again, Trevor was so touched by the simple genuineness of the moment and tried to pull up any memory of a time shared this way with his parents, but, yet again, he drew a blank.

Jackie was also lost in her own thoughts as she tried to remember when or if she had ever felt so comfortable and at ease with a man. She also came up empty.

Then the song "For the First Time in Forever" started playing. Emily started singing while Jackie looked at Trevor and each held the other's eyes as if they both felt the same exact thought. He put his arm around her, and they contently watched the rest of the movie with Emily now draped across their laps.

Once the movie ended, Jackie told Emily that it was time for bed and to say goodnight to Mr. Trevor. Emily stretched, yawned and said, "Yes, Mommy. I'm tired." She then wormed her way onto Trevor's lap and gave him a big hug saying, "Thank you again for the pizza, Mr. Trevor, and watching Frozen with us. It was a lot of fun having you over."

Trevor hugged her back while saying, "You're welcome, Miss Emily. Thank you for letting me visit you and your mom. I really liked the movie. Thanks for sharing it with me."

Emily squeezed him again and said, "I've got to go night-night now." She gave him a peck on the cheek and trotted off to her room.

Jackie looked at Trevor, smiled and said, "You're definitely on her good side now. I'm going to put her to bed. If you'd like to stay, it'll just be a bit."

Trevor thought, *There's no way in hell I'm going anywhere,* but instead said, "Sure, take your time."

Jackie got Emily changed and watched how incredibly cute she was as she stood on her stool and brushed her teeth. Then she tucked her in saying, "Thank you for being such a good girl during Mr. Trevor's visit."

Emily looked sleepily up at her mom and said, "He's nice."

Jackie smiled slightly and said, "Yes, my precious Em, he is. Now you go night-night and I'll see you in the morning. I love you most."

Emily rolled over and replied, "Goodnight, Mommy. I love you the mostest."

Jackie smoothed her hair, kissed her beloved daughter on the head and then left the room. When she got back to the living room, she found Trevor checking the numerous emails on his phone. She sat down next to him and said, "Trevor, I know how incredibly busy you are, so thank you so much for taking time to come over and spend some time with us."

Trevor closed his phone and replied, "Nonsense. The pleasure is all mine. As a matter of fact, I haven't had as much fun as we've had over the last few days in a very long time, and, if I'm being honest, maybe ever."

He patted the cushion on the couch for her to sit down and when she did, he took her hands and said, "Jackie, you've helped me in so many ways. Not just the aviary and work things, but real-life things that I had forgotten about. Like enjoying life." He hesitated a bit and added, "And each other."

They both came together and kissed and embraced. They were feeling so much desire, yet also a strong sense of security and calm. It was extremely difficult to restrain the want to delve further into their powerful attraction for each other, but they knew that there was a little girl in the other room, so they controlled themselves from going where they both desperately wanted to go.

Jackie finally found the resolve to pull away for a moment saying, "Trevor, remember, we both have to go to work tomorrow."

Trevor smiled shyly and said, "I know," and then kissed her once more. Jackie fell under the spell again and loved the feeling of his strong body against hers. Yet, his movements were so gentle, never anything too forward or abrupt. They continued to explore each other until, almost as one, they knew that things needed to end there. Otherwise, they might not stop. Still holding each other's hands, they stepped away from the temptation with Trevor saying, "Jackie, thank you so much for letting me enter your world."

She quietly laughed and replied, "Funny, I never thought it was anything especially great, certainly nothing exciting, particularly by Naples' standards."

Trevor looked at her and said seriously, "Believe me Jackie, what you and Emily have is truly something special. Unlike so much in this town, it's real. None of the Naples' BS where everyone is always trying to one-up each other, whether it's looks, money or all the rest of that crap."

Jackie looked at Trevor with a purposely quizzical expression and said, "Says the man who drives a Tesla sports car?"

Trevor blushed a bit and replied, "Touché, but I do really like the car, and it is environmentally friendly. Look Jackie, I'm not saying all material things are bad. I've worked very hard to get where I am and I'm certainly not ashamed, but you've opened up my view and helped me reassess what really matters. It looks like I'm indebted to you once again."

Jackie grinned and replied, "Well, Mr. Harding, I must thank you as well for helping me learn that all powerful and wealthy people aren't fake pompous asses."

Trevor laughed at her blunt assessment and said, "My pleasure." Then he pulled her close for one last kiss and said, "Time to take my less-than-pompous ass home, so we can both recharge before we're back at the grind tomorrow."

They embraced and kissed again, each time more passionately than the one before. Then Jackie reluctantly let go of him saying, "As much as I am enjoying this, you, Mr. Harding, are correct as usual. We both have a very busy day tomorrow, so it's best that we say goodnight."

He held her hands as he had done before, but this time he felt so much more emotion and, he realized, commitment.

"Good night, Jackie," he said somewhat regretfully and then added, "I would love to see you again very soon."

Jackie showed him her smile again that now had the effect

of melting his heart and said, "I would also love that very much."

With that he let go of her hands, closed the door, and another magical experience between them ended with both of them yearning for more.

Chapter Forty-Two

Tuesday was another workday filled with routine goings on. Jackie reviewed five new contracts and sent out introductory letters. She also made phone calls to various realtors, the sales team at Excelsior, and some buyers, who again had more of the same usual questions. She tracked all the purchasers who were obtaining financing and was generally pleased with how it all was progressing. She updated her spreadsheet as she did every day, not only to keep track for herself but also to present to Mr. Wright at the end of each week.

Trevor was also filling his time with his normal everyday functions—reading Pete's report, inspecting work sites, and monitoring sales.

He also had a very positive and productive Facetime call with Michael. He had received the plans back from him with all his ideas marked on the print, and they used the call to finish hammering out the logistics of how to implement them all. Each time Trevor spoke to Michael, it confirmed his decision to let him take the lead on the medical center. Dr. Michael

Worthington was so incredibly knowledgeable about geriatrics and elder care, and Trevor was always impressed by his ability to come up with better ways to arrange space and protocols to accommodate and meet patient needs. In a most heartfelt manner, Trevor thanked him at the end of their call by saying, "Michael, I so appreciate you spearheading this project. With your vision, the medical center is going to be the capstone of all of the amazing services that we will provide at Excelsior."

Michael was taken by Trevor's deferential manner and replied, "Thank you, Trevor. I do believe that we're going to transform the model and accomplish much for how elder care is viewed in this country. I very much appreciate you allowing me such a free hand in its development."

They said their goodbyes, and then Trevor reviewed the plan again exclaiming, "By God, yes, this facility is going to be awesome! I can hardly wait to tell Jackie."

Then, he allowed himself to break out of work mode and reflect back on last night and pictured her in his arms. He was a 39-year-old man and never had he felt the way he did when he was with her. Their times together were so different from what used to be the norm for him in the Naples social scene, and that's what made it so real and true. No airs or put-on graces. Just a day at the beach and a night on the couch. Instead of his usual halting approach to relationships and his feelings, he leaned back in his chair and admitted the obvious to himself by saying, "By God, I really think I'm falling in love."

Jackie also came to a break in her workday, and immediately her thoughts turned to Trevor and last night. She giggled, *Did I really say that I thought he would be a pompous ass?* She laughed some more. *He did take it in good humor, thank heavens, and God knows how incredibly wrong I was. I've never been with a man who has accepted and valued who I am so much. It's almost as if Emily and I are giving him something that he's been missing. Go figure.*

She then allowed herself to think about how wonderful she felt in his arms and how his kisses were so passionate yet caressing and tender. She got flushed and suddenly realized what was happening saying, "Oh Lord, am I actually falling in love?"

Trevor decided he wasn't going to wait any longer. *If this relationship was going to work out with Jackie, then she needed to know where I live, just like I learned about her home.* He also concluded that he had to come clean and explain how he had watched her all this time. He thought about the difficulty of that. *I have to convince her that this isn't some grand cooked-up scheme—just blessed fate.*

He knew he had his work cut out for him but resolved to meet her on the beach that evening. He would set up his newly purchased umbrella and chairs, pack the cooler with a bottle of champagne, and pray that she would believe and understand.

When the time came, he sat there as nervous as a student waiting to see the principal while waiting for her inevitable appearance. At 5:20, he spotted her walking toward him. She took his breath away as he watched her beautiful light brown hair blowing in the breeze and her magnificent legs constricting as she dug her feet into each step. Then he started to panic, *Oh God, Trevor! What if she's offended? You still have time to pack up and run.* As soon as the thought crossed his mind, he remembered her kiss and admitted, *No, this has to be.*

She was about twenty feet away from him and he couldn't stand it any longer, so he got up and walked toward her. She was visibly shocked to see him and said, "My goodness Trevor, what in the world are you doing here?"

He looked around and replied with the first thing that came into his head, "Well, I did say I wanted to see you again soon."

Jackie was still unnerved and replied, "Yes, but how on earth did you know that I'd be here?"

Trevor reached for her hand and answered, "I know it must seem very odd, if not unsettling, but I hope you'll let me explain." He led her to the chairs and said, "I know this is going to sound crazy, but I'm asking you to trust me. I don't know how or why we got to where we are now, so I guess it's best to just start at the beginning. But first, will you join me in a glass of champagne?"

Jackie sat down but was still startled by the interruption to her sacred walk. On the other hand, she did trust Trevor, so she replied, "Not my normal Tuesday evening beverage, but why not?"

She watched Trevor pour two glasses of champagne, took the glass that he offered and touched his outstretched one as he toasted saying, "Jackie, please know that I've never been this happy. Thank you for letting me into your world. Now, I'd like to welcome you to mine. I so hope that they might become one."

Jackie was touched by his sentiments, but confused because she couldn't figure out where this was going, so she just nodded.

Trevor swallowed hard and took a sip of champagne. *It's now or never.* Then he gently explained to her how he had noticed her months ago and had admired her from afar. He continued, telling her that he had absolutely no idea that she worked for the law firm and was in a complete state of shock when she appeared there. He added, "But, truth be told, I was also very thrilled to meet you and hear your lovely voice for the first time."

Jackie listened to him, and although his story could be cause for alarm, she still felt an uncanny sense of safety with him. She asked, "But, where were you?"

He sipped again hoping the champagne was truly liquid courage and replied, "Well, you know that house that you always pass by and look at?"

Jackie met his eyes and firmly said, "Are you kidding me?"

Trevor tried to reassure her with a smile and replied, "No Jackie, I'm not kidding you. That is my house and I'd love to show it to you."

Jackie sprang to her feet, abruptly handed him her glass and said angrily, "So, let me see if I have this straight. Not only were you spying on me, but you were doing it from your rich-ass mansion!?"

Trevor looked genuinely wounded and answered, "I'm afraid so."

Jackie suddenly looked at her phone, realized how late it was and said, "Look Trevor, I know this is not good timing, but, as you well know, I don't have the luxury of spending hours on the beach. I have a three-year-old that I have to get home to. Plus, I need time to wrap my brain around what you just dropped on me."

Trevor nodded as if he had just been scolded and said, "Yes, of course. I know you have to go home to Emily and I'm sorry to lay all of this on you, but I care about you so much, I couldn't keep it from you any longer. Please try to understand, Jackie.

This is my house, and whatever you think about it, it really is no different than yours. It's where I live and dream. However, to be completely honest, yours has way more life and love in it. That, I envy and hope to have one day."

She couldn't help but feel for him, so she gave him a quick kiss on the cheek and said, "We'll talk soon." She turned and started walking very quickly down the beach and then broke out into a run.

She got to her car and gave Maria a call saying, "I'm so sorry I'm late. Something came up, but I'm on my way. I'll be there in five minutes."

Maria heard the distress in Jackie's voice and responded, "It's OK Jackie. I was just getting worried. Is everything all right?"

Jackie started her car and backed out of her parking space while replying, "I'm fine. It's just that I learned something pretty shocking about Trevor."

Maria was immediately concerned and said, "Mon Dios. He had better not have hurt you."

Jackie quickly said, "No, it's nothing like that. I'll explain when I get home."

"OK, my dear," Maria said, even though she was still concerned.

Jackie opened the door to the usual shouts of "Mommy, Mommy" from Emily. She reached down, picked her up and gave her an extra-long hug and a big kiss saying, "Oh my Em. What would I do without you? You are my very special girl."

Emily looked at Jackie, smiled wide and said, "Well, you are my bestest Mom!"

They both giggled and then Jackie caught Maria's eye, which had the look of a mother's worry and concern. She asked Emily to go watch TV, which Emily happily skipped off to do.

Jackie sat down to tell Maria what had happened as briefly as possible. "Oh Maria," she started. "I have so many emotions going on right now. I really don't know what to think or feel."

Maria looked at Jackie lovingly and said, "What happened, my dear? You seemed so content and happy this morning."

"Yes, Maria" Jackie agreed. "But tonight … on the beach … he was there."

Maria smiled and said, "I'm sure it was quite a surprise, but that's a nice coincidence, yes?"

Jackie shook her head a bit and replied, "Yes, except it wasn't a coincidence."

Maria chuckled and said, "So, this man wants to see you and took the time to be there. You should be flattered."

Jackie was struggling with the disconnect between her feelings about what had just happened and Maria's take on it, so she continued, "I know, Maria. But it's more than that. It wasn't just tonight—he's been watching me for months."

"Aayyy!" Maria said as she understood. "He was a secret admirer. I'm sure many men admire you from afar. Perhaps, my dear, it's destino, yes, fate that you two have met and are meant to be together."

Jackie digested this thought and then said, "There's more"

Maria smiled assuredly and said, "Go on."

Jackie started nervously wringing her hands together and continued, "Remember that enormous house on the beach that I'm always talking about?"

Maria nodded and replied, "Of course."

Jackie wrung her hands some more, swallowed and blurted out, "It's his!"

Now it was Maria's turn to be shocked. "Que?" she said loudly.

"I know. I can't believe it either. He wanted me to come inside and see it. I'm afraid I said some rude things to him about spying and being rich."

Maria waved her hands and said, "This is too much to believe."

"Yes," Jackie agreed. "But he said it's just his house. Just like this is ours and that he actually envies Emily and me. Now that I think about it, he's right, you know. I was so worried about him judging us because of where we live and now I'm guilty of doing it to him. He was so open and accepting of our world and then I go and condemn him for his. I've got to apologize."

Maria looked at her watch and said, "This sort of apology must be made face to face. I'll call my husband and tell him to fend for himself for a change. You call Trevor and then go make your peace with him."

Jackie felt tears streaming down her cheeks and said, "Really Maria?"

"Absolutamente," Maria confidently replied and then added, "Do not waste another minute."

Jackie got up and came around to Maria and gave her a heartfelt kiss saying, "If I say it a million times, it isn't enough. I don't know what I'd do without you."

She went into her bedroom and dialed Trevor's number. He answered quickly and asked with concern in his voice, "Jackie?"

She breathed deep to try to sound calm and replied, "Yes, Trevor, it's me. I'm so sorry I said those things about you, and I'm sorry that I had to run off."

Trevor was cautiously optimistic and said, "No, Jackie. It's all right. I know it's a lot to take in. I'm sorry I made you late."

Jackie knew that he was being completely honest, so she continued saying, "I was wondering if your offer to see your house is still open?"

Trevor was taken back a bit, but thrilled that she seemed to be coming around, so he answered, "Of course. When would you like to come by?"

Jackie quickly answered, "How about now?"

Trevor was taken off guard, but figured there's no time like the present, so he said, "Sure. What about Emily?"

Jackie was touched that he wanted to include her, but responded saying, "No, no. My dear babysitter, Maria, has offered to stay late for me, so it will just be me."

Trevor flushed with anticipation and said, "Sounds wonderful. I'll leave your name at the guard gate. Just drive straight and then make a left at the stop sign. My house is on the right. I'll be waiting out front."

"OK," Jackie said, "I'll see you soon, and if you have any of that champagne left, I'll take some. I never even took a sip of it earlier."

Trevor chuckled and said, "Yes, you were somewhat pre-occupied. I'll have a glass waiting. See you in a bit."

Jackie hung up the phone and went into the living room where Emily was engrossed in an episode of Paw Patrol. Jackie put her hand on her shoulder and said, "Em, I need to go out for a little while. Great news is Maria is going to watch you some more. Be a good girl for Mommy, OK?"

Emily barely broke her gaze from the silliness going on in her show, but said, "OK, Mommy. I'll see you later."

Jackie thought about fixing her hair and makeup but decided that Trevor had already seen her this way today, so she muttered, "What the hell."

She went back into the kitchen where Maria had started

cooking some rice and beans. She smiled at Jackie and said, "I saw you have some leftover chicken in the fridge, so it will go perfectly with my famous rice and beans. You go and be with your intended. Be apologetic, but don't go too far. He has some responsibility in this misunderstanding, too. Learn about his world and, who knows, it just might be your destiny."

Jackie hugged her and merely said, "Yes, Maria."

* * *

She pulled up to the neighborhood guard gate where some cop-school flunky looked suspiciously at her and her beat-up Honda. She smiled and handed him her license while saying, "Mr. Trevor Harding is expecting me."

The guard smirked and punched his computer, which confirmed her admittance. He handed back her license saying, "Funny, I've never known Mr. Harding to have visitors, especially this time of the night."

Jackie snatched her license from him and said, "Well, I'm happy I could provide a little change of plans to the norm," and then hurriedly pulled away.

She followed the directions and saw Trevor standing outside his enormous house, waving like he was trying to hail a cab. She smiled, pulled into the driveway and put the car in park. She was somewhat startled when he opened the door for her, saying, "So glad you found it OK." He held out his hand to assist her in getting out of the car. Jackie gladly reached out and felt his comforting hand while replying, "It wasn't exactly like finding the holy grail. Even I can manage 'go straight and make a left.'" They both laughed and then she looked up at the huge house that stood in front of them and couldn't resist announcing, "Oh

Trevor, this is absolutely magnificent!"

Trevor put his arm around her and replied, "Yes, I guess it is. Honestly, I always pull right into the garage, so I never get to see the front of the house. Isn't that crazy?"

Jackie tried to visualize his world. Work, come home, eat, work again and repeat. She tenderly replied, "Yes, it is a bit odd, but when you're as busy as you are, I can imagine that there's not much time to enjoy all of this."

Trevor nodded and said, "Exactly! My world has been so filled with projects, plans and deadlines, this house has pretty much become just a place where I eat and sleep." He held up his hand and said, "However, I do exercise and swim every day."

She looked at him, giggled and said, "Well, I guess that's getting your money's worth. Sorta."

Trevor was about to lead her inside when Jackie stopped and turned to him saying, "Trevor, I want to apologize again. Some of the things I said earlier were hurtful and I'm very sorry. I was just … "

Trevor covered her mouth with his fingers and gently said, "No need to apologize and I mean it. I dropped a bombshell on you. You had every right to be upset. Now, let me show you my 'rich-ass mansion.'"

They were both laughing as they walked into the top-of-the-line kitchen where Andre was in the middle of preparing a salmon filet.

Trevor stopped and said, "Andre, I'm sorry, but I'll be somewhat late for dinner. May I introduce you to Ms. Jackie Summerville."

Andre was at first taken aback and a bit disturbed by the change of plans, but once he looked up from his cutting board and saw Jackie and the happiness exuding from Trevor, he just smiled and said, "Of course, Mr. Harding. It's a pleasure to meet you, Ms. Summerville." Then he extended his hand to shake.

Jackie took his hand and replied, "So nice meeting you as well. I'm sorry if my visit is interrupting your dinner preparations."

Andre could tell that she was sincere and not just giving him lip service, so he kissed her hand and said, "No, it's no problem at all. It's so nice to have a visitor. Can you stay for dinner? I can certainly prepare enough for two."

Jackie appreciated the courtesy and responded, "Thank you so much, but, no. I can't stay long."

Trevor interrupted their exchange by saying, "Well, I can at least get you that champagne that you missed out on earlier."

Andre was confused by the reference to earlier, but dutifully opened the refrigerator, poured two glasses of bubbly and handed them each one. Then, much to Andre's surprise, Trevor took Jackie's hand and led her on a tour of his house.

They went from one room to the next to the next with Jackie taking it all in. *I might as well be in a museum. Everything is so planned and perfect. No sign of real life or people.* She didn't want to be rude, though, and definitely didn't want to hurt his feelings, so she picked the safest comment she could come up with and said, "This is all so beautiful."

Trevor looked at her a bit suspiciously and said, "Do you really like it? I think it's all a bit overkill and there's no personal connection like what I felt when I was at your house. Truth be told, just like everything else I've done, I bought this as an investment. It's obviously much too big for a single man, but it has increased in value by twenty percent."

Jackie looked at him and replied, "OK, now that we're

being truthful, it is a lot and seems like a designer has staged everything. However, twenty percent is quite the return on your money. Another remarkable success by Trevor Harding."

They walked out to the pool area and patio where his balcony was. He smiled and said, "Oh right, there is one other thing I do when I'm home. Three days a week I stand over there and get the gift of watching the most beautiful woman in the world walk the beach."

Then he stopped, turned to her and gently held her hands while saying, "Yes, Jackie, I am very successful and certainly not ashamed of it, but I've been missing something just as important, if not more."

Jackie knew he was trying to get something off his chest so she remained quiet and he continued on, "I was so caught up in the world of developing, building and making money that I never allowed myself to see outside of it. Yes, I was infatuated with you on the beach, but since meeting you everything has changed. I now realize how narrow and confining my life was."

Again, Jackie stayed silent so he could get all his thoughts out. He went on asking, "Who would think that a legal assistant with a great talent for presentations, an incredibly observant eye for burrowing owls, and a crazy idea to build an aviary would change my existence?"

Then he looked at her lovingly yet squarely in the eyes and tenderly said, "I can't thank you enough and, Jackie, I might as well just say it—I am hopelessly in love with you."

Jackie was digesting all that Trevor had just proclaimed as she looked out over the sand and gulf waters that lay below this unbelievable setting. The reddish sun was just about to slip below the horizon, and then the day would slide into darkness.

She thought about how magical and restoring the beach always was, but to see it from this height made it even more miraculous and calming, yet not so different. She continued to scan the soothing waters and waves until Trevor interrupted her thoughts by asking, "Jackie, are you all right?"

She broke her gaze, turned to him and gently answered, "Yes, Trevor, I'm fine. As a matter of fact, I'm perfect. I was just taking in the view from your world. Yes, it's spectacular, but really not so much different than what I experience down there."

"Yes," Trevor said urgently. "But did you hear me? I love you and want both of our worlds to be one. You, me and Emily."

Jackie reached out, pulled him to her and kissed him passionately saying, "Yes, Trevor. One world. I am so in love with you, too."

Chapter Forty-Three

Trevor and Mr. Wright were standing under the canopy that had been erected on his expansive pool deck. As always, Mr. Wright was wearing a conservative pinstriped suit while Trevor was in a formfitting navy one. He knew that most grooms wore tuxedos, but his aversion to them because of the Naples elite made him stick with an everyday, albeit formal suit.

Trevor wasn't nervous because he was so supremely confident that Jackie was the best thing to happen to him in all his life. Forget all the business successes, forget all the money he had made and things he had acquired. His relationship and love with this one extraordinary woman were really the ingredients for becoming a true success.

As calm as he felt, he couldn't help fidgeting with the ring that was nestled in his right pocket. Even though he was her son and would never wear her jewelry himself, his mother was always telling him that she wanted to give him some of her keepsakes. He would respond by protesting lightly, saying, "Mom, that is such a sweet gesture, but what will I do with them?"

Once she received her diagnosis, she put an end to this question and insisted on giving him the ring that was now in his pocket and some of her other treasured items. As she did, she looked at him with the loving and knowing eyes of a mother and said, "Trevor, my dear, believe me, one of these days you will find the right girl. I just know it, and I want you to have a few things of mine to give her. Just because I won't be there doesn't mean I can't give a bit of myself to your special love."

Trevor put his hand in his pocket again and felt the beautiful platinum and diamond ring. *Thank you so much, Mom. I so wish you could be here, but I know you are in your own very special way. And yes, Jackie is definitely that special love that you so wisely knew would come into my life.*

He almost lost his composure but found the strength to collect himself and turn his attention to Mr. Wright. Their eyes met, and Trevor sincerely said, "Alan, first, thank you so much for officiating today. Secondly, I know I promised not to steal Jackie from you in a professional capacity, but I do believe that a personal contract between Jackie and me is exempt."

Mr. Wright smiled broadly and replied, "Yes, Trevor, indeed, you are correct. The truth of it is, however, I have never been so pleased about losing such a valued employee. I know the two of you will be very happy together. Something about inspiration, if I remember correctly."

Trevor shook his hand and said, "Yes, ours is truly a very inspired relationship. I thank you so much."

Trevor then walked over to his father who was sitting in the first row, took his hand and said, "Thank you for coming, Father. It means a lot."

Pierce Harding shook his son's hand and said, "Well, Trevor, just like everything else you've done, this wedding is a bit on the rash side, but if it's as successful as your other endeavors, you'll have a long and happy marriage ahead of you. I sincerely wish you both well."

Trevor got choked up again and simply mouthed the words "Thank you" to his father.

He went back to where Mr. Wright was standing as the music started to play. He pivoted and looked down the aisle to see the gathering of people who represented both halves of their worlds—Jackie's colleagues from work and his from Excelsior and Prestigious Properties all waiting to witness the melding of Trevor and Jackie's lives and their very different worlds. He had never been happier or surer of anything in his life.

Then his eye caught sight of little Emily with Maria holding her hand, and he couldn't help but smile. She was dressed in a pale pink dress and was gently throwing pink rose petals as Maria guided her down the aisle. Maria looked beautiful in a darker pink dress and kept wiping tears from her eyes as she escorted Emily.

Just then, his eyes were drawn to the image of Jackie at the end of the walkway, and it took his breath away. He fiddled with the ring again while whispering "Oh my God" as she was about to start walking toward him. *How in the world could I be so lucky and blessed to have this exquisite woman as my wife?*

Jackie's wedding dress was simple yet flowing. It was cinched at the waist with what appeared to be a beaded belt, so it showed off her amazing figure. It was sleeveless with more lace and beading around her shoulders. Her hair was up so it highlighted her feminine neckline, and the only jewelry she wore were some silver drop earrings and her mother's platinum ring on her right hand.

She rubbed her fingers over the pearls as she had done a million times as a good luck charm. This time, however, she didn't need luck because she already felt like the luckiest girl in the world. Instead, she was stroking the ring and reflecting about her mother. *Oh, Mom. I would give anything for you to be here and share in this amazing moment. I've never been happier. I know you would just love Trevor and he would be crazy about you, too. I know you'll be watching and sending your love, but I miss and love you so much.* She looked down at her ring, gave it a gentle kiss and wiped a tear from her eye. Then she turned her focus back to the here and now.

She didn't have an engagement ring on because they had both decided they didn't need an engagement. They had waited so long to find each other, they didn't want to waste any more precious time.

She inhaled deeply and then took her first step while looking down to make sure Emily was doing her part correctly. Once she was sure the rose petals were being tossed bit by bit and not one giant shower, she looked up and saw Trevor. Her heart skipped a beat at the sight of him. Handsome and strong, but so kind and gentle. She started to get emotional thinking about how much she loved him but told herself, *Jackie, keep it together and just keep walking.*

She made her way to the front where Trevor took her hand and gave it one of his now familiar gentle squeezes. Mr. Wright looked kindly at Jackie and started the ceremony.

Instead of exchanging vows in the usual way with one saying their entire speech first then the other, they alternated lines.

Jackie started by saying, "Trevor, when you entered my world, I never knew where it would lead, but I always knew you were a very special man who I will now have the honor of calling my husband."

Then Trevor said, "Jackie, I have always considered myself a lucky guy, but when you came into my world, I finally knew what lucky really meant. I am more than honored to be your husband, and I'm incredibly blessed to have you as my wife."

They continued until the last lines, which they said together, "From this day forward, in the spirit of our love that has no bounds, we, Jackie and Trevor, are combining our worlds into one, and from this moment on we will be one until we are on this earth no more."

Mr. Wright then asked Trevor to put his mother's precious ring on Jackie's finger and pronounced them husband and wife. They looked at each other bursting with love and shared a long and tender kiss, oblivious to the clapping that surrounded them, because they were cherishing the first moments of the long-awaited love that they both had been destined to share and were reveling in anticipation of the future upon which they were about to embark together.

About the Author

Born and raised in Manhasset, NY, Nancy Molloy-Geiman was, and still is, an athlete. She is a tennis pro in Naples, Florida where she has lived since 1987. She is also a high school tennis and springboard diving coach since 1999.

Nancy does not have the typical author pedigree, but, back in the day, she was a legal assistant in a very busy real estate law firm and has drawn from that experience, and many walks on the beach, to create her first novel.

She has always had a love of the written word and decided to put that passion into writing *Beach Walk Treasures*, a story meant to be uplifting, regardless of the times, but especially for those times in which we have been living.

Made in the USA
Columbia, SC
30 October 2021